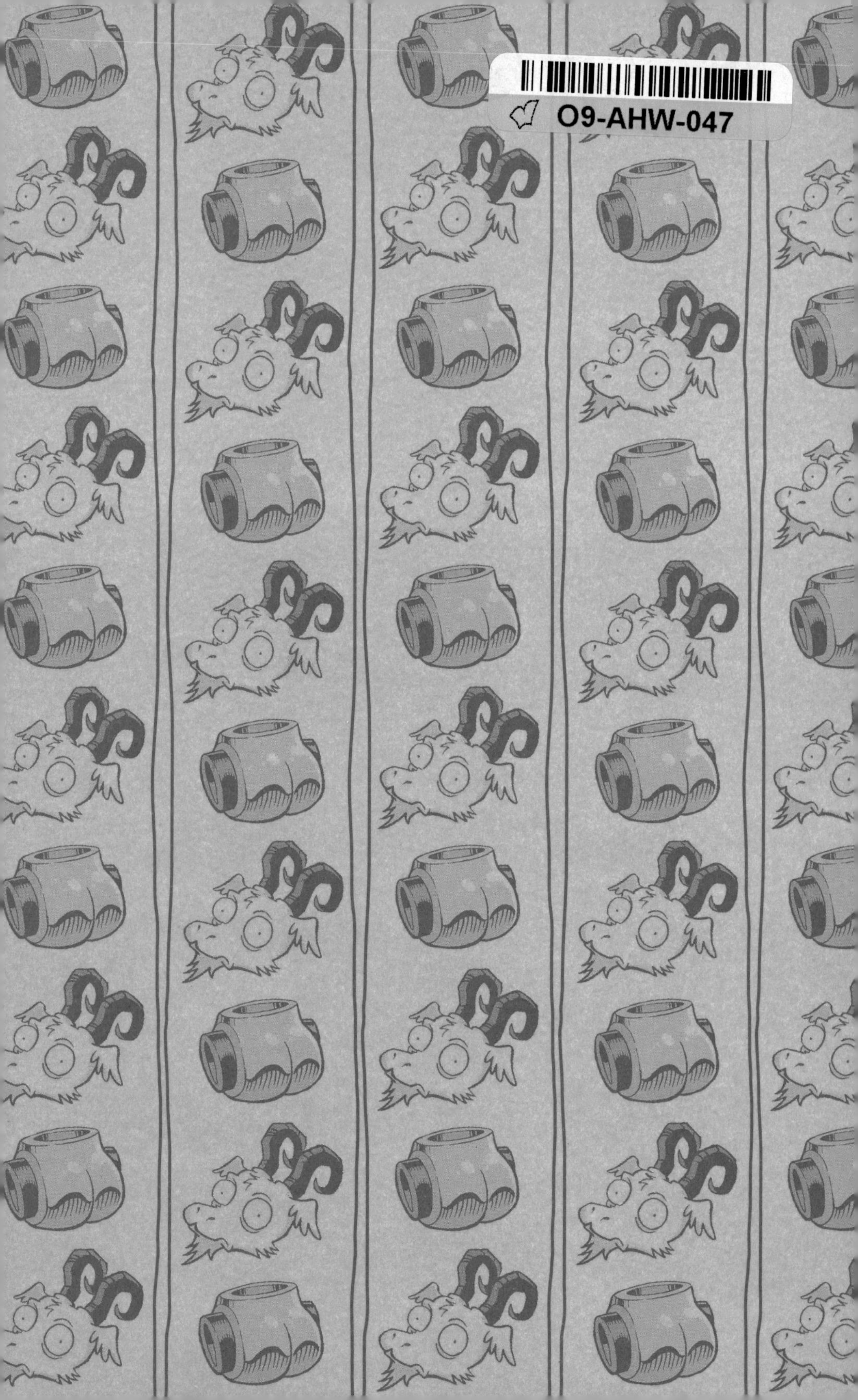

PLANTS VS. ZOMBIES™
GARDEN WARFARE

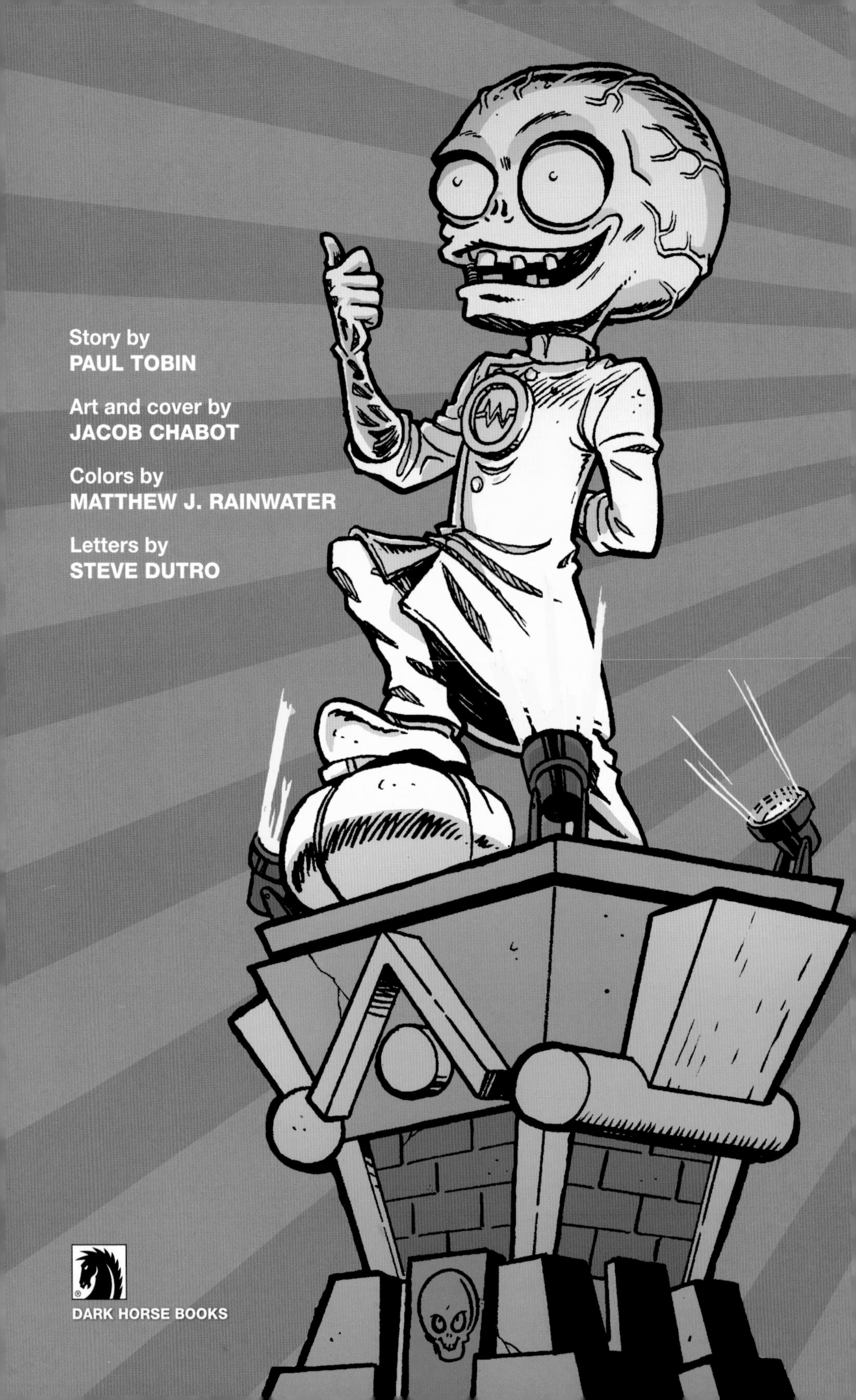

Story by
PAUL TOBIN

Art and cover by
JACOB CHABOT

Colors by
MATTHEW J. RAINWATER

Letters by
STEVE DUTRO

DARK HORSE BOOKS

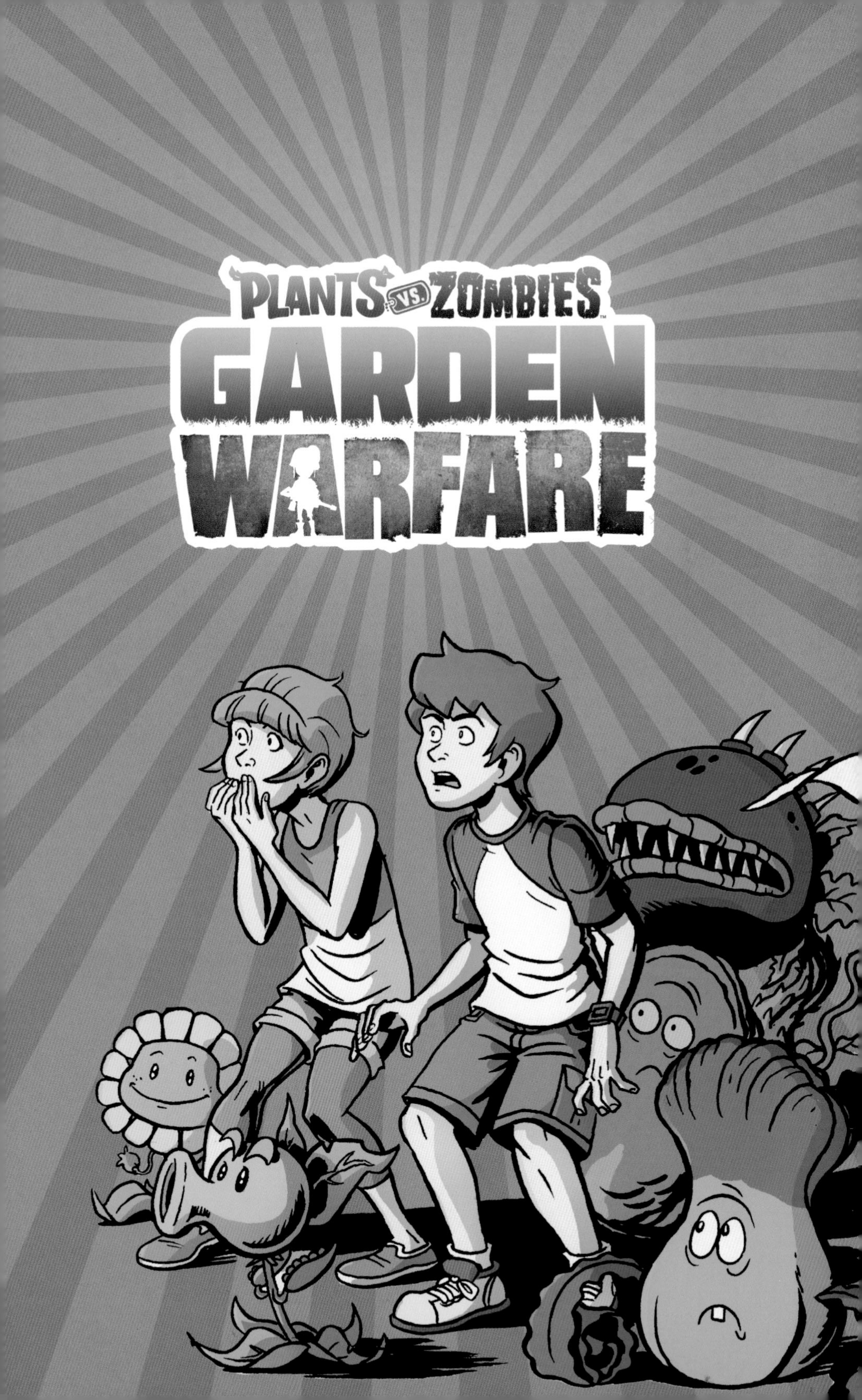
PLANTS VS. ZOMBIES™
GARDEN
WARFARE

Publisher **MIKE RICHARDSON**
Editor **PHILIP R. SIMON**
Assistant Editor **ROXY POLK**
Designer **JIMMY PRESLER**
Digital Art Technician **CHRISTINA McKENZIE**

Special thanks to **LEIGH BEACH, GARY CLAY,
SHANA DOERR, A.J. RATHBUN, KRISTEN STAR,
JEREMY VANHOOZER,** and everyone at PopCap Games.

First edition: January 2016
ISBN 978-1-61655-946-5

10 9 8 7 6 5
Printed China

DarkHorse.com | PopCap.com

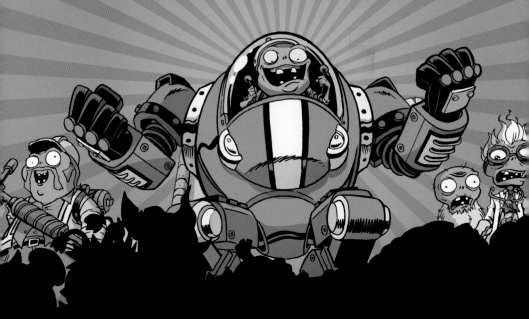

▷ No plants were harmed in the making of this comic. Numerous zombies
and various zombie-focused mecha, however, definitely were.

NEIL HANKERSON Executive Vice President **TOM WEDDLE** Chief Financial Officer **RANDY STRADLEY** Vice President of Publishing
MICHAEL MARTENS Vice President of Book Trade Sales **MATT PARKINSON** Vice President of Marketing **DAVID SCROGGY** Vice
President of Product Development **DALE LaFOUNTAIN** Vice President of Information Technology **CARA NIECE** Vice President of
Production and Scheduling **KEN LIZZI** General Counsel **DAVEY ESTRADA** Editorial Director **DAVE MARSHALL** Editor in Chief
SCOTT ALLIE Executive Senior Editor **CHRIS WARNER** Senior Books Editor **CARY GRAZZINI** Director of Print and Development

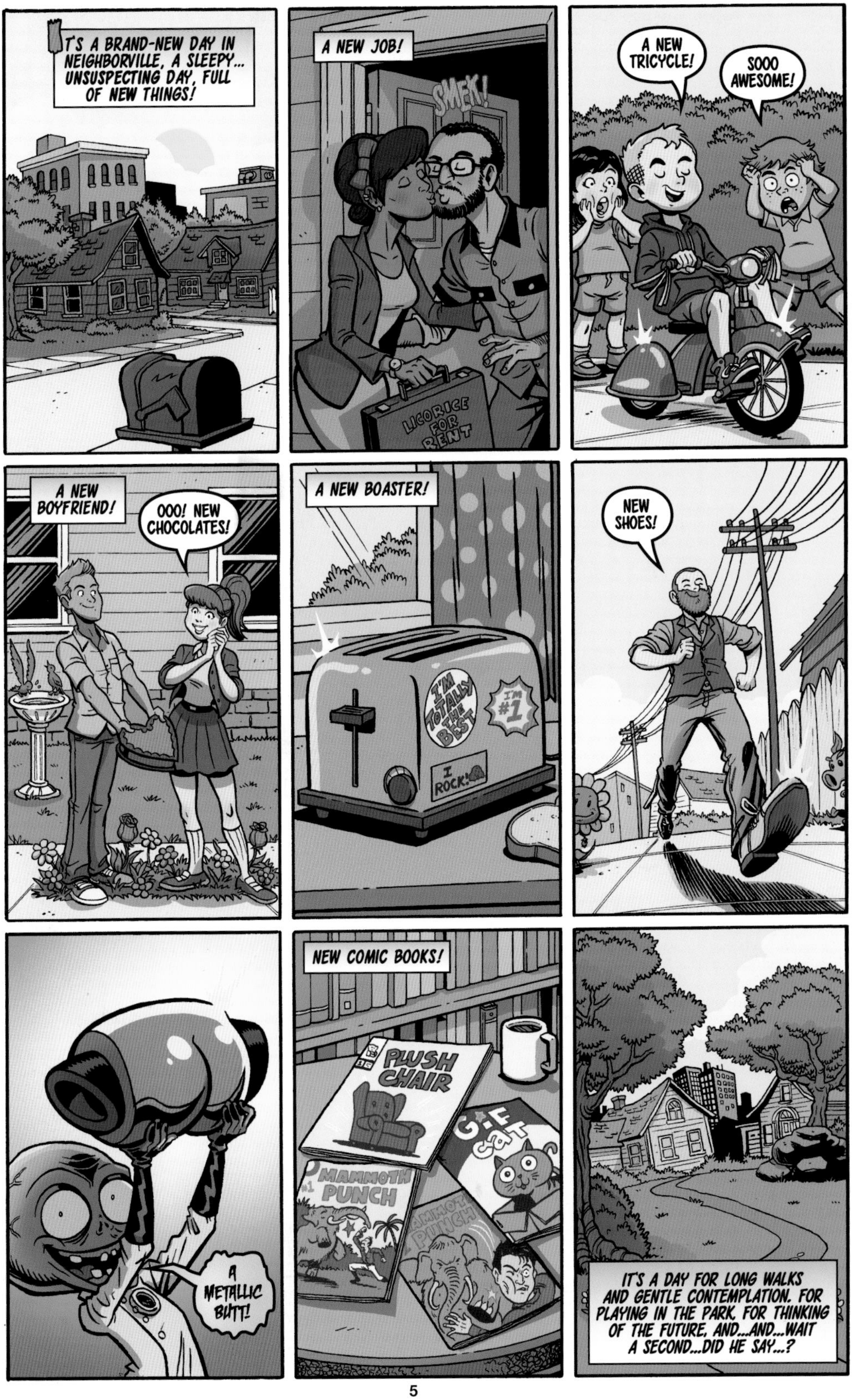
IT'S A BRAND-NEW DAY IN NEIGHBORVILLE, A SLEEPY... UNSUSPECTING DAY, FULL OF NEW THINGS!
A NEW JOB!
SMEK!
LICORICE FOR RENT
A NEW TRICYCLE!
SOOO AWESOME!
A NEW BOYFRIEND!
OOO! NEW CHOCOLATES!
A NEW BOASTER!
I'M TOTALLY THE BEST
I'M #1
I ROCK!
NEW SHOES!
A METALLIC BUTT!
NEW COMIC BOOKS!
PLUSH CHAIR
G.I. CAT
MAMMOTH PUNCH
IT'S A DAY FOR LONG WALKS AND GENTLE CONTEMPLATION. FOR PLAYING IN THE PARK, FOR THINKING OF THE FUTURE, AND...AND...WAIT A SECOND...DID HE SAY...?

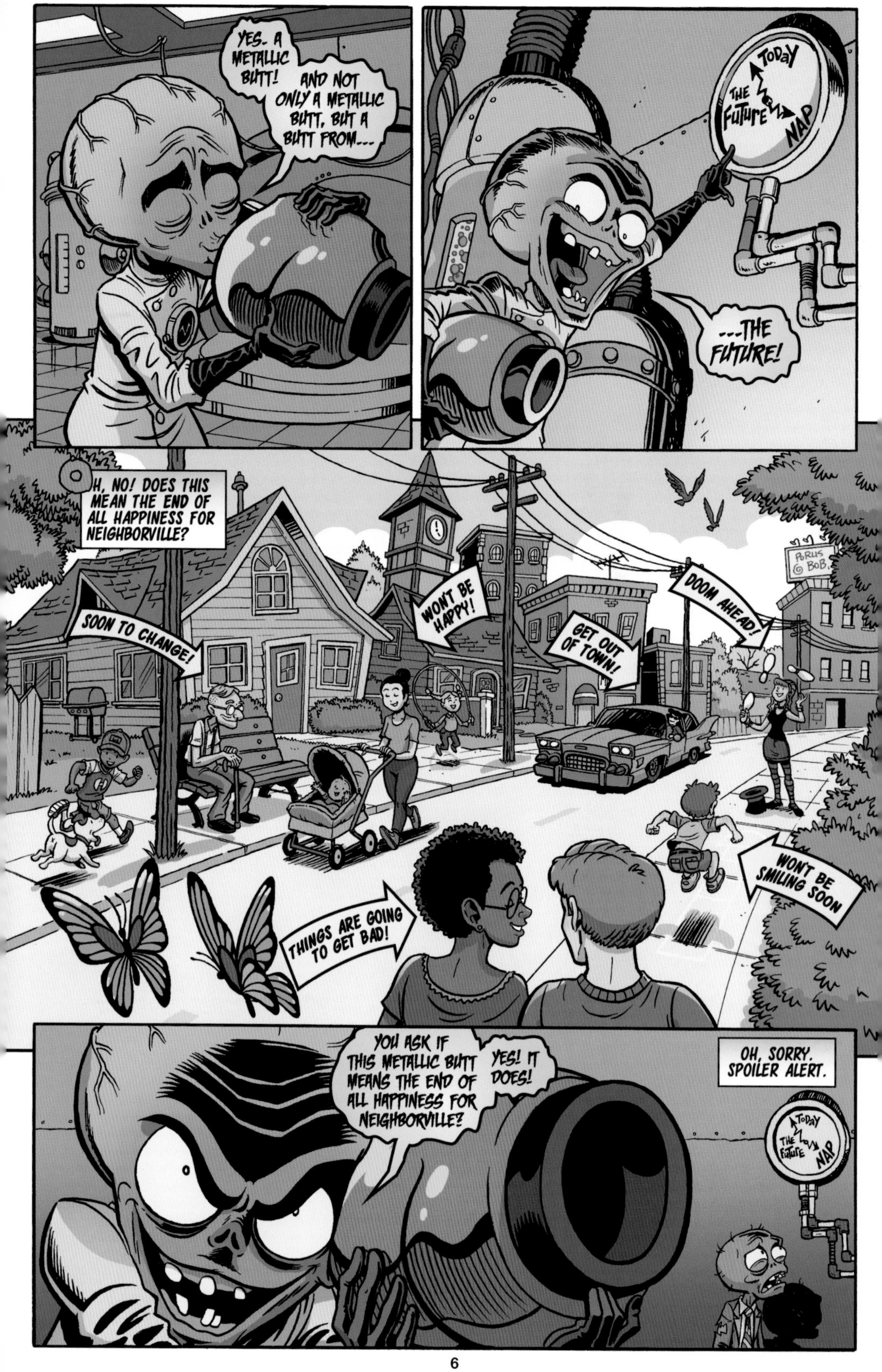
YES. A METALLIC BUTT!
AND NOT ONLY A METALLIC BUTT, BUT A BUTT FROM...
TODAY
THE FUTURE
NAP
...THE FUTURE!
OH, NO! DOES THIS MEAN THE END OF ALL HAPPINESS FOR NEIGHBORVILLE?
SOON TO CHANGE!
WON'T BE HAPPY!
GET OUT OF TOWN!
DOOM AHEAD!
PORUS BOB
WON'T BE SMILING SOON
THINGS ARE GOING TO GET BAD!
YOU ASK IF THIS METALLIC BUTT MEANS THE END OF ALL HAPPINESS FOR NEIGHBORVILLE?
YES! IT DOES!
OH, SORRY. SPOILER ALERT.
TODAY
THE FUTURE
NAP

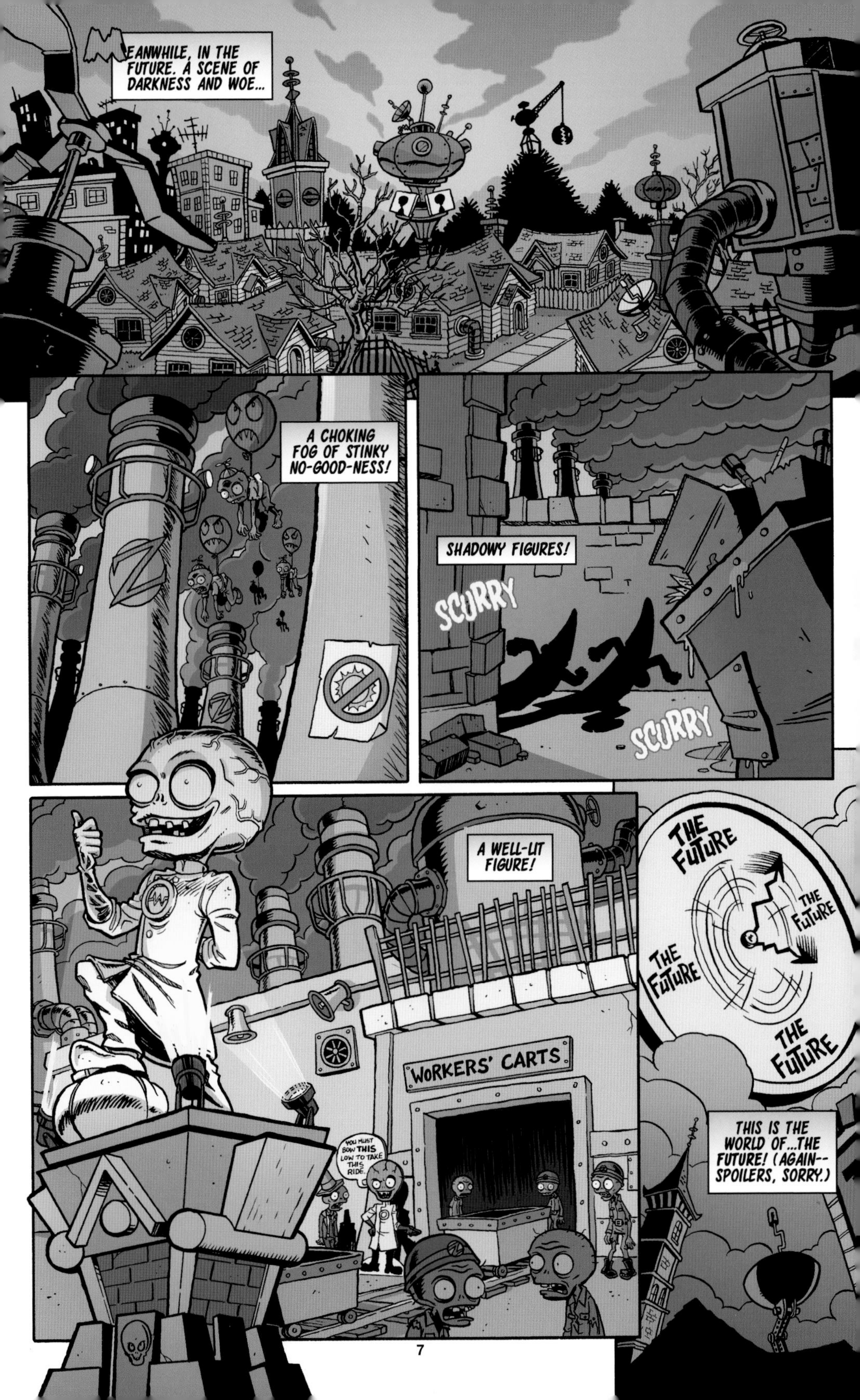
MEANWHILE, IN THE FUTURE. A SCENE OF DARKNESS AND WOE...
A CHOKING FOG OF STINKY NO-GOOD-NESS!
SHADOWY FIGURES!
SCURRY
SCURRY
A WELL-LIT FIGURE!
YOU MUST BOW THIS LOW TO TAKE THIS RIDE.
WORKERS' CARTS
THE FUTURE
THE FUTURE
THE FUTURE
THE FUTURE
THIS IS THE WORLD OF...THE FUTURE! (AGAIN--SPOILERS, SORRY.)

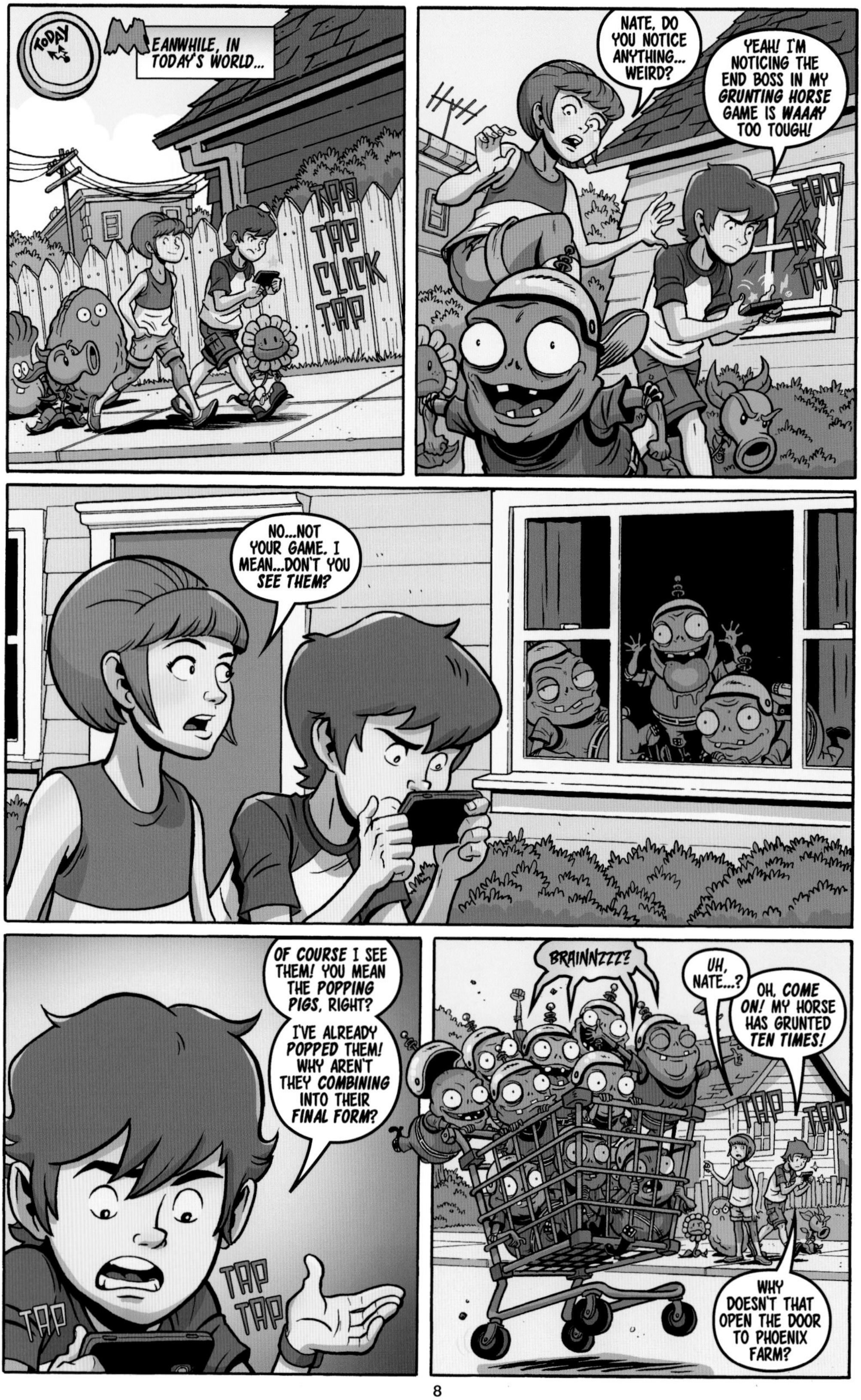
TODAY
MEANWHILE, IN TODAY'S WORLD...
TAP TAP CLICK TAP
NATE, DO YOU NOTICE ANYTHING... WEIRD?
YEAH! I'M NOTICING THE END BOSS IN MY GRUNTING HORSE GAME IS WAAAY TOO TOUGH!
TAP TIK TAP
NO...NOT YOUR GAME. I MEAN...DON'T YOU SEE THEM?
OF COURSE I SEE THEM! YOU MEAN THE POPPING PIGS, RIGHT?
I'VE ALREADY POPPED THEM! WHY AREN'T THEY COMBINING INTO THEIR FINAL FORM?
TAP TAP TAP
BRAINNZZZ?
UH, NATE...?
OH, COME ON! MY HORSE HAS GRUNTED TEN TIMES!
TAP TAP
WHY DOESN'T THAT OPEN THE DOOR TO PHOENIX FARM?

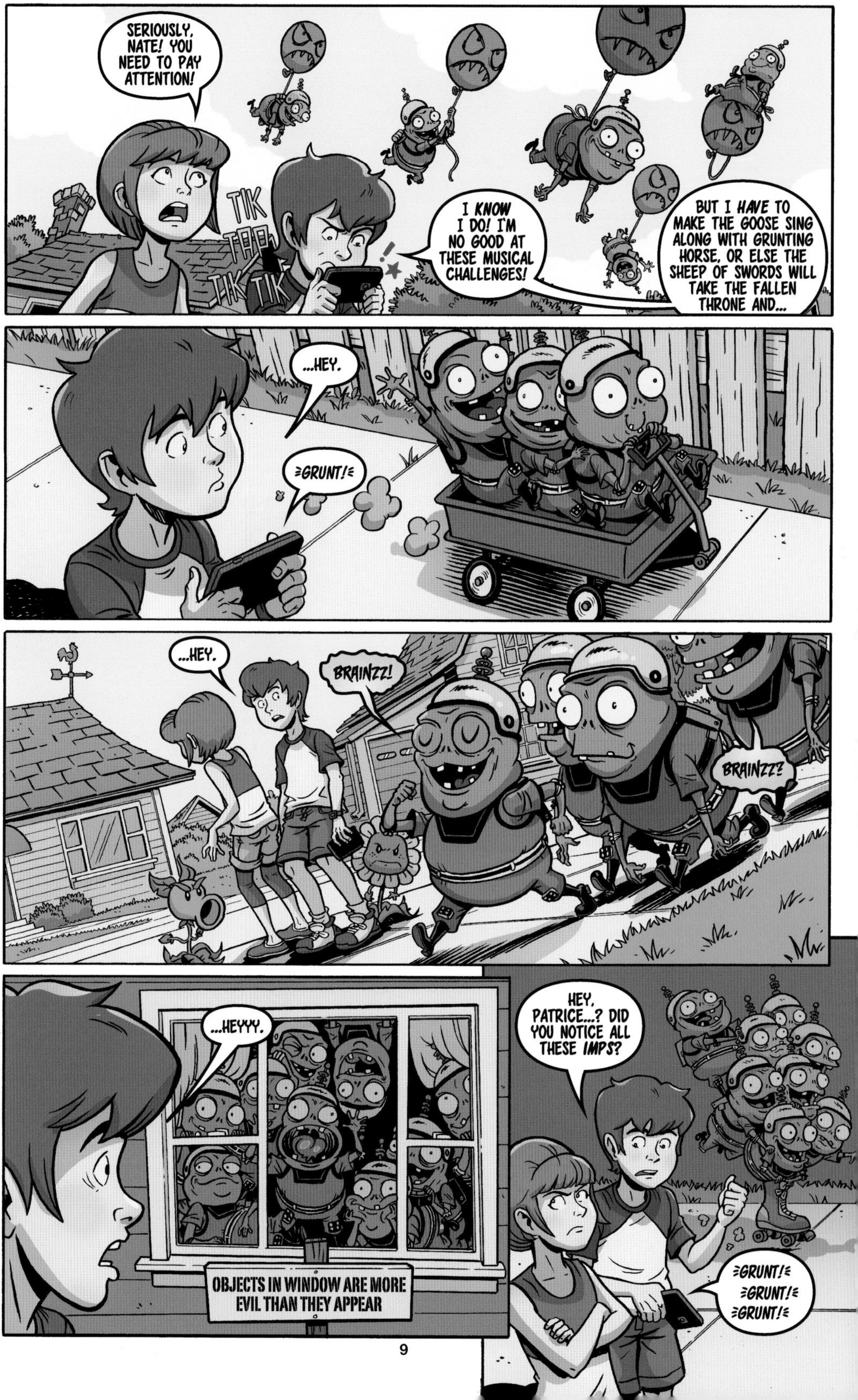
SERIOUSLY, NATE! YOU NEED TO PAY ATTENTION!
TIK TAP TIK TIK
I KNOW I DO! I'M NO GOOD AT THESE MUSICAL CHALLENGES!
BUT I HAVE TO MAKE THE GOOSE SING ALONG WITH GRUNTING HORSE, OR ELSE THE SHEEP OF SWORDS WILL TAKE THE FALLEN THRONE AND...
...HEY.
GRUNT!
...HEY.
BRAINZZ!
BRAINZZ?
...HEYYY.
OBJECTS IN WINDOW ARE MORE EVIL THAN THEY APPEAR
HEY, PATRICE...? DID YOU NOTICE ALL THESE IMPS?
GRUNT!
GRUNT!
GRUNT!

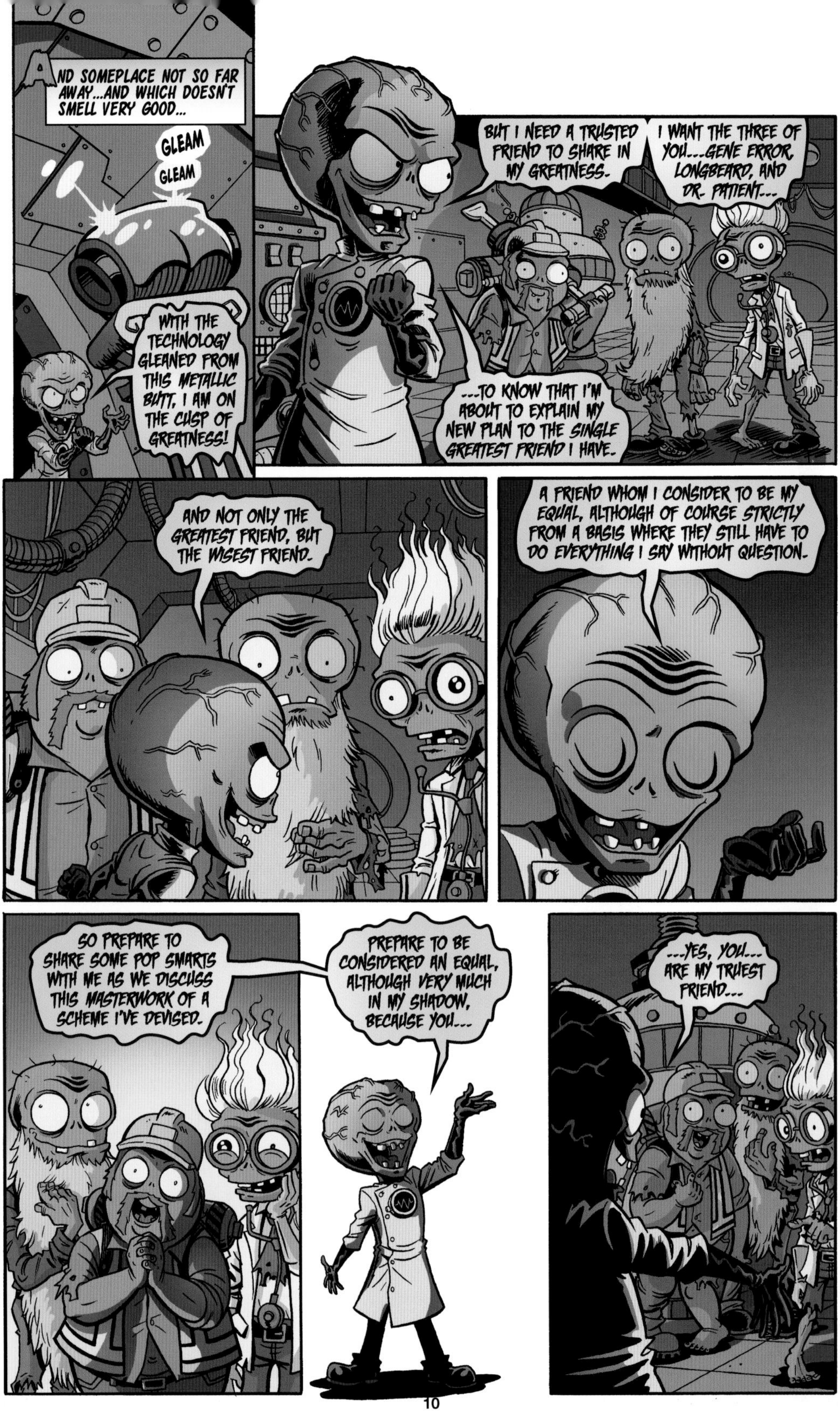
AND SOMEPLACE NOT SO FAR AWAY...AND WHICH DOESN'T SMELL VERY GOOD...
GLEAM
GLEAM
WITH THE TECHNOLOGY GLEANED FROM THIS METALLIC BUTT, I AM ON THE CUSP OF GREATNESS!
BUT I NEED A TRUSTED FRIEND TO SHARE IN MY GREATNESS.
I WANT THE THREE OF YOU...GENE ERROR, LONGBEARD, AND DR. PATIENT...
...TO KNOW THAT I'M ABOUT TO EXPLAIN MY NEW PLAN TO THE SINGLE GREATEST FRIEND I HAVE.
AND NOT ONLY THE GREATEST FRIEND, BUT THE WISEST FRIEND.
A FRIEND WHOM I CONSIDER TO BE MY EQUAL, ALTHOUGH OF COURSE STRICTLY FROM A BASIS WHERE THEY STILL HAVE TO DO EVERYTHING I SAY WITHOUT QUESTION.
SO PREPARE TO SHARE SOME POP SMARTS WITH ME AS WE DISCUSS THIS MASTERWORK OF A SCHEME I'VE DEVISED.
PREPARE TO BE CONSIDERED AN EQUAL, ALTHOUGH VERY MUCH IN MY SHADOW, BECAUSE YOU...
...YES, YOU... ARE MY TRUEST FRIEND...

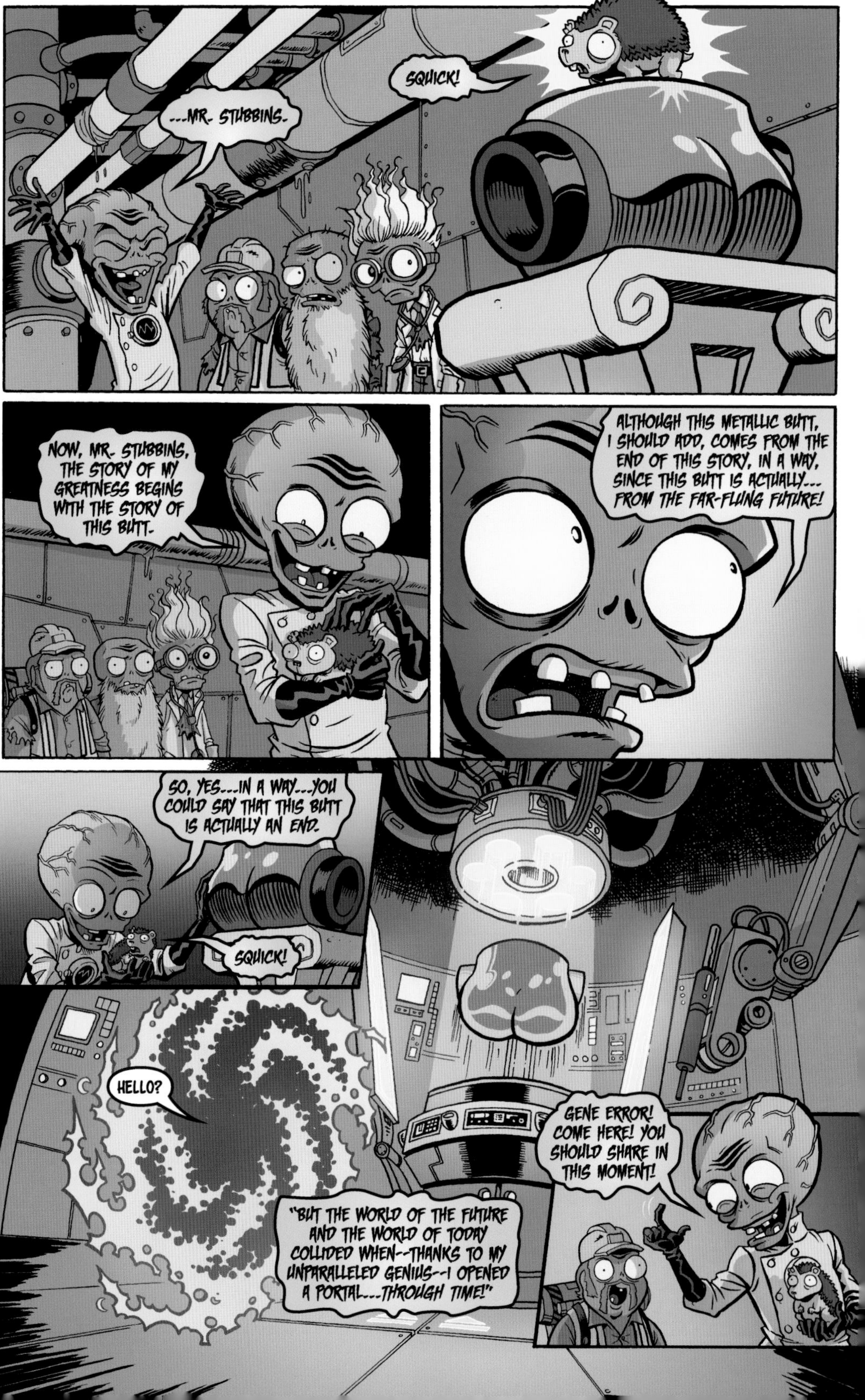
...MR. STUBBINS.
SQUICK!
NOW, MR. STUBBINS, THE STORY OF MY GREATNESS BEGINS WITH THE STORY OF THIS BUTT.
ALTHOUGH THIS METALLIC BUTT, I SHOULD ADD, COMES FROM THE END OF THIS STORY, IN A WAY, SINCE THIS BUTT IS ACTUALLY... FROM THE FAR-FLUNG FUTURE!
SO, YES...IN A WAY...YOU COULD SAY THAT THIS BUTT IS ACTUALLY AN END.
SQUICK!
HELLO?
GENE ERROR! COME HERE! YOU SHOULD SHARE IN THIS MOMENT!
"BUT THE WORLD OF THE FUTURE AND THE WORLD OF TODAY COLLIDED WHEN--THANKS TO MY UNPARALLELED GENIUS--I OPENED A PORTAL...THROUGH TIME!"

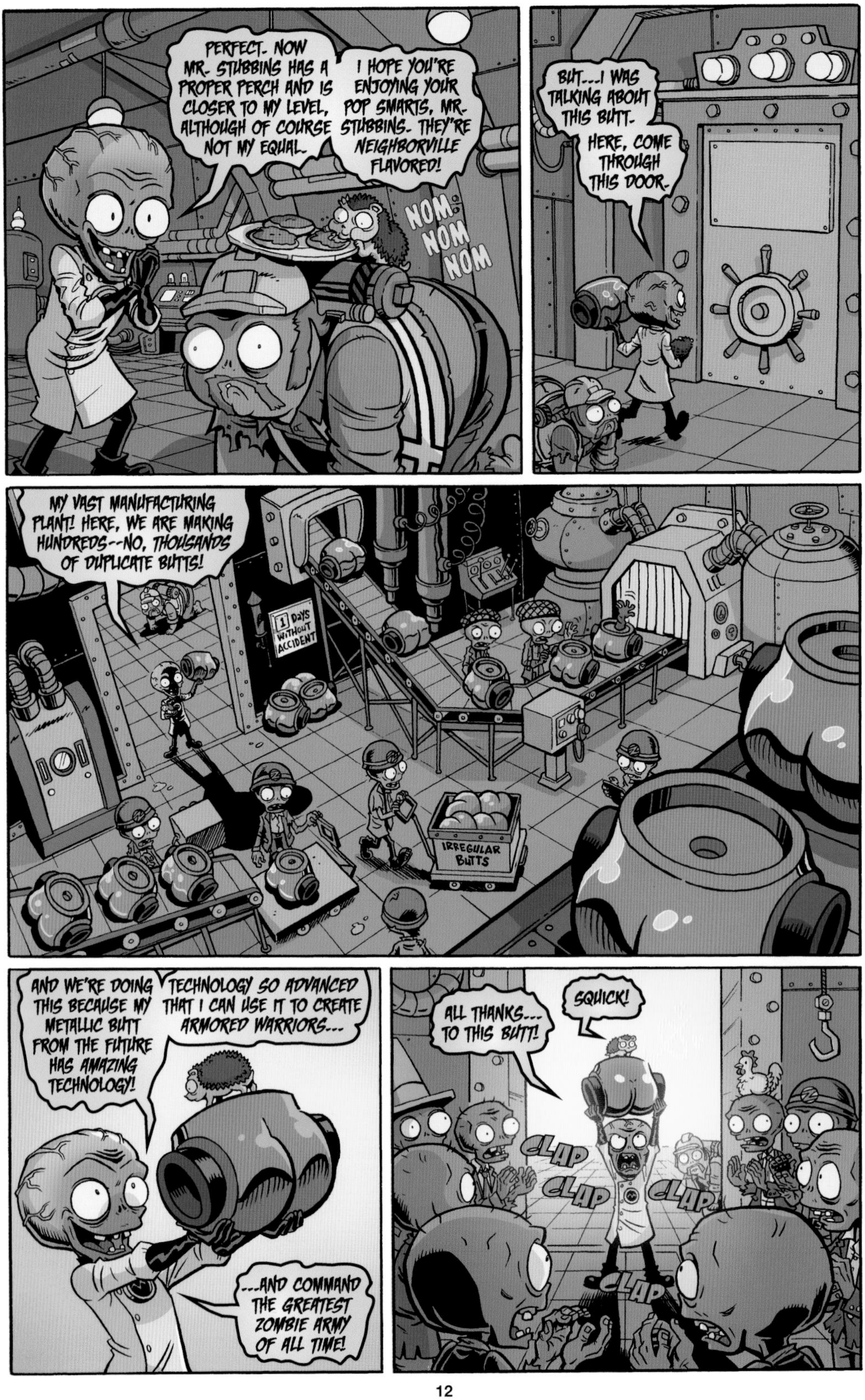
PERFECT. NOW MR. STUBBINS HAS A PROPER PERCH AND IS CLOSER TO MY LEVEL, ALTHOUGH OF COURSE NOT MY EQUAL.
I HOPE YOU'RE ENJOYING YOUR POP SMARTS, MR. STUBBINS. THEY'RE NEIGHBORVILLE FLAVORED!
NOM NOM NOM
BUT...I WAS TALKING ABOUT THIS BUTT.
HERE, COME THROUGH THIS DOOR.
MY VAST MANUFACTURING PLANT! HERE, WE ARE MAKING HUNDREDS--NO, THOUSANDS OF DUPLICATE BUTTS!
1 DAYS WITHOUT ACCIDENT
IRREGULAR BUTTS
AND WE'RE DOING THIS BECAUSE MY METALLIC BUTT FROM THE FUTURE HAS AMAZING TECHNOLOGY!
TECHNOLOGY SO ADVANCED THAT I CAN USE IT TO CREATE ARMORED WARRIORS...
...AND COMMAND THE GREATEST ZOMBIE ARMY OF ALL TIME!
ALL THANKS... TO THIS BUTT!
SQUICK!
CLAP
CLAP
CLAP
CLAP

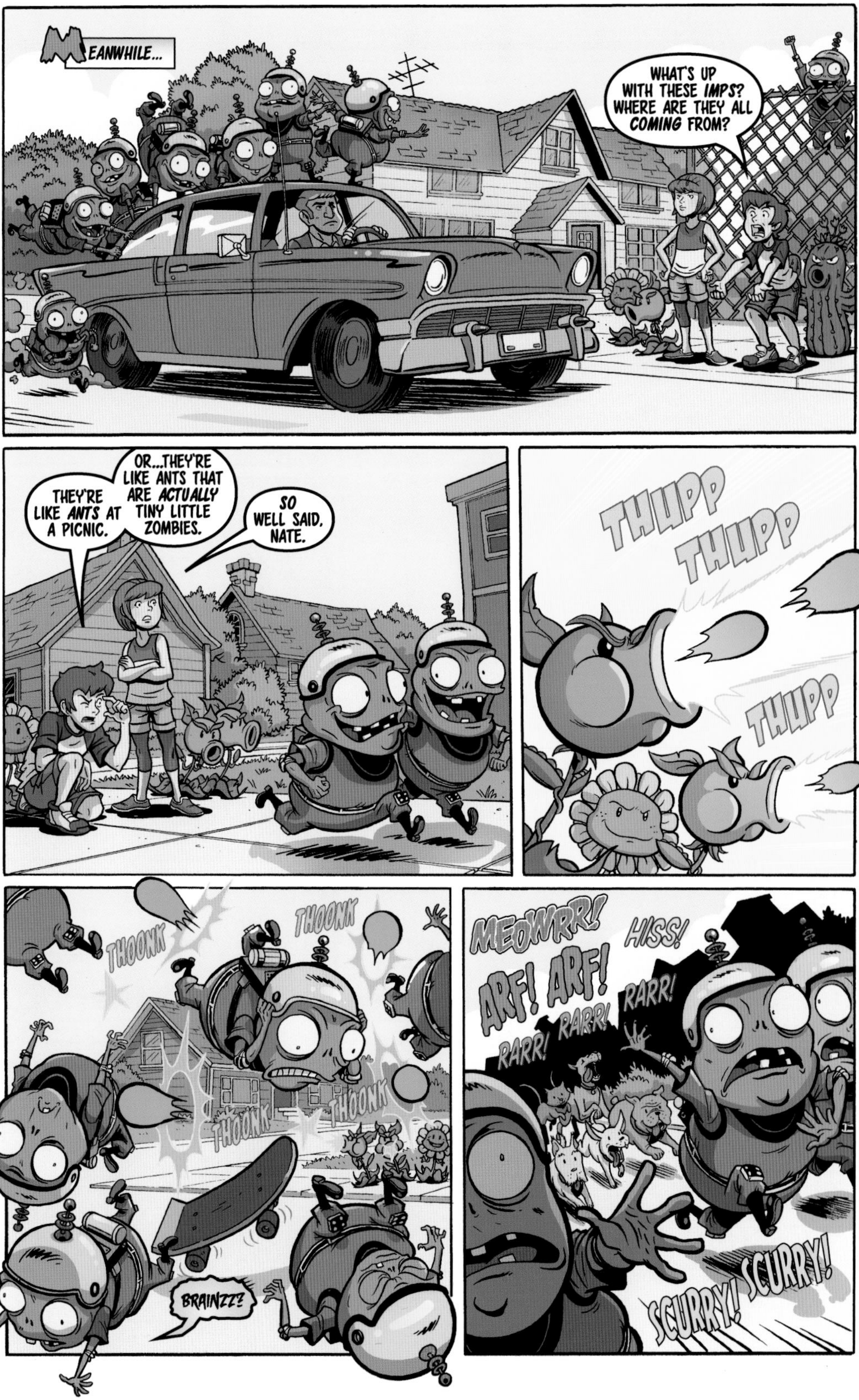
MEANWHILE...
WHAT'S UP WITH THESE IMPS? WHERE ARE THEY ALL COMING FROM?
THEY'RE LIKE ANTS AT A PICNIC.
OR...THEY'RE LIKE ANTS THAT ARE ACTUALLY TINY LITTLE ZOMBIES.
SO WELL SAID, NATE.
THUPP
THUPP
THUPP
THOONK
THOONK
THOONK
THOONK
BRAINZZ?
MEOWRR!
HISS!
ARF! ARF!
RARR!
RARR!
RARR!
SCURRY! SCURRY!

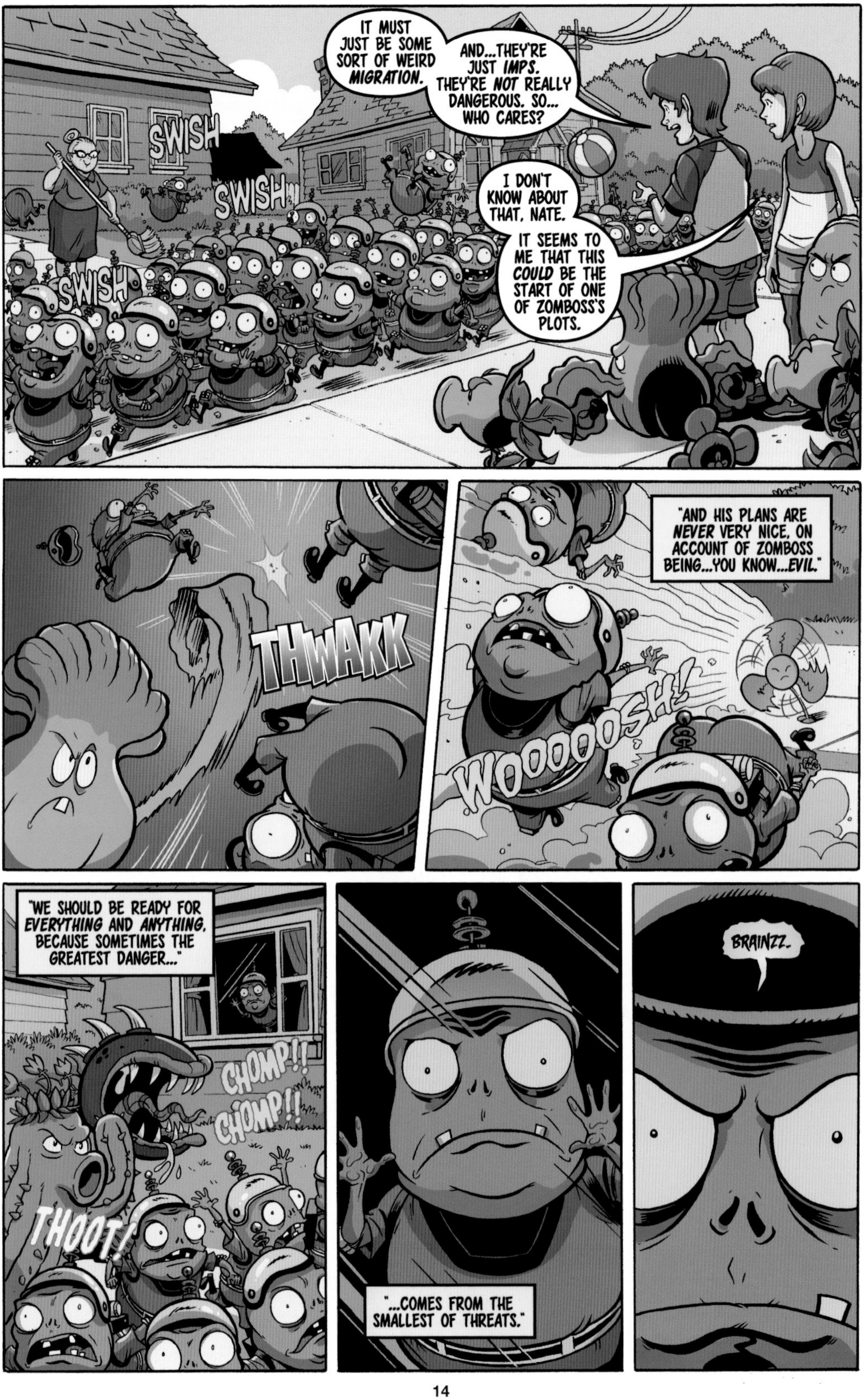
IT MUST JUST BE SOME SORT OF WEIRD MIGRATION.
AND...THEY'RE JUST IMPS. THEY'RE NOT REALLY DANGEROUS. SO... WHO CARES?
SWISH
SWISH
SWISH
I DON'T KNOW ABOUT THAT, NATE.
IT SEEMS TO ME THAT THIS COULD BE THE START OF ONE OF ZOMBOSS'S PLOTS.
THWAKK
"AND HIS PLANS ARE NEVER VERY NICE, ON ACCOUNT OF ZOMBOSS BEING...YOU KNOW...EVIL."
WOOOOOOSH!
"WE SHOULD BE READY FOR EVERYTHING AND ANYTHING, BECAUSE SOMETIMES THE GREATEST DANGER..."
CHOMP!!
CHOMP!!
THOOT!
"...COMES FROM THE SMALLEST OF THREATS."
BRAINZZ.

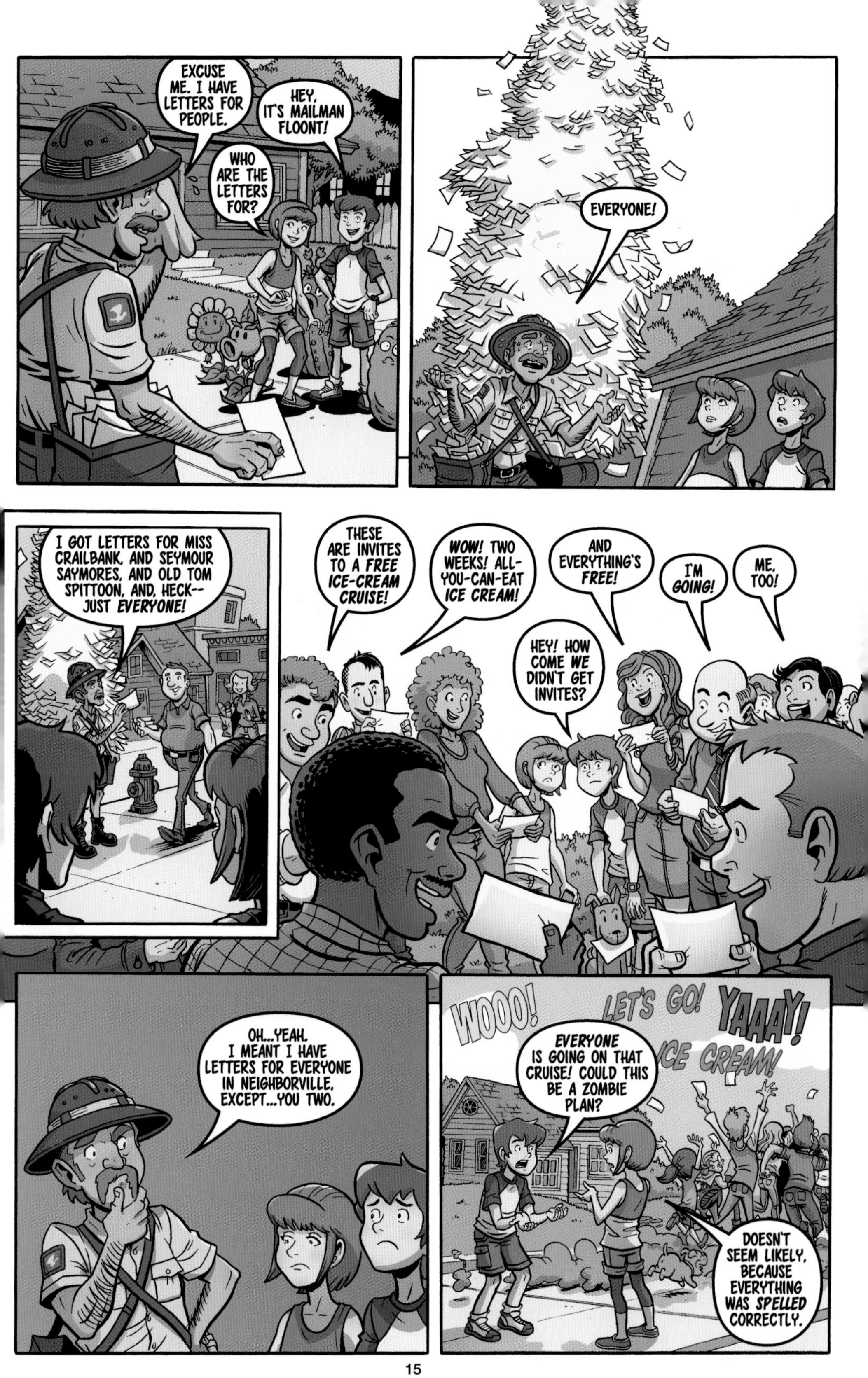
EXCUSE ME. I HAVE LETTERS FOR PEOPLE.
HEY, IT'S MAILMAN FLOONT!
WHO ARE THE LETTERS FOR?
EVERYONE!
I GOT LETTERS FOR MISS CRAILBANK, AND SEYMOUR SAYMORES, AND OLD TOM SPITTOON, AND, HECK-- JUST *EVERYONE!*
THESE ARE INVITES TO A *FREE ICE-CREAM CRUISE!*
WOW! TWO WEEKS! ALL-YOU-CAN-EAT *ICE CREAM!*
AND EVERYTHING'S *FREE!*
I'M *GOING!*
ME, TOO!
HEY! HOW COME *WE* DIDN'T GET INVITES?
OH...YEAH. I MEANT I HAVE LETTERS FOR EVERYONE IN NEIGHBORVILLE, EXCEPT...YOU TWO.
WOOO!
LET'S GO!
YAAAY!
ICE CREAM!
EVERYONE IS GOING ON THAT CRUISE! COULD THIS BE A ZOMBIE PLAN?
DOESN'T SEEM LIKELY, BECAUSE EVERYTHING WAS *SPELLED* CORRECTLY.

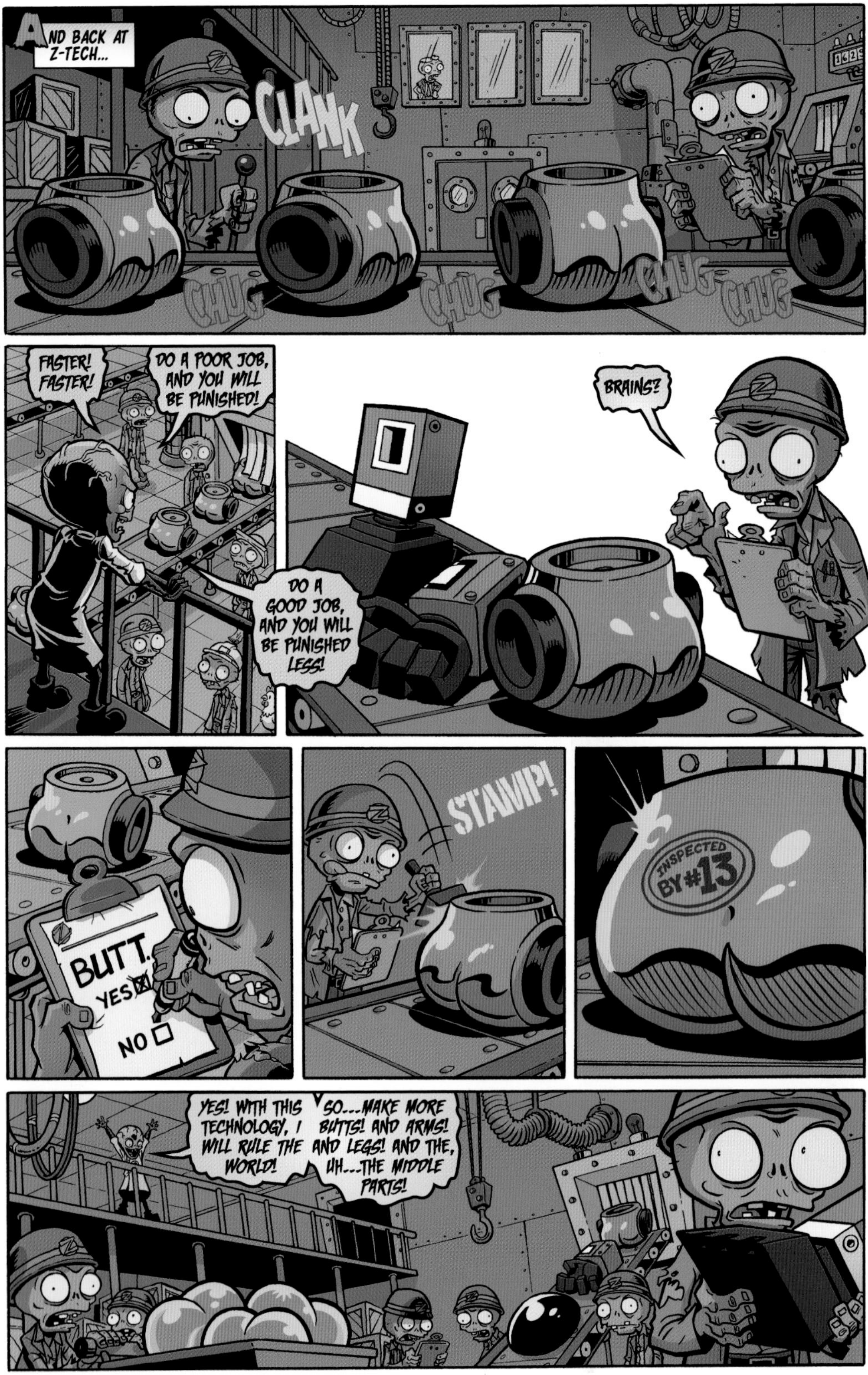
AND BACK AT Z-TECH...
CLANK
CHUG
CHUG
CHUG
CHUG
FASTER! FASTER!
DO A POOR JOB, AND YOU WILL BE PUNISHED!
DO A GOOD JOB, AND YOU WILL BE PUNISHED LESS!
BRAINS?
BUTT.
YES
NO
STAMP!
INSPECTED BY #13
YES! WITH THIS TECHNOLOGY, I WILL RULE THE WORLD!
SO...MAKE MORE BUTTS! AND ARMS! AND LEGS! AND THE, UH...THE MIDDLE PARTS!

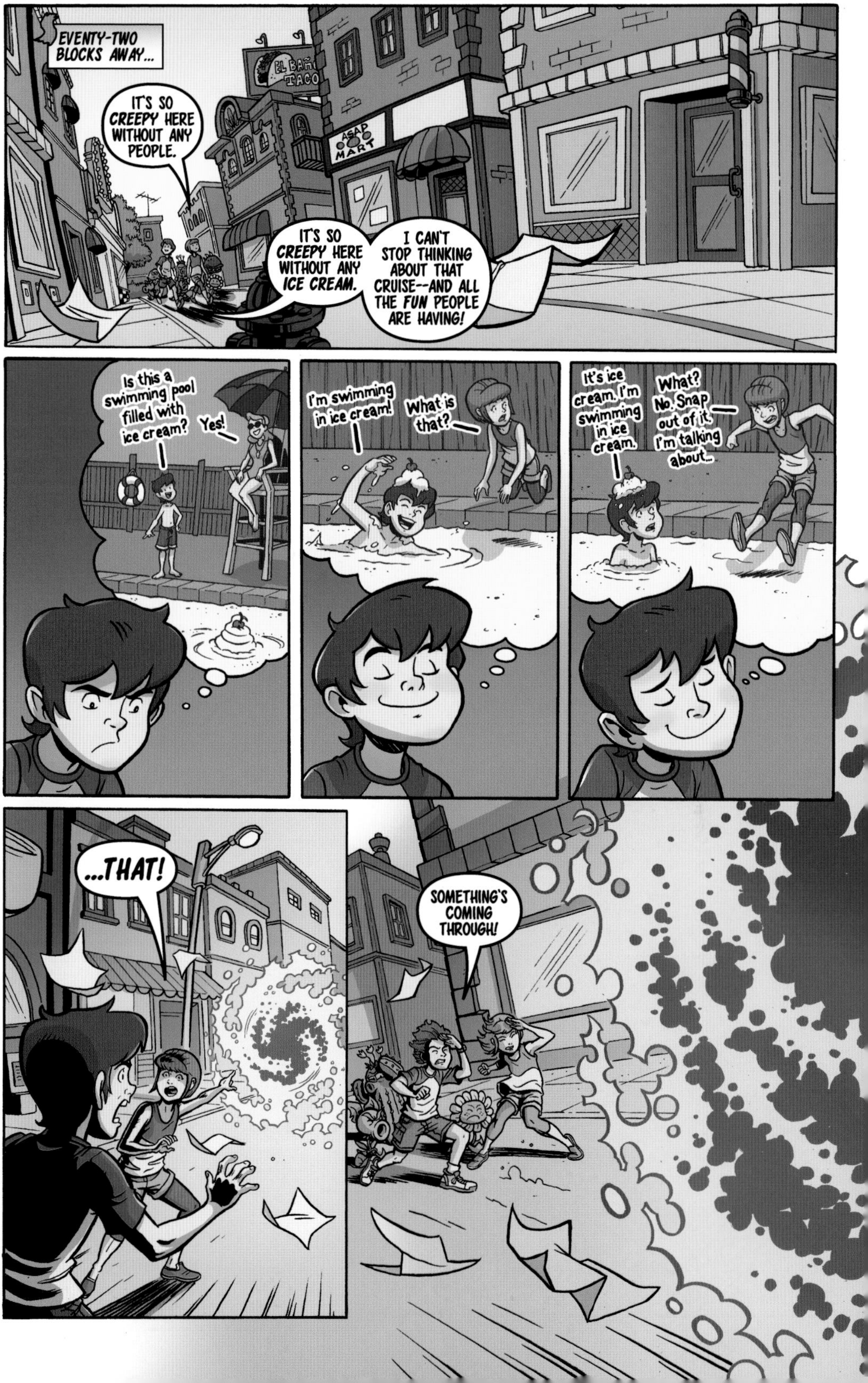
EVENTY-TWO BLOCKS AWAY...
IT'S SO CREEPY HERE WITHOUT ANY PEOPLE.
EL BAÑO TACO
ASAP MART
IT'S SO CREEPY HERE WITHOUT ANY ICE CREAM.
I CAN'T STOP THINKING ABOUT THAT CRUISE--AND ALL THE FUN PEOPLE ARE HAVING!
Is this a swimming pool filled with ice cream?
Yes!
I'm swimming in ice cream!
What is that?
It's ice cream. I'm swimming in ice cream.
What? No. Snap out of it. I'm talking about...
...THAT!
SOMETHING'S COMING THROUGH!

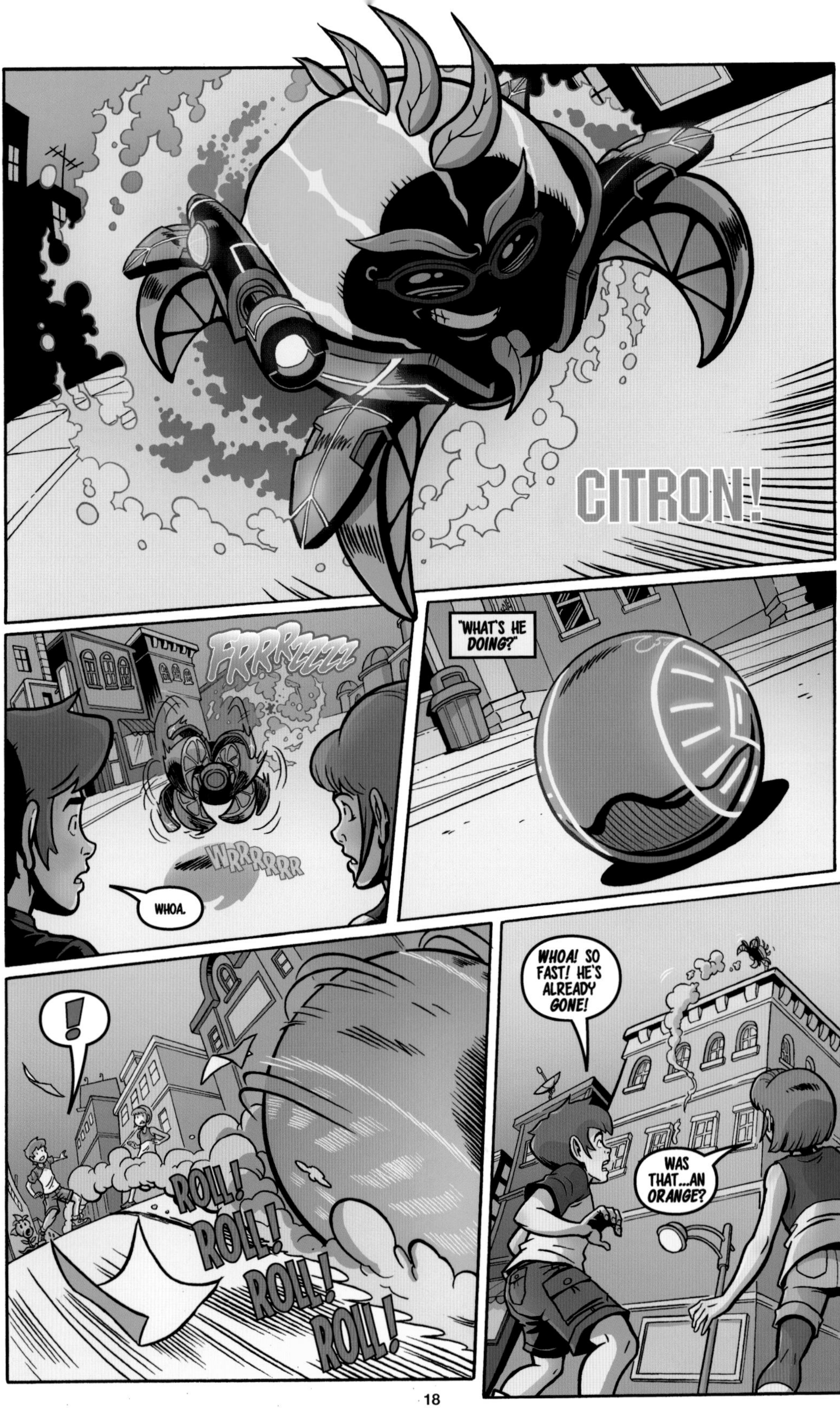
CITRON!
FRRRZZZZZ
WRRRRRR
WHOA.
"WHAT'S HE DOING?"
!
ROLL! ROLL! ROLL! ROLL!
WHOA! SO FAST! HE'S ALREADY GONE!
WAS THAT...AN ORANGE?

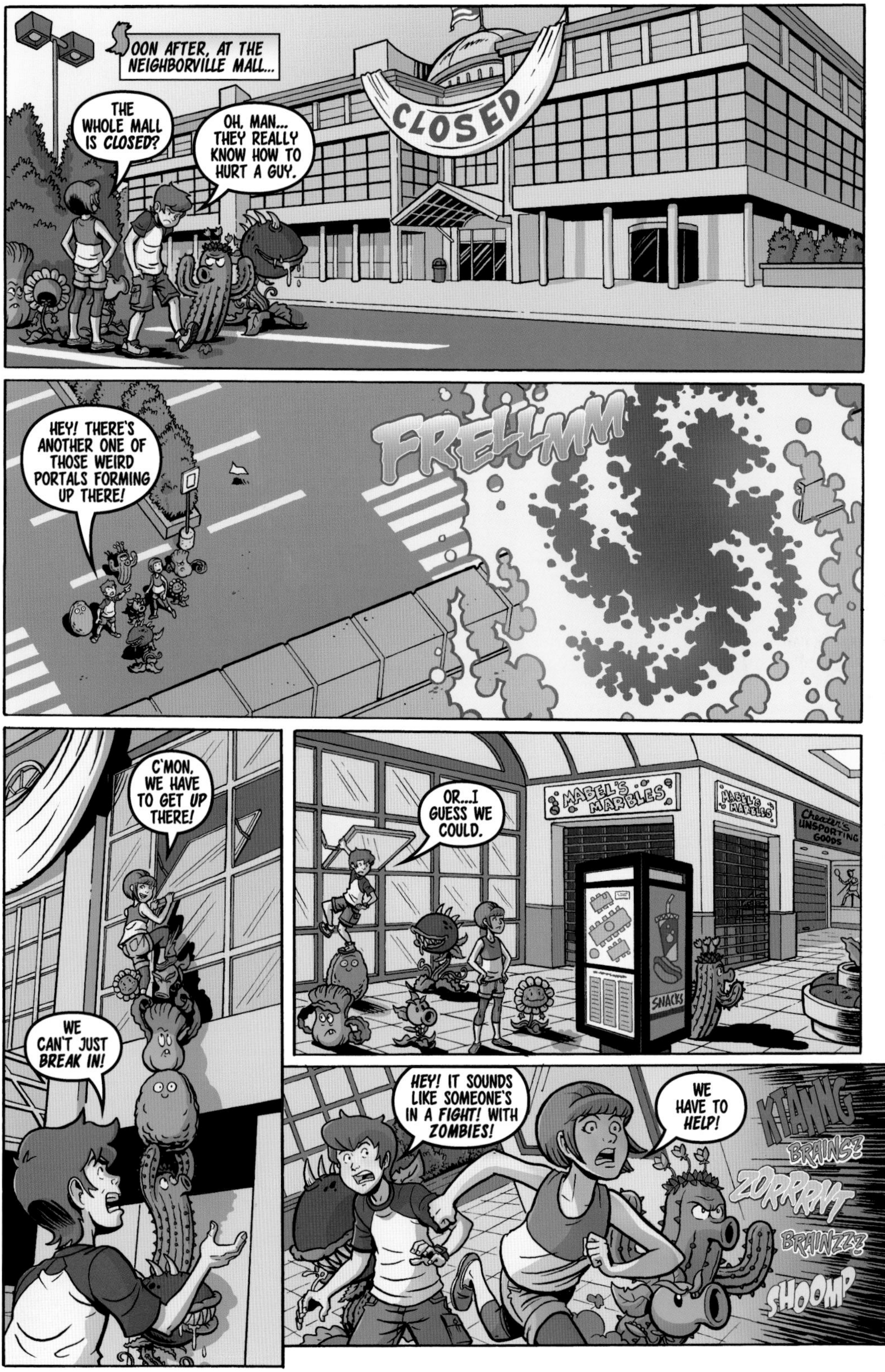
SOON AFTER, AT THE NEIGHBORVILLE MALL...
CLOSED
THE WHOLE MALL IS CLOSED?
OH, MAN... THEY REALLY KNOW HOW TO HURT A GUY.
HEY! THERE'S ANOTHER ONE OF THOSE WEIRD PORTALS FORMING UP THERE!
FRELLMM
C'MON, WE HAVE TO GET UP THERE!
WE CAN'T JUST BREAK IN!
OR...I GUESS WE COULD.
MABEL'S MARBLES
MABEL'S MARBLES
Chester's UNSPORTING GOODS
SNACKS
HEY! IT SOUNDS LIKE SOMEONE'S IN A FIGHT! WITH ZOMBIES!
WE HAVE TO HELP!
KTANNG
BRAINSZ
ZORRRNT
BRAINZZZ
SHOOMP

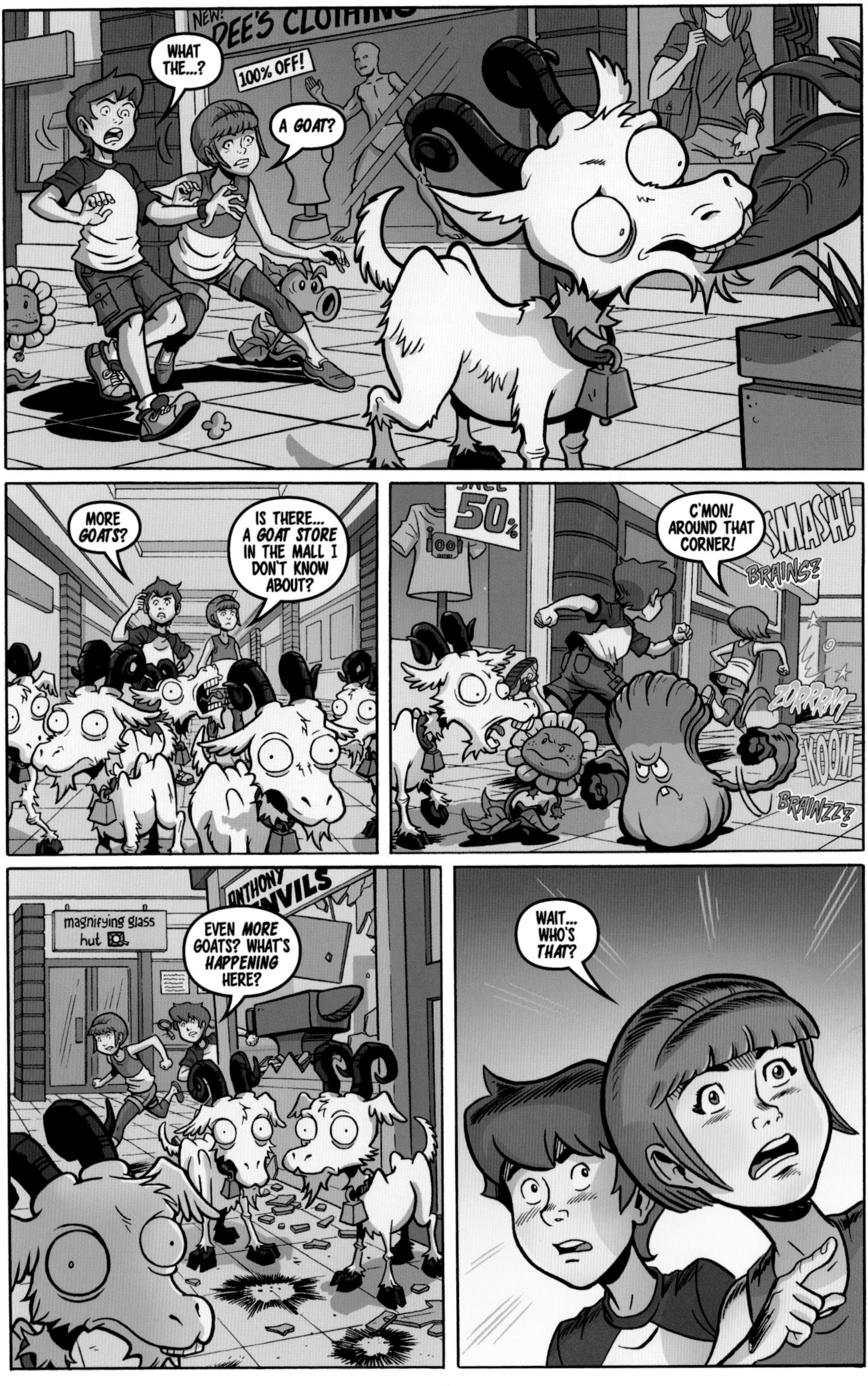
NEW! DEE'S CLOTHING
100% OFF!
WHAT THE...?
A GOAT?
MORE GOATS?
IS THERE... A GOAT STORE IN THE MALL I DON'T KNOW ABOUT?
50%
C'MON! AROUND THAT CORNER!
SMASH!
BRAINS?
ZORRRNT
KOOM
BRAINZZZ?
magnifying glass hut
ANTHONY ANVILS
EVEN MORE GOATS? WHAT'S HAPPENING HERE?
WAIT... WHO'S THAT?

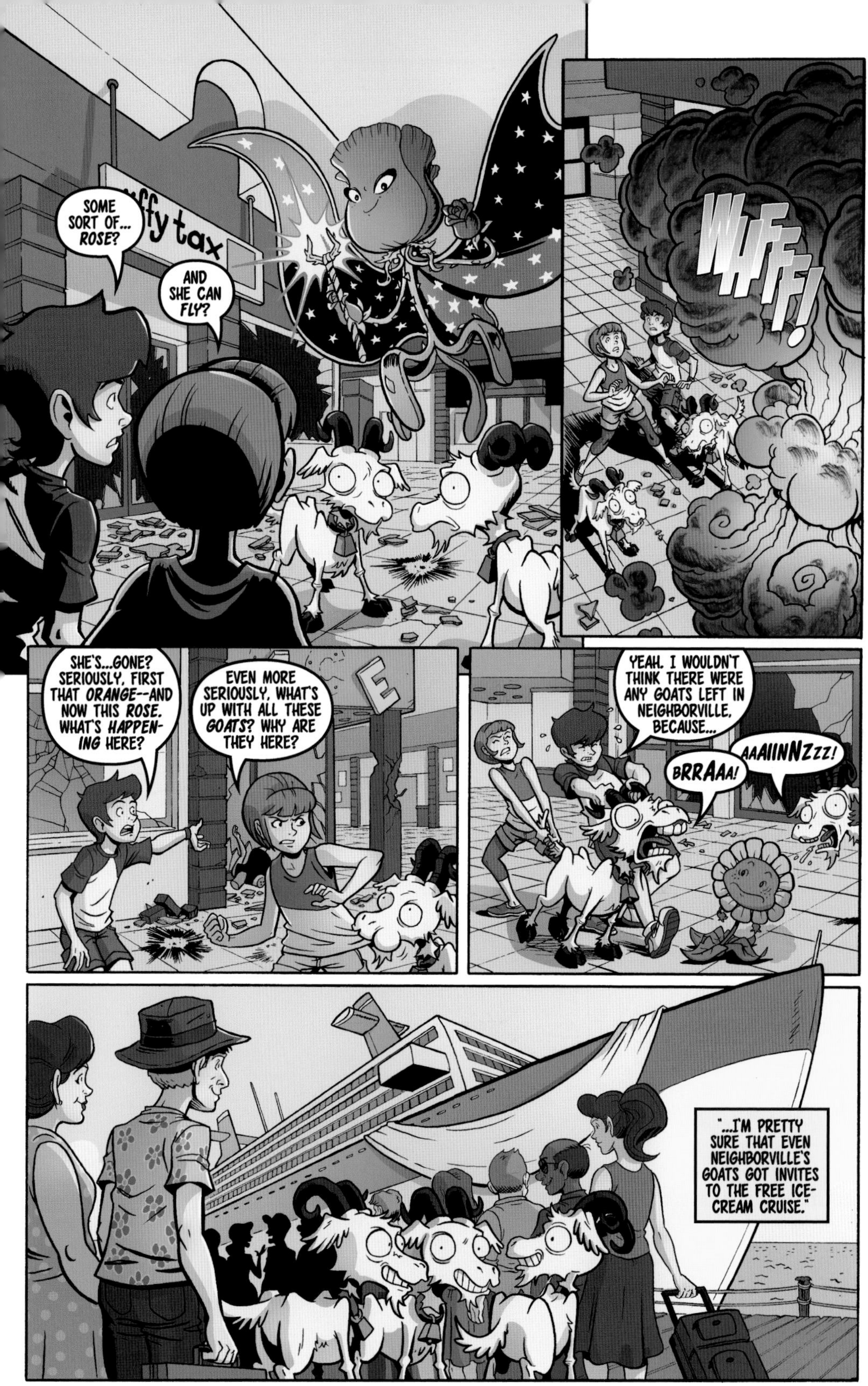
ffy tax
SOME SORT OF... ROSE?
AND SHE CAN FLY?
WHFFF!
SHE'S...GONE? SERIOUSLY, FIRST THAT ORANGE--AND NOW THIS ROSE. WHAT'S HAPPENING HERE?
E
EVEN MORE SERIOUSLY, WHAT'S UP WITH ALL THESE GOATS? WHY ARE THEY HERE?
YEAH. I WOULDN'T THINK THERE WERE ANY GOATS LEFT IN NEIGHBORVILLE, BECAUSE...
BRRAAA!
AAAIINNZzz!
"...I'M PRETTY SURE THAT EVEN NEIGHBORVILLE'S GOATS GOT INVITES TO THE FREE ICE-CREAM CRUISE."

WITH ALL THIS WEIRDNESS, THERE'S *NO WAY* THE ZOMBIES AREN'T INVOLVED SOMEHOW--AND THAT'S *ALWAYS* BAD.

I BETTER CALL MY UNCLE.

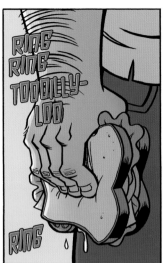

RING RING TOODILLY-LOO RING

GROBBLE?

UNCLE DAVE! IT'S PATRICE!

WHERE ARE YOU?

SOMETHING WEIRD IS GOING ON IN NEIGHBORVILLE, AND WE NEED YOU!

UNCLE DAVE, WE NEED YOU!

FREE ICE CREAM

FREE ICE CREAM

MUNCH

MUNCH

MUNCH

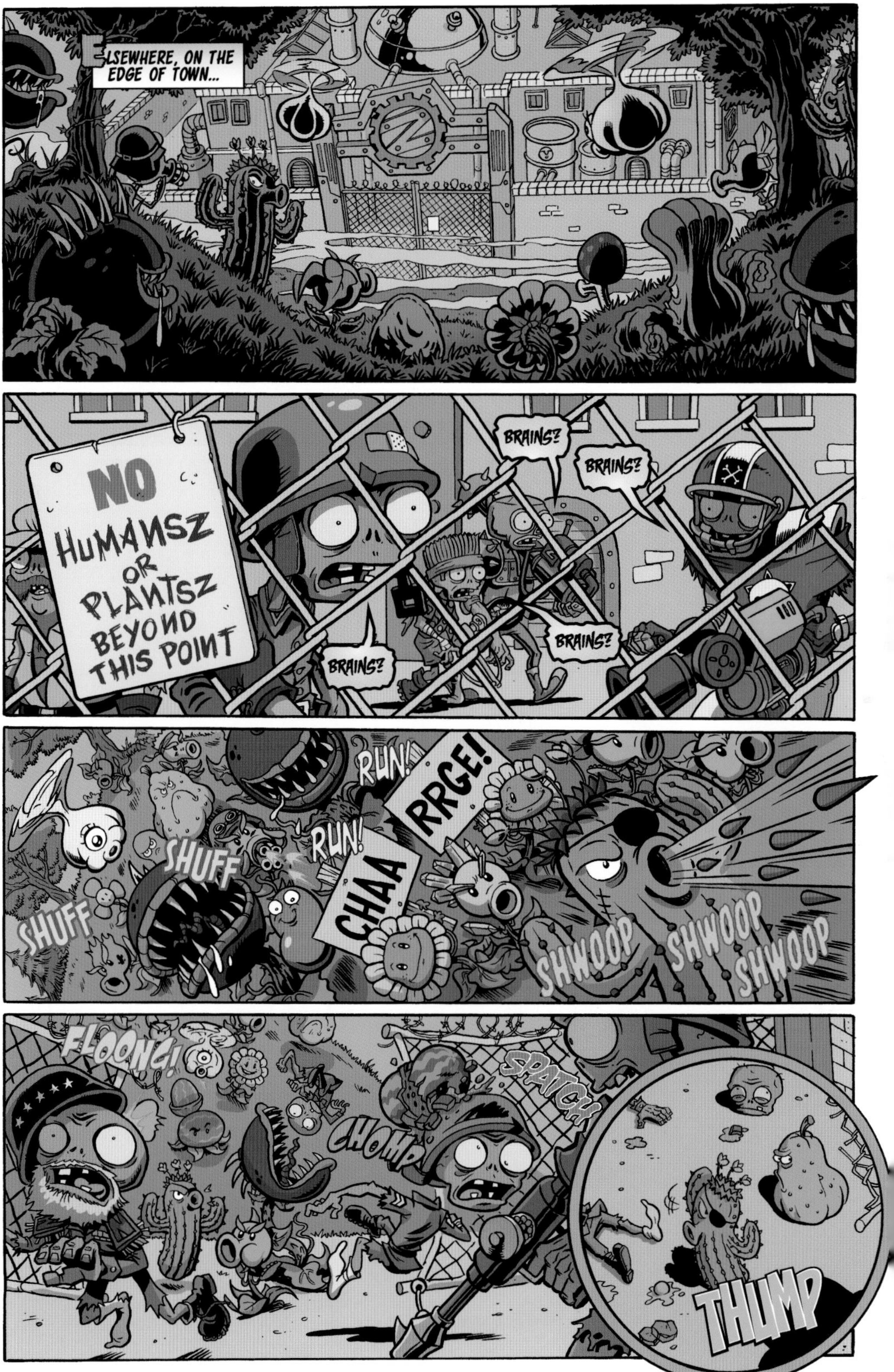
ELSEWHERE, ON THE EDGE OF TOWN...
NO HUMANSZ OR PLANTSZ BEYOND THIS POINT
BRAINS?
BRAINS?
BRAINS?
BRAINS?
RUN!
RUN!
CHAA RRGE!
SHUFF
SHUFF
SHWOOP
SHWOOP
SHWOOP
FLOONG!
SPATCH
CHOMP
THUMP

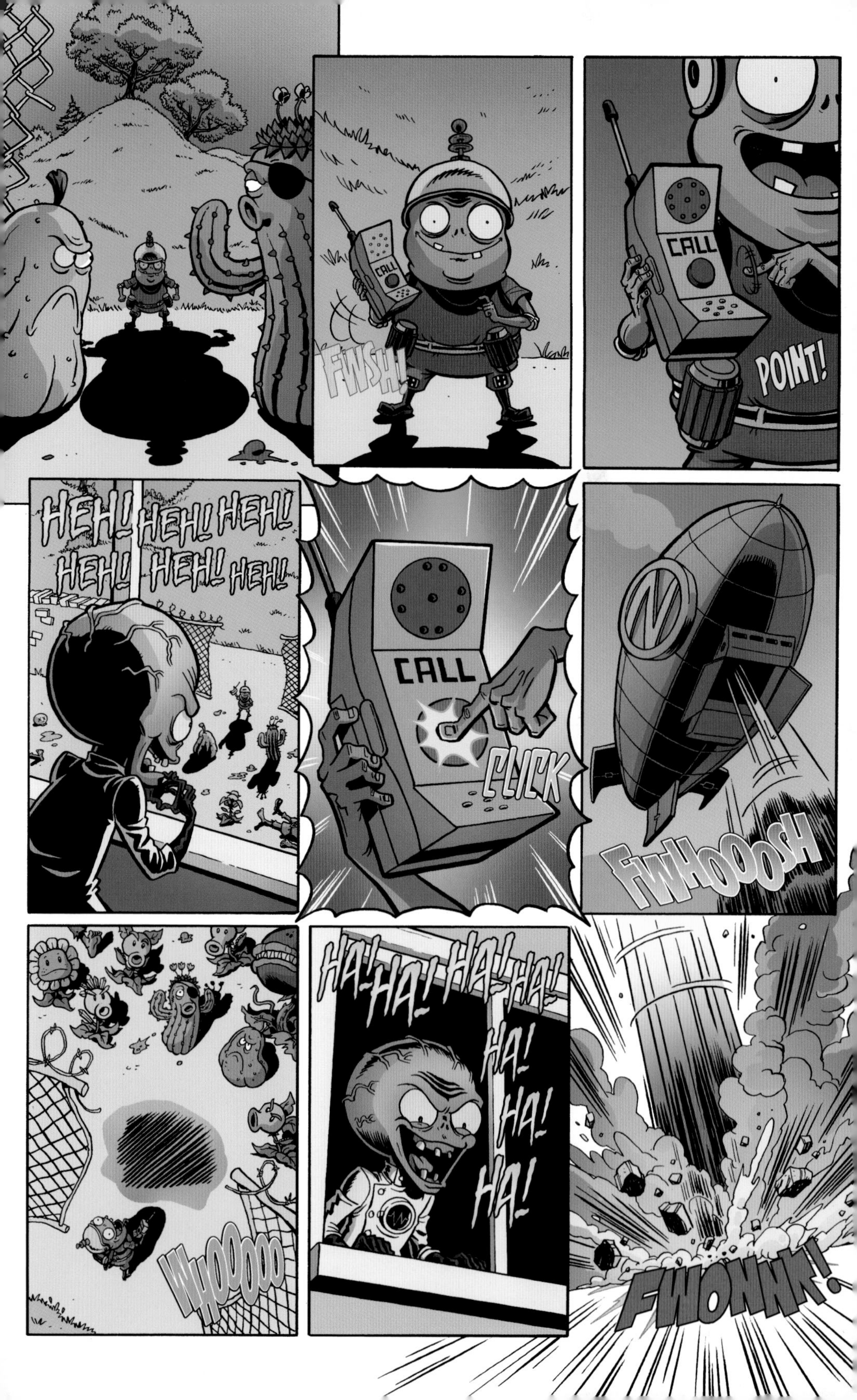
CALL
FWSH!
CALL
POINT!
HEH! HEH! HEH!
HEH! HEH! HEH!
CALL
CLICK
FWHOOOSH
WHOOOOO
HA! HA! HA! HA!
HA!
HA!
HA!
FWONK!

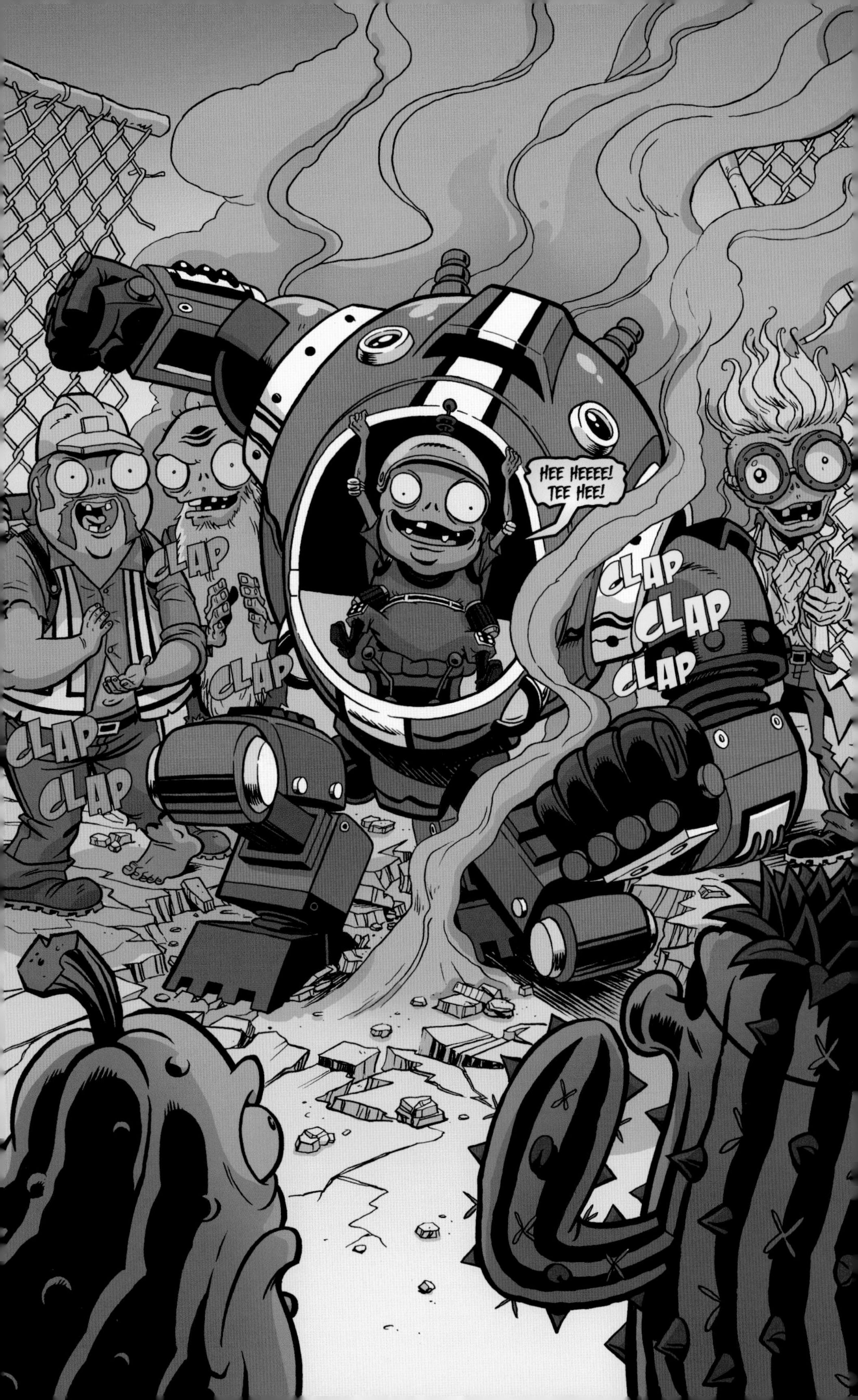
HEE HEEEE!
TEE HEE!
CLAP
CLAP
CLAP
CLAP
CLAP
CLAP
CLAP
CLAP

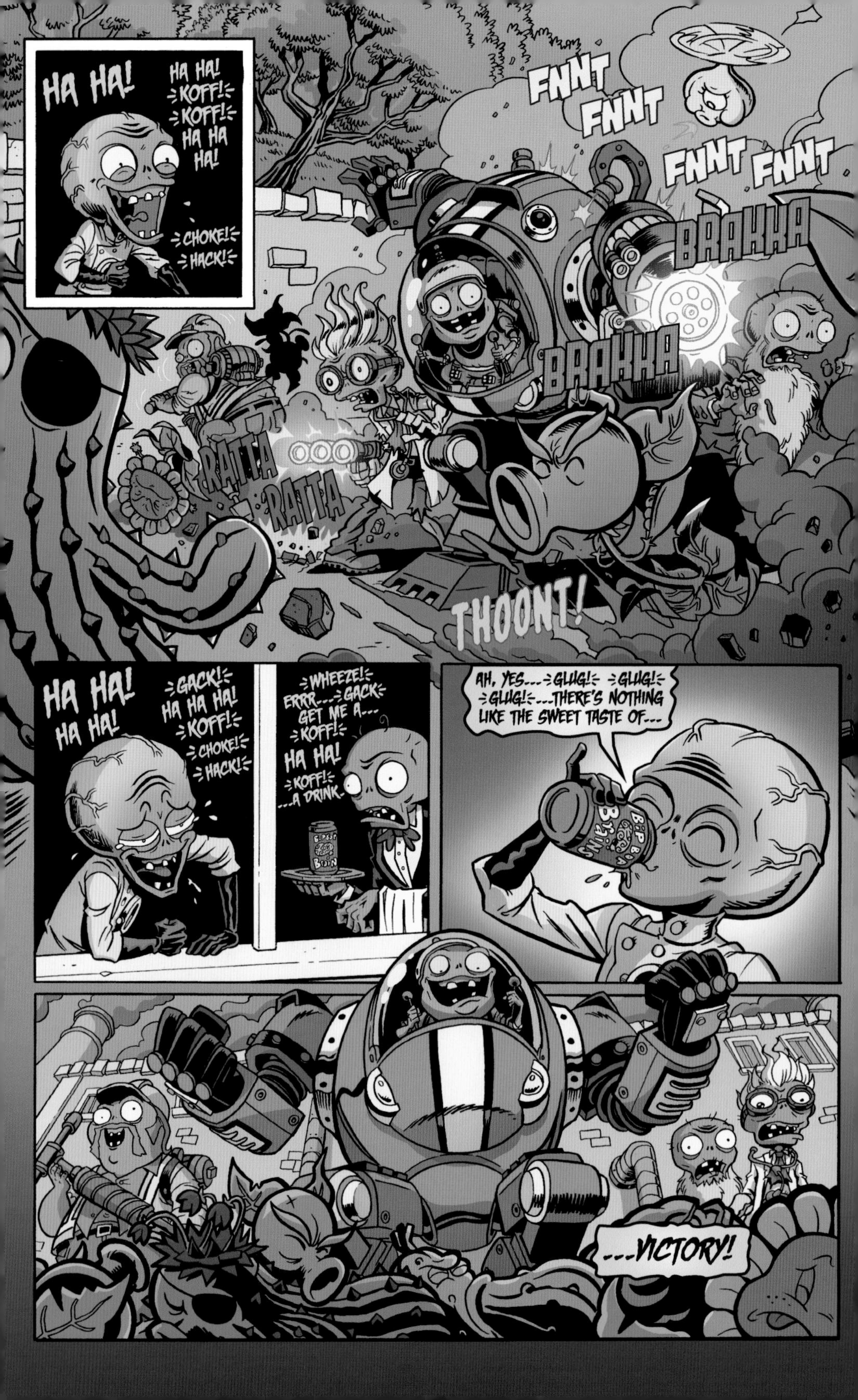
HA HA!
HA HA! KOFF! KOFF! HA HA HA!
CHOKE! HACK!
FNNT FNNT
FNNT FNNT
BRAKKA
BRAKKA
RATTA RATTA
THOONT!
HA HA! HA HA!
GACK! HA HA HA! KOFF! CHOKE! HACK!
WHEEZE! ERRR... GACK GET ME A... KOFF!
HA HA!
KOFF! ...A DRINK.
AH, YES... GLUG! GLUG! GLUG! ...THERE'S NOTHING LIKE THE SWEET TASTE OF...
...VICTORY!

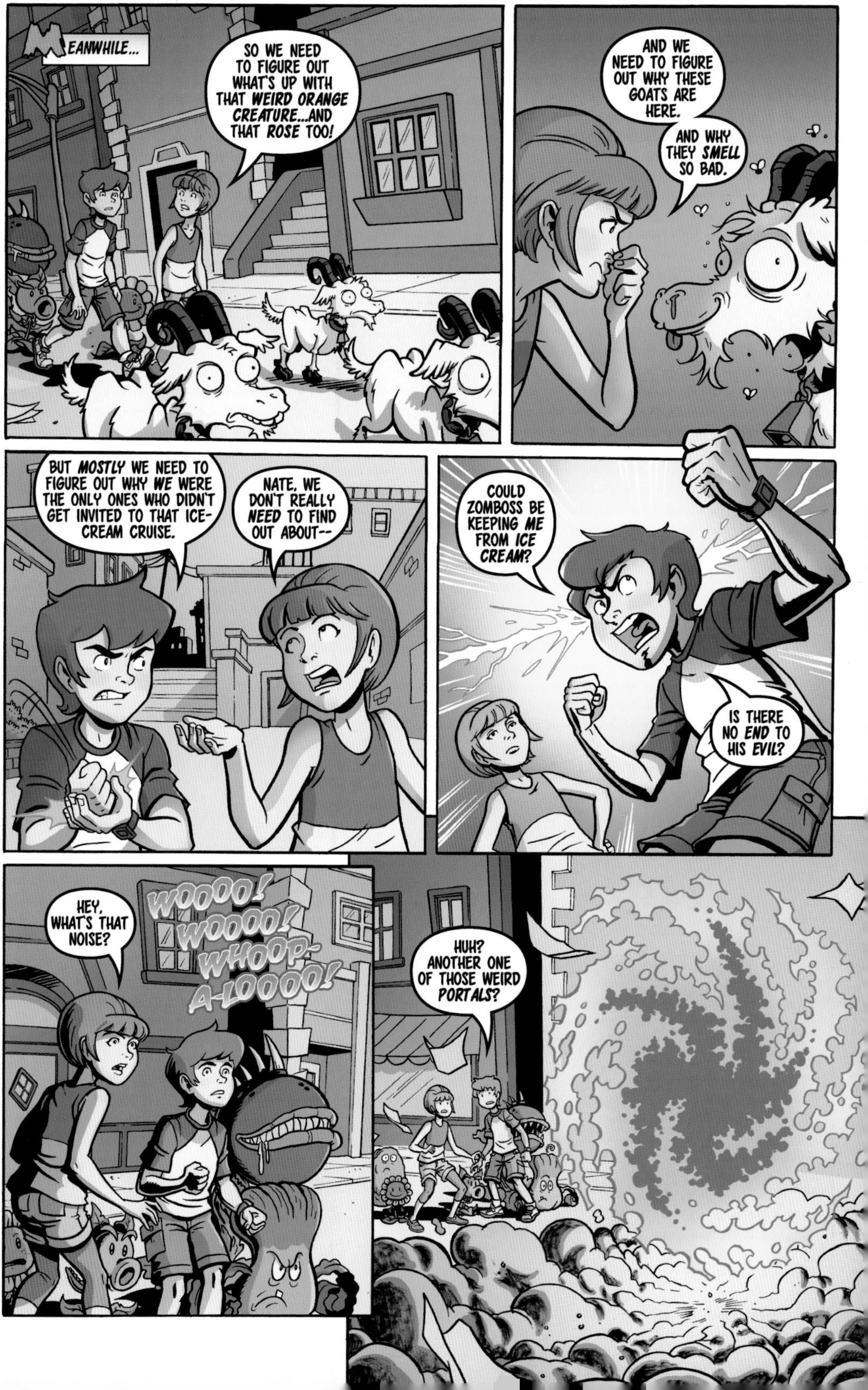
MEANWHILE...
SO WE NEED TO FIGURE OUT WHAT'S UP WITH THAT WEIRD ORANGE CREATURE...AND THAT ROSE TOO!
AND WE NEED TO FIGURE OUT WHY THESE GOATS ARE HERE.
AND WHY THEY SMELL SO BAD.
BUT MOSTLY WE NEED TO FIGURE OUT WHY WE WERE THE ONLY ONES WHO DIDN'T GET INVITED TO THAT ICE-CREAM CRUISE.
NATE, WE DON'T REALLY NEED TO FIND OUT ABOUT--
COULD ZOMBOSS BE KEEPING ME FROM ICE CREAM?
IS THERE NO END TO HIS EVIL?
HEY, WHAT'S THAT NOISE?
WOOOO! WOOOO! WHOOP-A-LOOOO!
HUH? ANOTHER ONE OF THOSE WEIRD PORTALS?

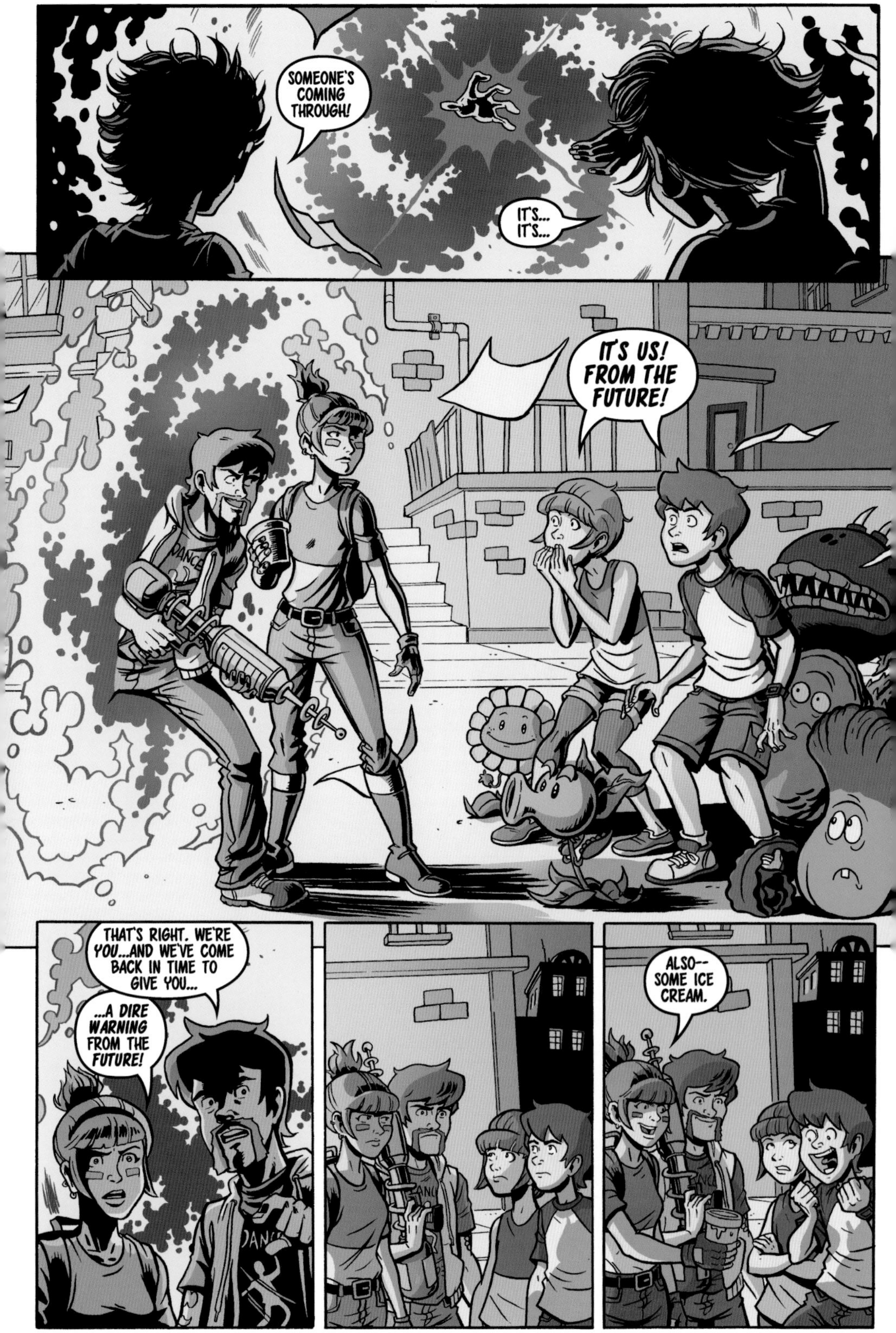
SOMEONE'S COMING THROUGH!
IT'S... IT'S...
IT'S US! FROM THE FUTURE!
THAT'S RIGHT. WE'RE YOU...AND WE'VE COME BACK IN TIME TO GIVE YOU...
...A DIRE WARNING FROM THE FUTURE!
ALSO-- SOME ICE CREAM.

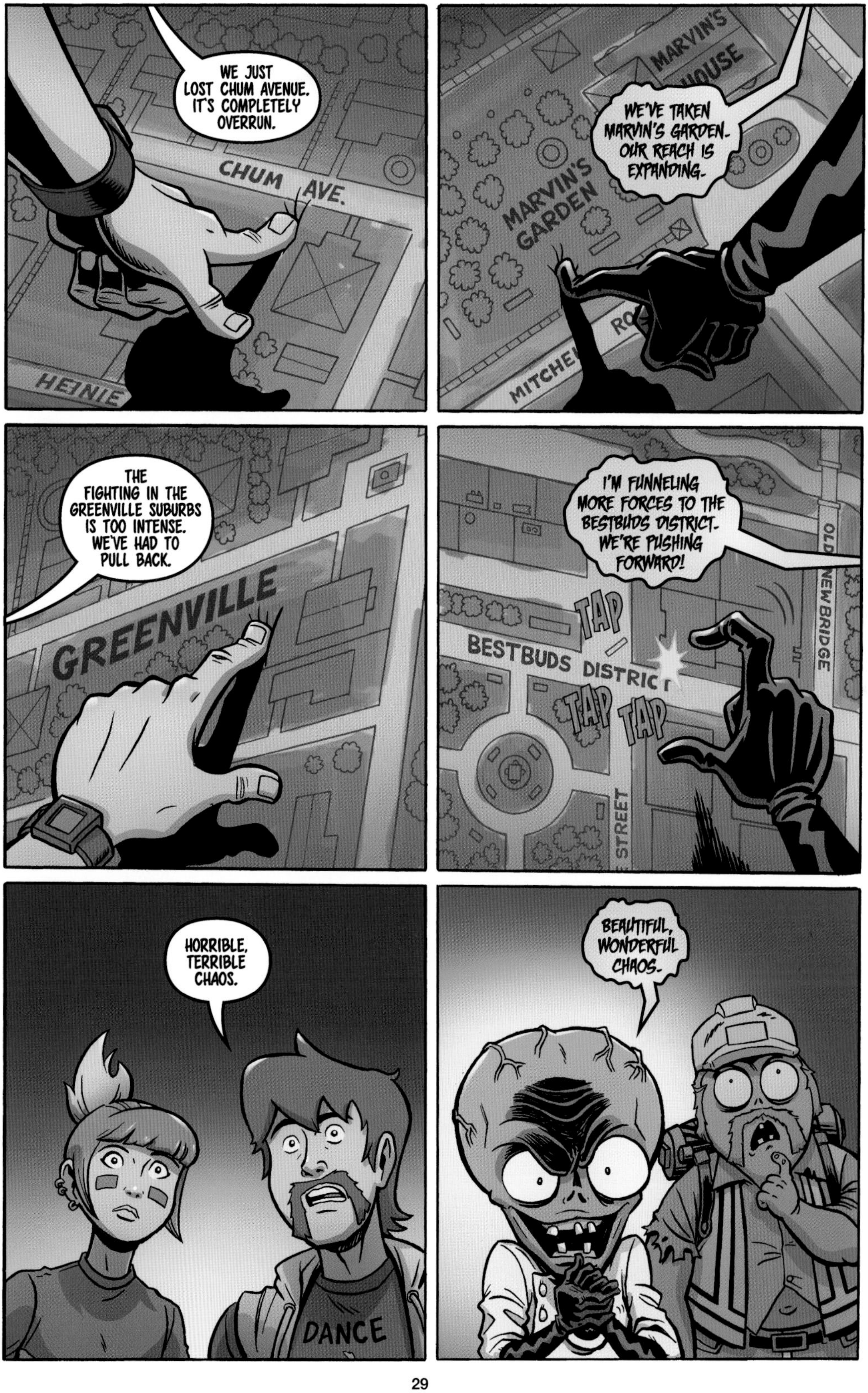
WE JUST LOST CHUM AVENUE. IT'S COMPLETELY OVERRUN.
CHUM AVE.
HEINIE
MARVIN'S HOUSE
WE'VE TAKEN MARVIN'S GARDEN. OUR REACH IS EXPANDING.
MARVIN'S GARDEN
MITCHE
RO
THE FIGHTING IN THE GREENVILLE SUBURBS IS TOO INTENSE. WE'VE HAD TO PULL BACK.
GREENVILLE
I'M FUNNELING MORE FORCES TO THE BESTBUDS DISTRICT. WE'RE PUSHING FORWARD!
OLD NEWBRIDGE
TAP
BESTBUDS DISTRICT
TAP TAP
STREET
HORRIBLE, TERRIBLE CHAOS.
DANCE
BEAUTIFUL, WONDERFUL CHAOS.

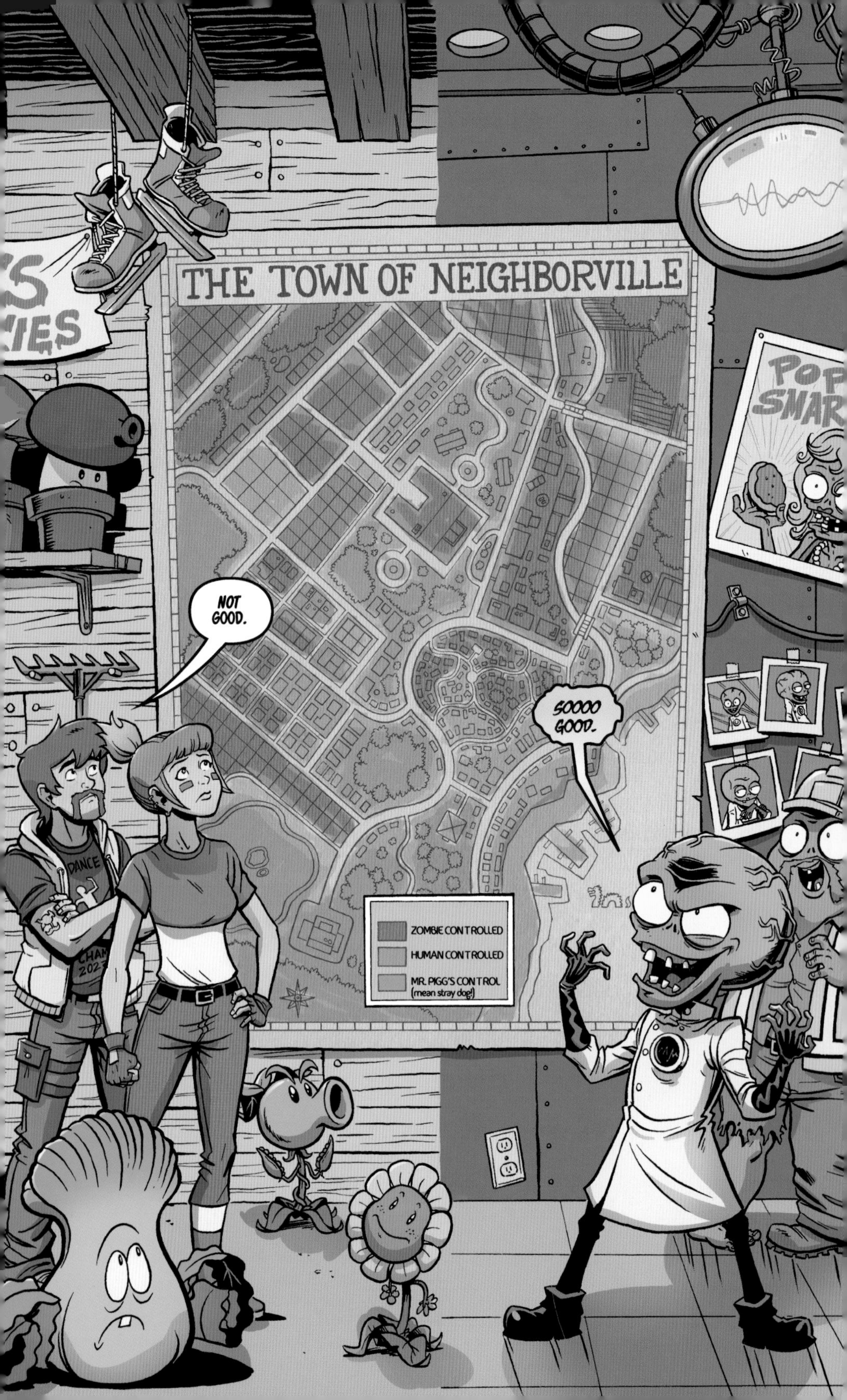
THE TOWN OF NEIGHBORVILLE
ZOMBIE CONTROLLED
HUMAN CONTROLLED
MR. PIGG'S CONTROL (mean stray dog!)
NOT GOOD.
SOOOO GOOD.
DANCE

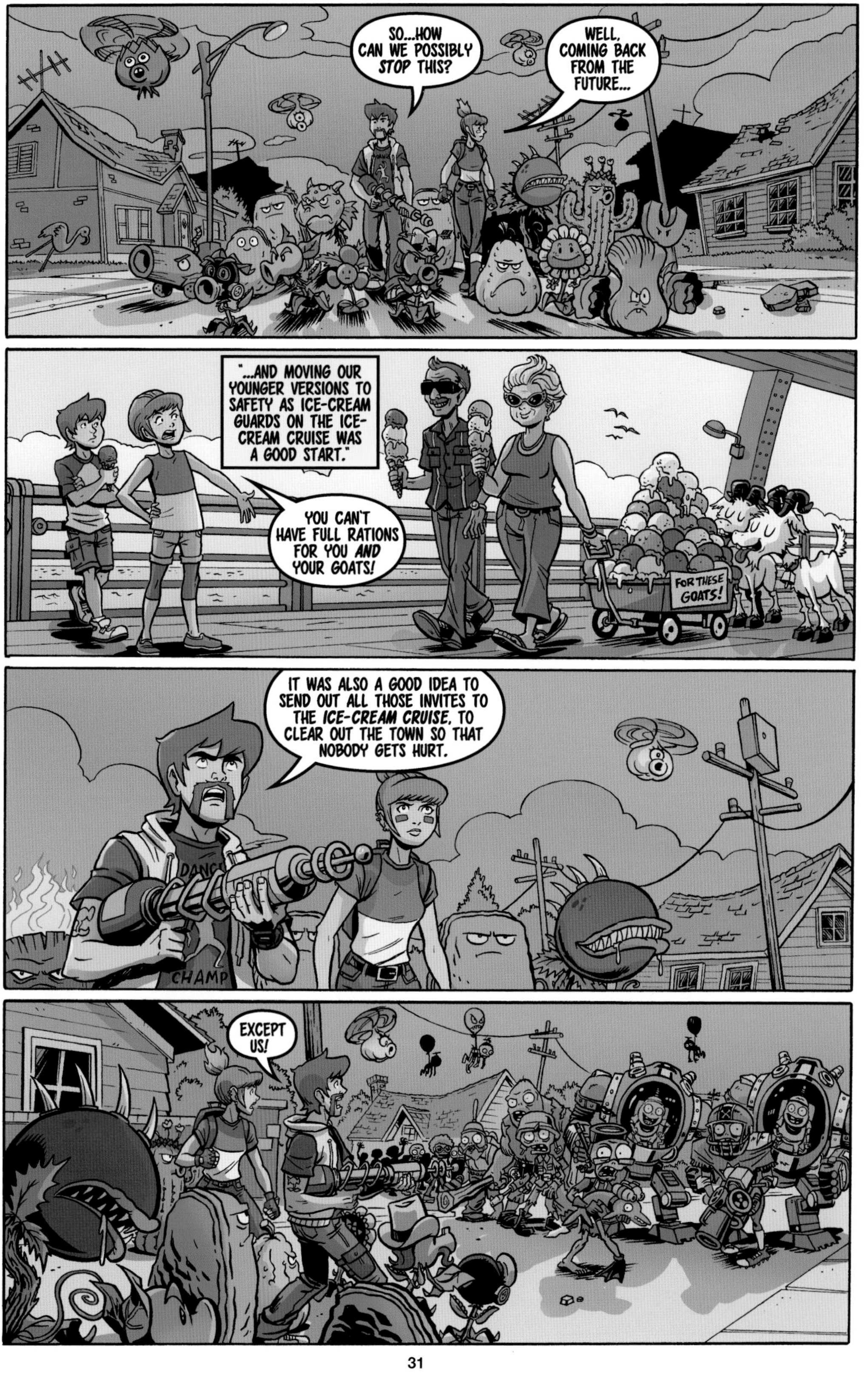
SO...HOW CAN WE POSSIBLY STOP THIS?
WELL, COMING BACK FROM THE FUTURE...
"...AND MOVING OUR YOUNGER VERSIONS TO SAFETY AS ICE-CREAM GUARDS ON THE ICE-CREAM CRUISE WAS A GOOD START."
YOU CAN'T HAVE FULL RATIONS FOR YOU AND YOUR GOATS!
FOR THESE GOATS!
IT WAS ALSO A GOOD IDEA TO SEND OUT ALL THOSE INVITES TO THE ICE-CREAM CRUISE, TO CLEAR OUT THE TOWN SO THAT NOBODY GETS HURT.
CHAMP
EXCEPT US!

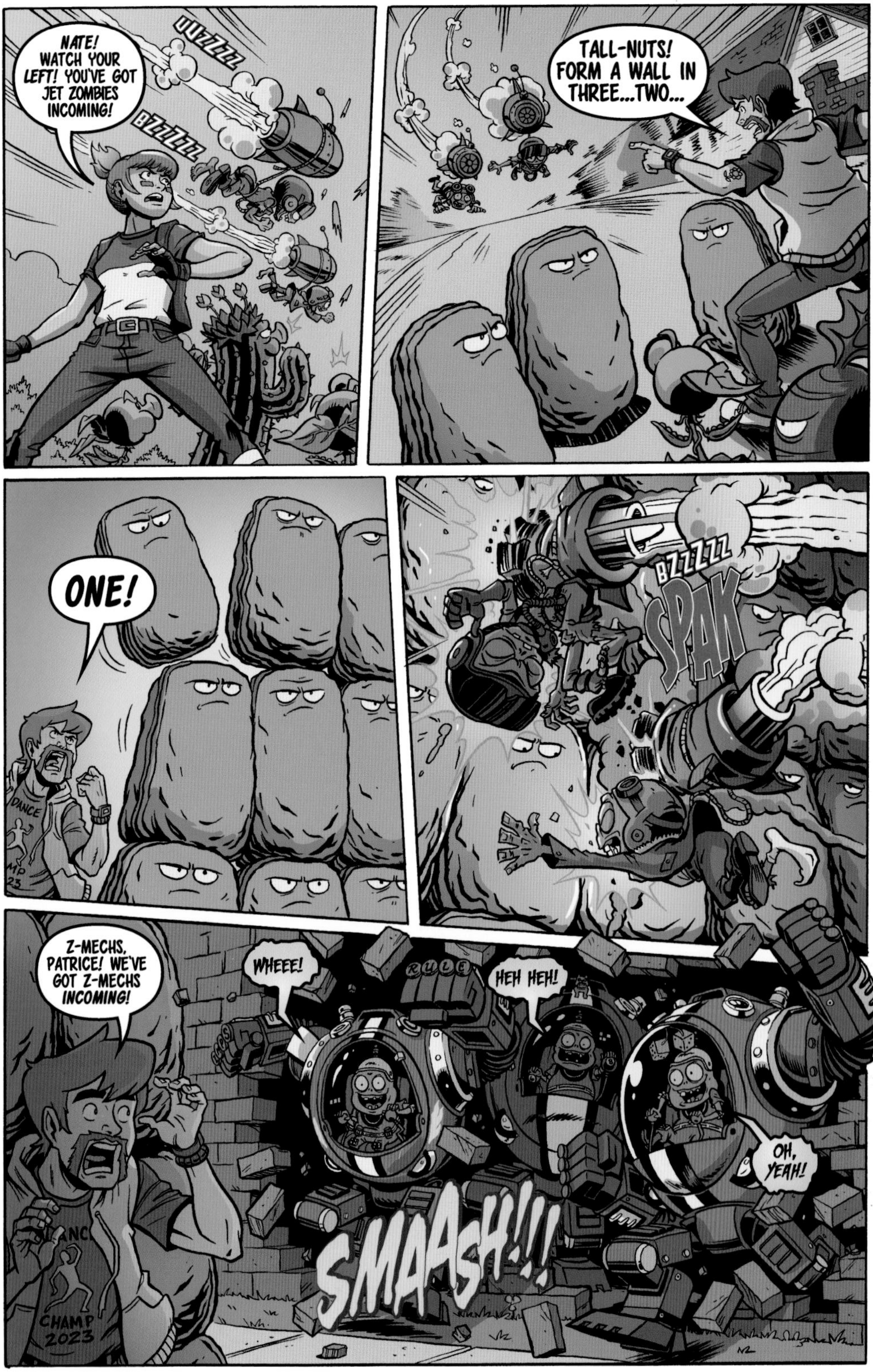
NATE! WATCH YOUR LEFT! YOU'VE GOT JET ZOMBIES INCOMING!
BZZZZZ
BZZZZZ
TALL-NUTS! FORM A WALL IN THREE...TWO...
ONE!
DANCE
BZZZZZ
SPAK
Z-MECHS, PATRICE! WE'VE GOT Z-MECHS INCOMING!
WHEEE!
HEH HEH!
OH, YEAH!
SMAASH!!!
CHAMP 2023

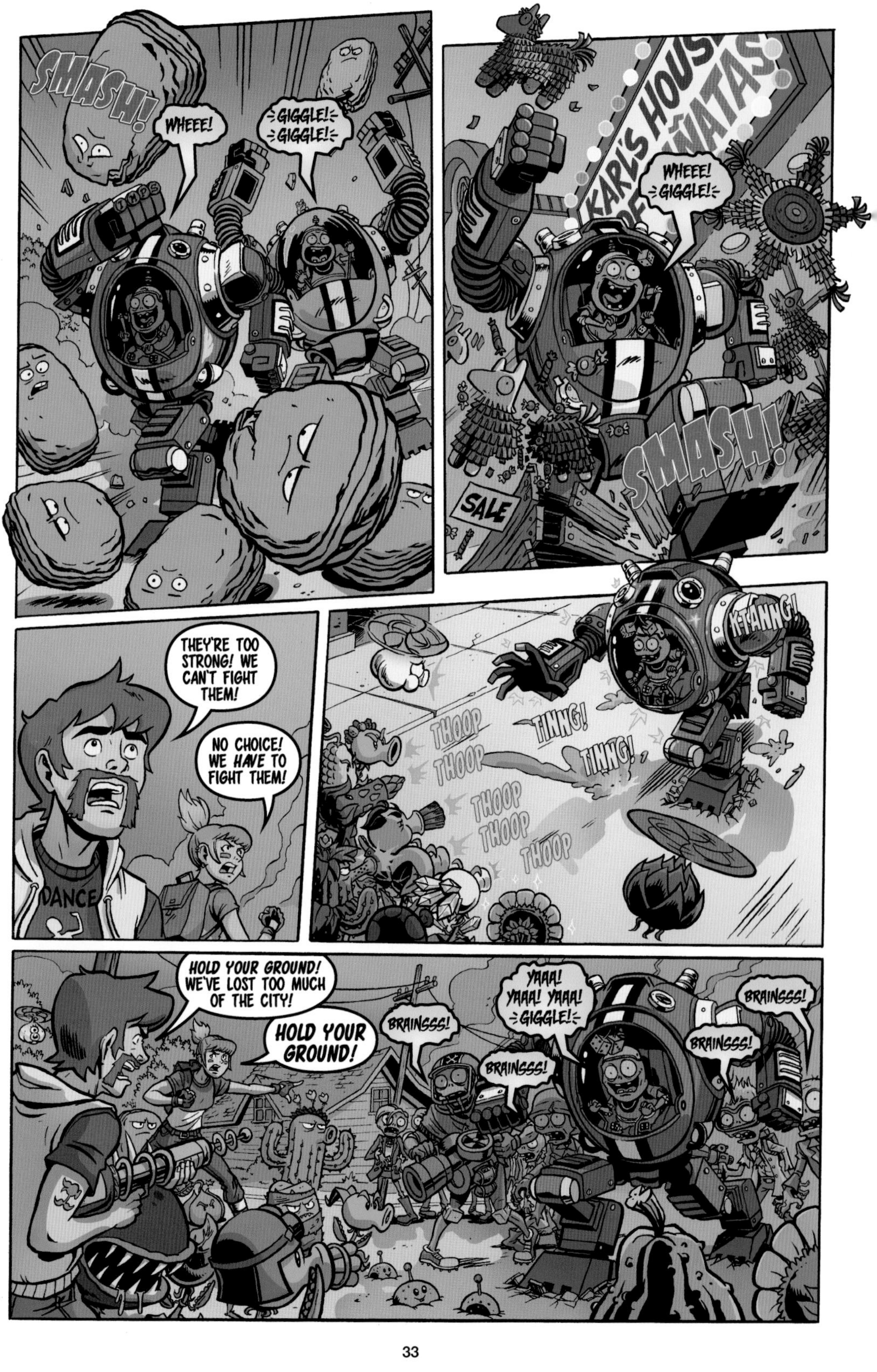
SMASH!
WHEEE!
GIGGLE! GIGGLE!
KARL'S HOUS
WHEEE! GIGGLE!
SMASH!
SALE
THEY'RE TOO STRONG! WE CAN'T FIGHT THEM!
NO CHOICE! WE HAVE TO FIGHT THEM!
DANCE
K-TANNG!
THOOP THOOP
TINNG!
TINNG!
THOOP THOOP THOOP
HOLD YOUR GROUND! WE'VE LOST TOO MUCH OF THE CITY!
HOLD YOUR GROUND!
BRAINSSS!
BRAINSSS!
YAAA! YAAA! YAAA! GIGGLE!
BRAINSSS!
BRAINSSS!

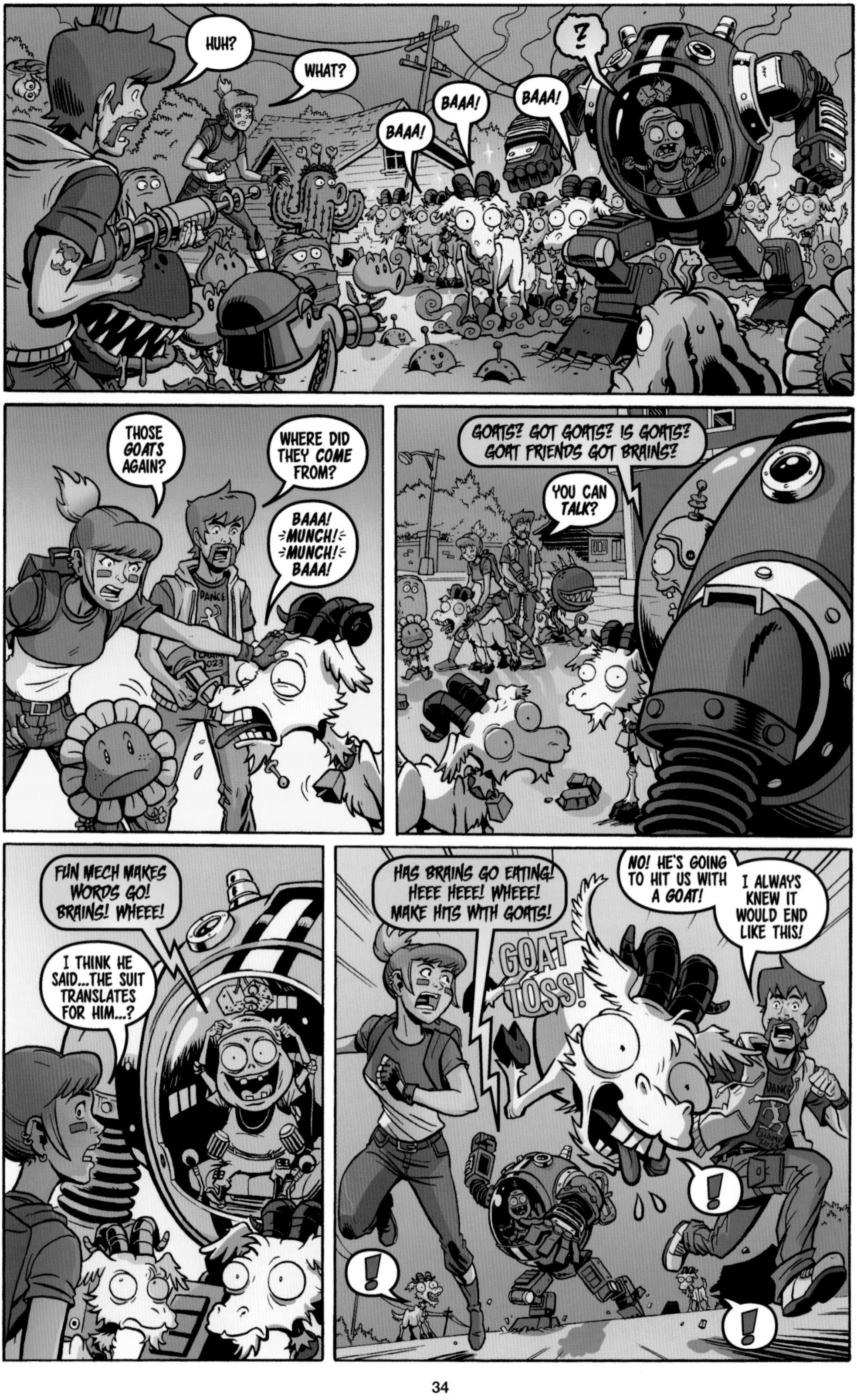
HUH?
WHAT?
BAAA!
BAAA!
BAAA!
?
THOSE GOATS AGAIN?
WHERE DID THEY COME FROM?
BAAA! MUNCH! MUNCH! BAAA!
GOATS? GOT GOATS? IS GOATS? GOAT FRIENDS GOT BRAINS?
YOU CAN TALK?
FUN MECH MAKES WORDS GO! BRAINS! WHEEE!
I THINK HE SAID...THE SUIT TRANSLATES FOR HIM...?
HAS BRAINS GO EATING! HEEE HEEE! WHEEE! MAKE HITS WITH GOATS!
NO! HE'S GOING TO HIT US WITH A GOAT!
I ALWAYS KNEW IT WOULD END LIKE THIS!
GOAT TOSS!
!
!
!

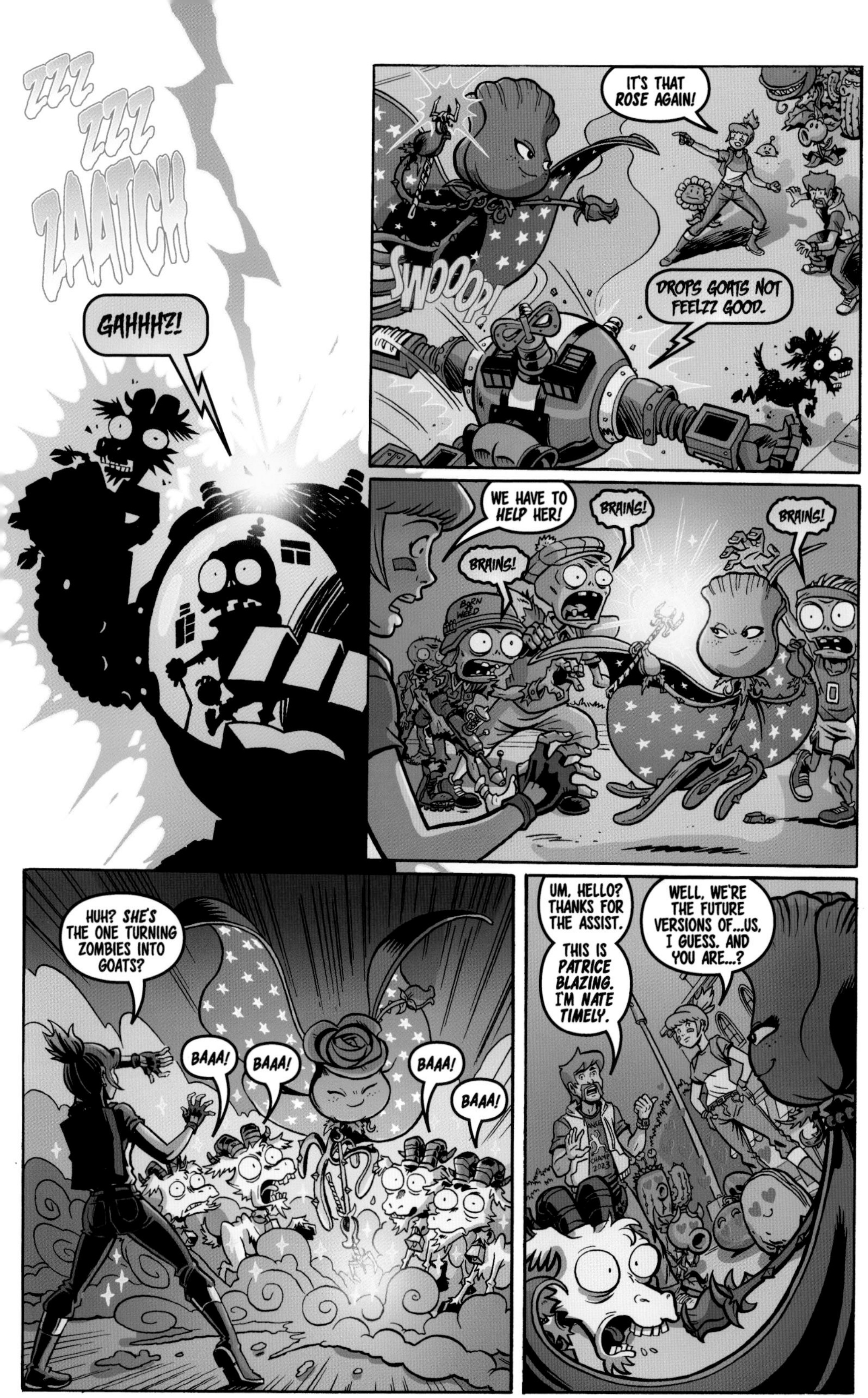
ZZZ ZZZ ZAATCH
GAHHHZ!
IT'S THAT ROSE AGAIN!
SWOOOP!
DROPS GOATS NOT FEELZZ GOOD.
WE HAVE TO HELP HER!
BRAINS!
BRAINS!
BRAINS!
HUH? SHE'S THE ONE TURNING ZOMBIES INTO GOATS?
BAAA!
BAAA!
BAAA!
BAAA!
UM, HELLO? THANKS FOR THE ASSIST.
THIS IS PATRICE BLAZING. I'M NATE TIMELY.
WELL, WE'RE THE FUTURE VERSIONS OF...US, I GUESS. AND YOU ARE...?

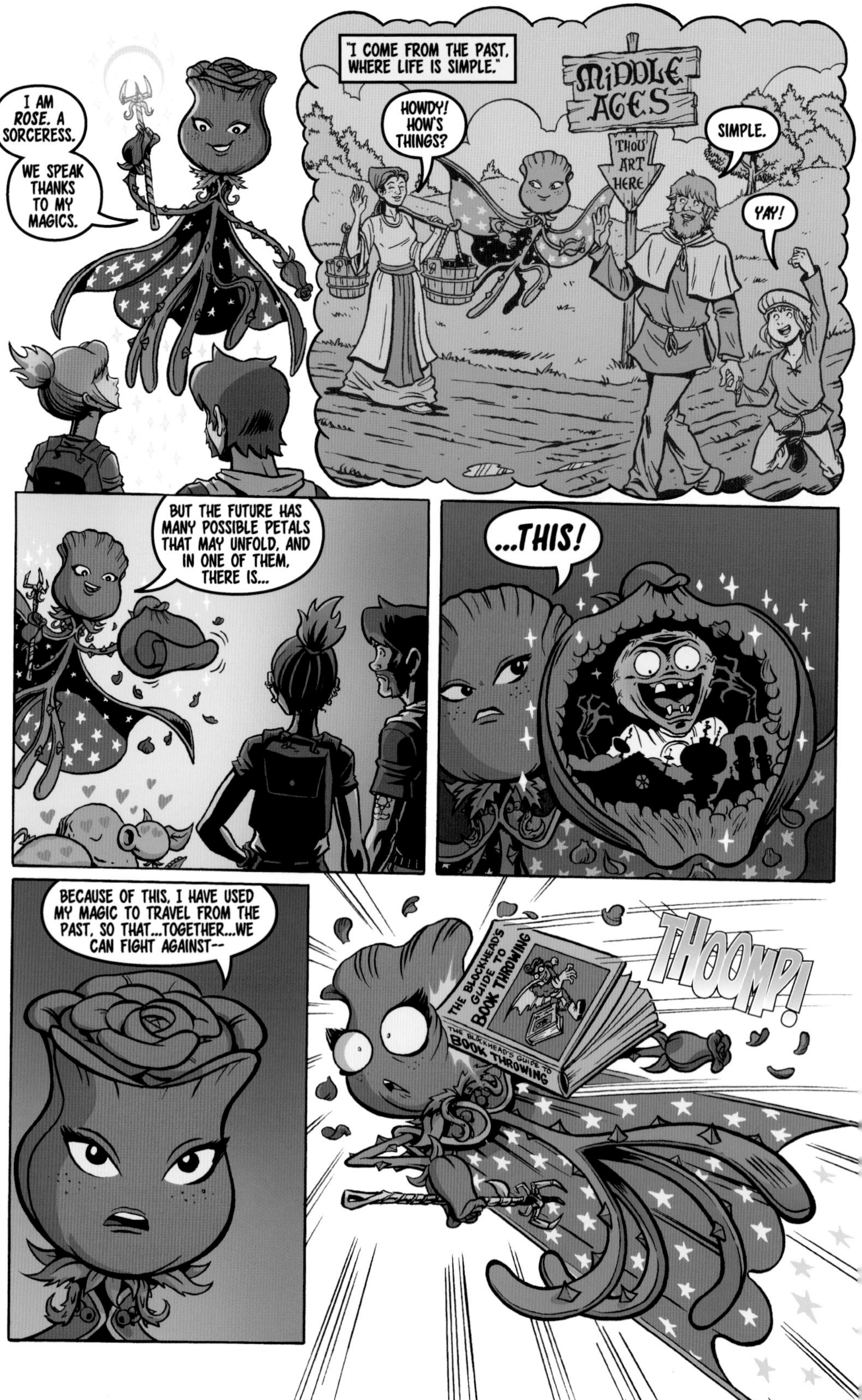
I AM ROSE. A SORCERESS.
WE SPEAK THANKS TO MY MAGICS.
"I COME FROM THE PAST, WHERE LIFE IS SIMPLE."
MIDDLE AGES
HOWDY! HOW'S THINGS?
THOU ART HERE
SIMPLE.
YAY!
BUT THE FUTURE HAS MANY POSSIBLE PETALS THAT MAY UNFOLD, AND IN ONE OF THEM, THERE IS...
...THIS!
BECAUSE OF THIS, I HAVE USED MY MAGIC TO TRAVEL FROM THE PAST, SO THAT...TOGETHER...WE CAN FIGHT AGAINST--
THE BLOCKHEAD'S GUIDE TO BOOK THROWING
THE BLOCKHEAD'S GUIDE TO BOOK THROWING
THOOMP!

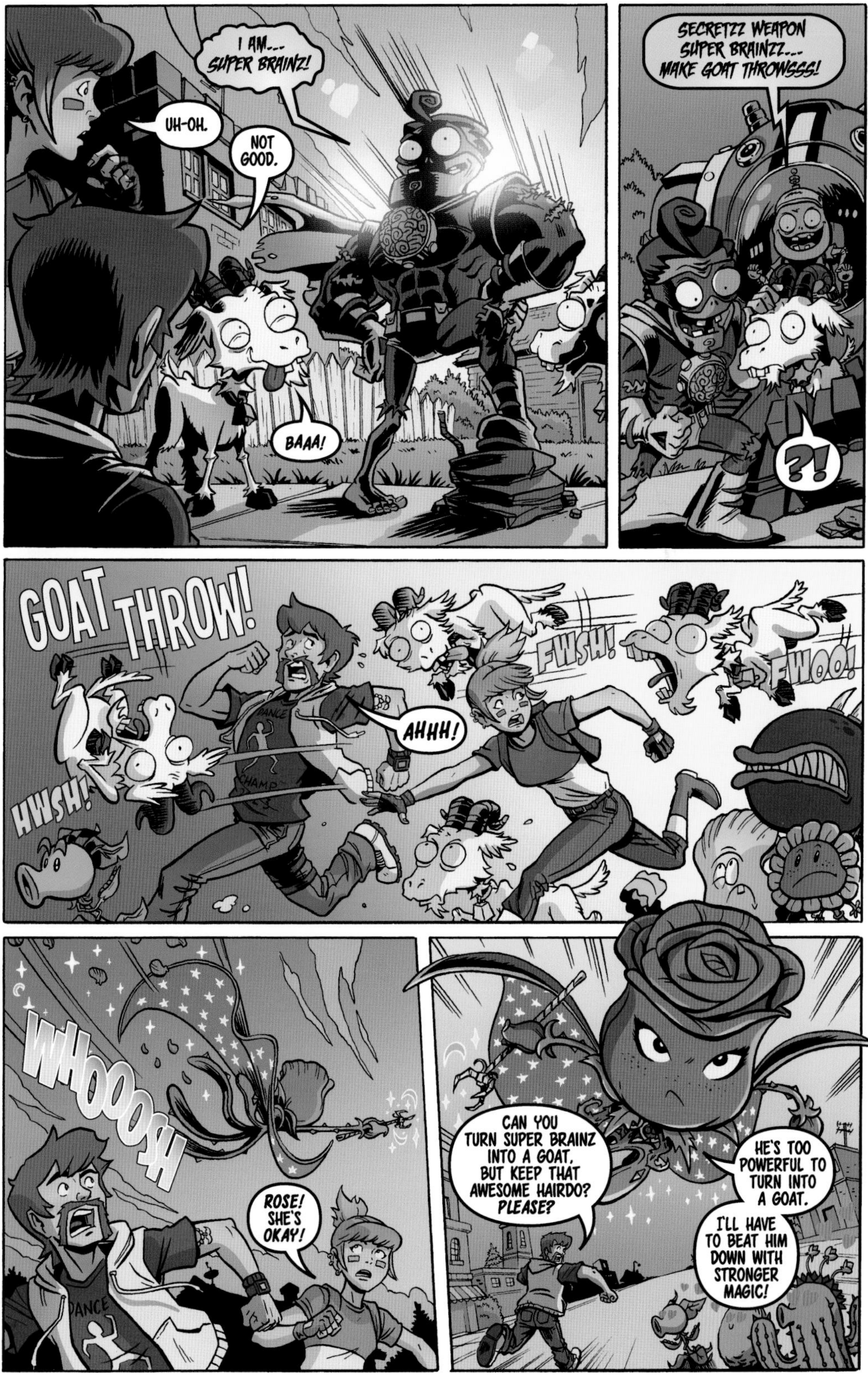
I AM... SUPER BRAINZ!
UH-OH.
NOT GOOD.
BAAA!
SECRETZZ WEAPON SUPER BRAINZZ... MAKE GOAT THROWSSS!
?!
GOAT THROW!
HWSH!
DANCE CHAMP
AHHH!
FWSH!
FWOO!
WHOOOOSH
ROSE! SHE'S OKAY!
DANCE
CAN YOU TURN SUPER BRAINZ INTO A GOAT, BUT KEEP THAT AWESOME HAIRDO? PLEASE?
HE'S TOO POWERFUL TO TURN INTO A GOAT.
I'LL HAVE TO BEAT HIM DOWN WITH STRONGER MAGIC!

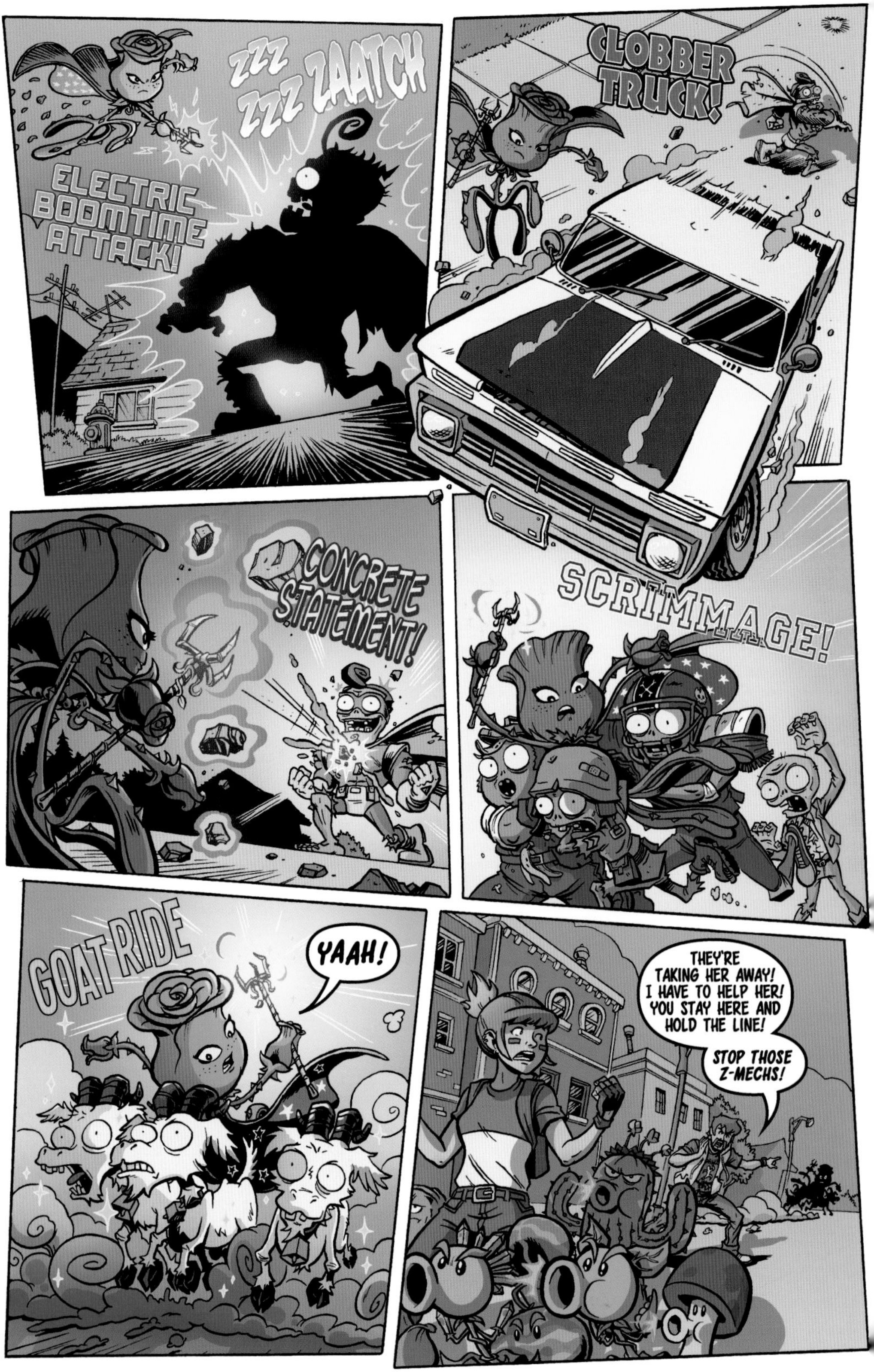
ZZZ ZZZ ZAATCH
ELECTRIC BOOMTIME ATTACK!
CLOBBER TRUCK!
CONCRETE STATEMENT!
SCRIMMAGE!
GOAT RIDE
YAAH!
THEY'RE TAKING HER AWAY! I HAVE TO HELP HER! YOU STAY HERE AND HOLD THE LINE!
STOP THOSE Z-MECHS!

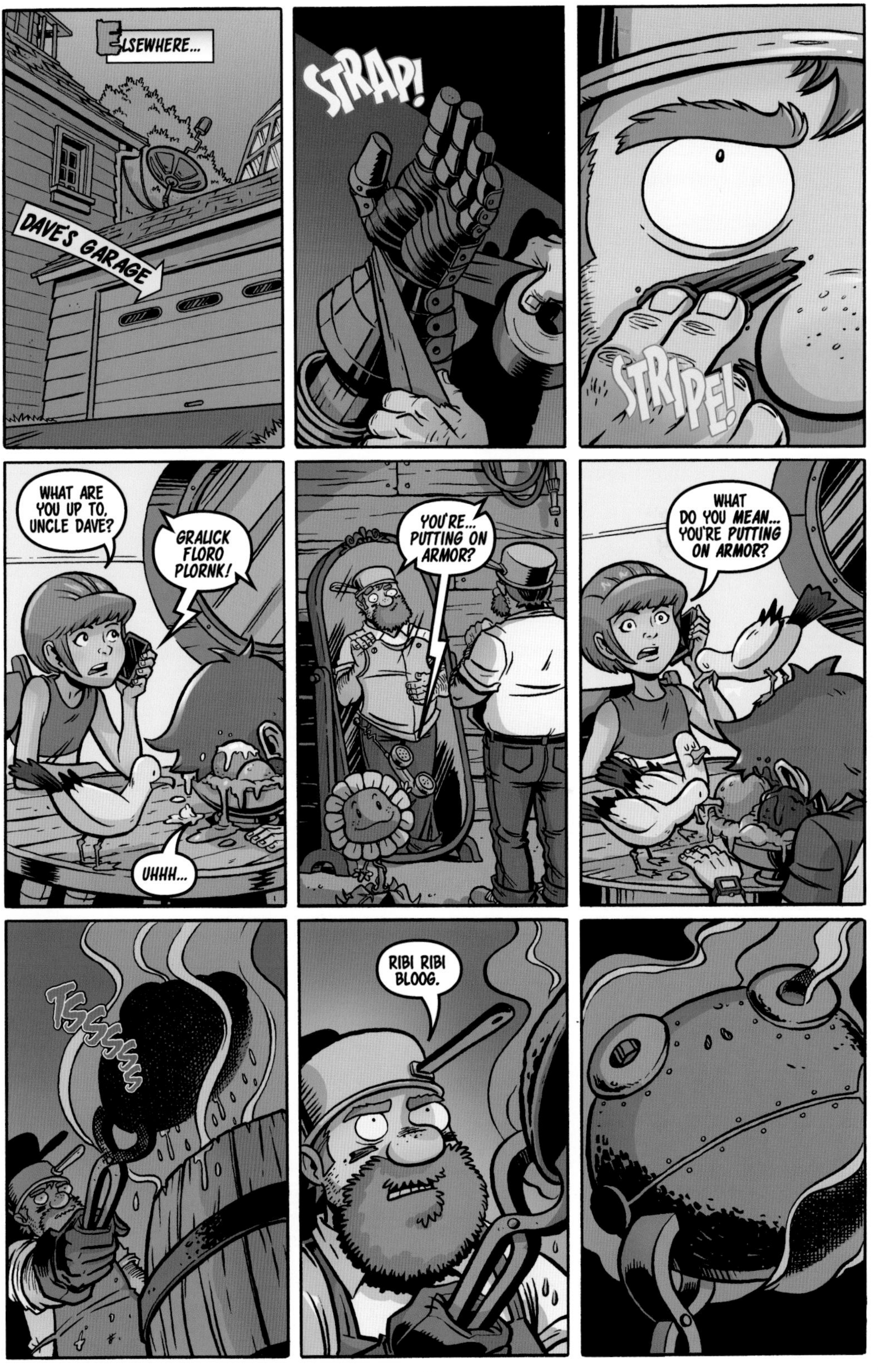
ELSEWHERE...
DAVE'S GARAGE
STRAP!
STRIPE!
WHAT ARE YOU UP TO, UNCLE DAVE?
GRALICK FLORO PLORNK!
UHHH...
YOU'RE... PUTTING ON ARMOR?
WHAT DO YOU MEAN... YOU'RE PUTTING ON ARMOR?
TSSSSSS
RIBI RIBI BLOOG.

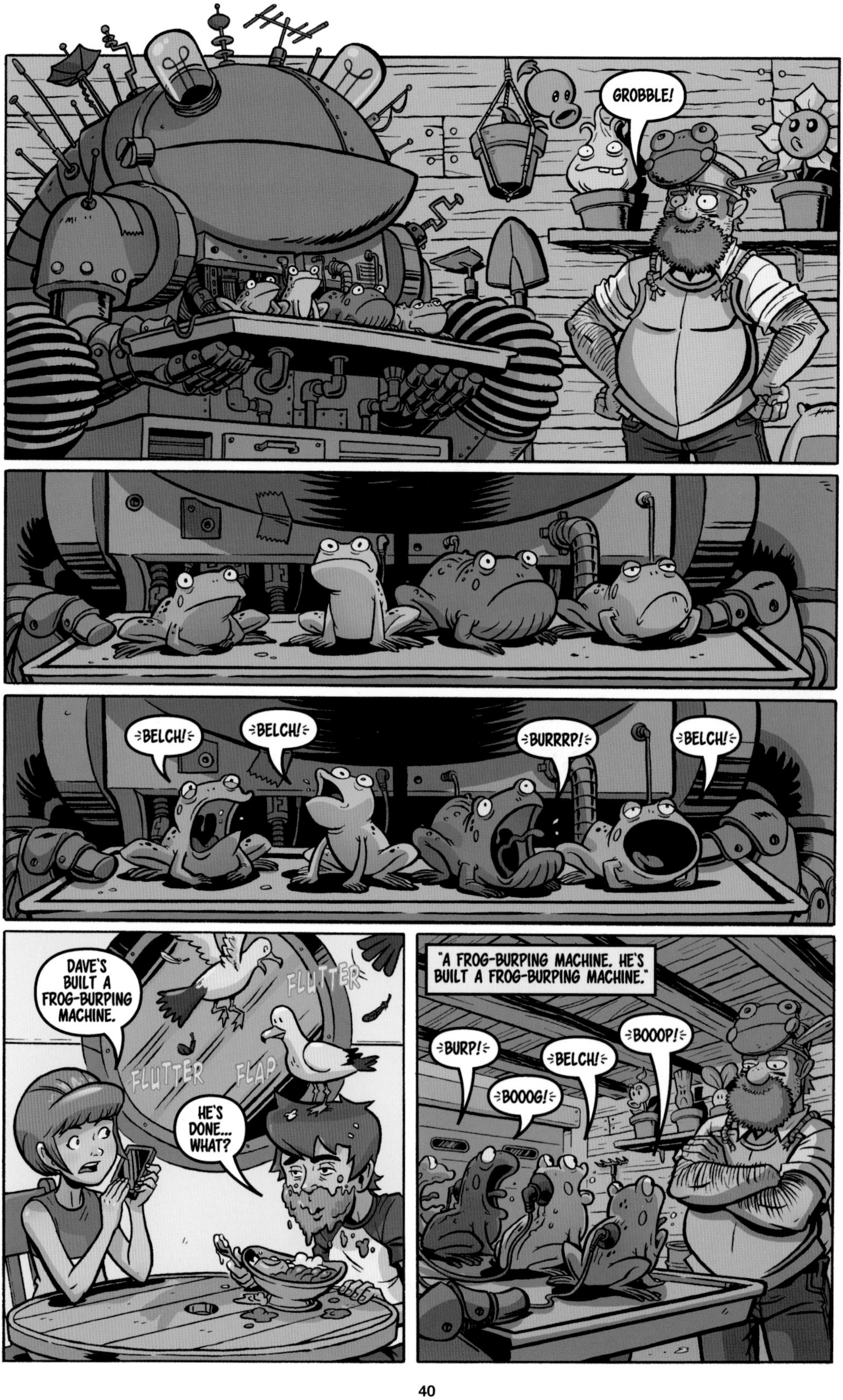

GROBBLE!
BELCH!
BELCH!
BURRRP!
BELCH!
DAVE'S BUILT A FROG-BURPING MACHINE.
FLUTTER
FLUTTER
FLAP
HE'S DONE... WHAT?
"A FROG-BURPING MACHINE. HE'S BUILT A FROG-BURPING MACHINE."
BURP!
BOOOG!
BELCH!
BOOOP!

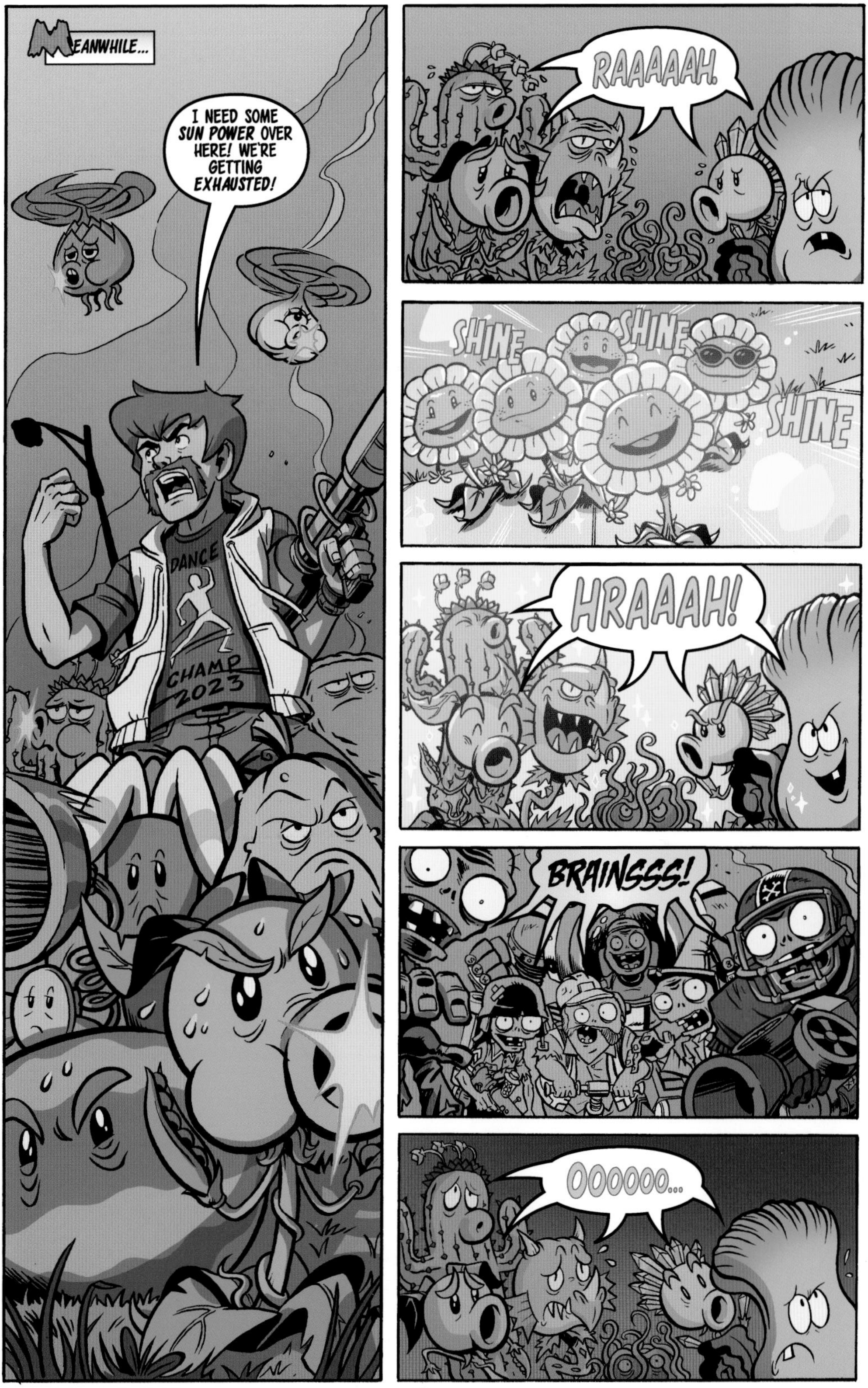
MEANWHILE...
I NEED SOME SUN POWER OVER HERE! WE'RE GETTING EXHAUSTED!
DANCE CHAMP 2023
RAAAAAH.
SHINE
SHINE
SHINE
HRAAAH!
BRAINSSS!
OOOOOO...

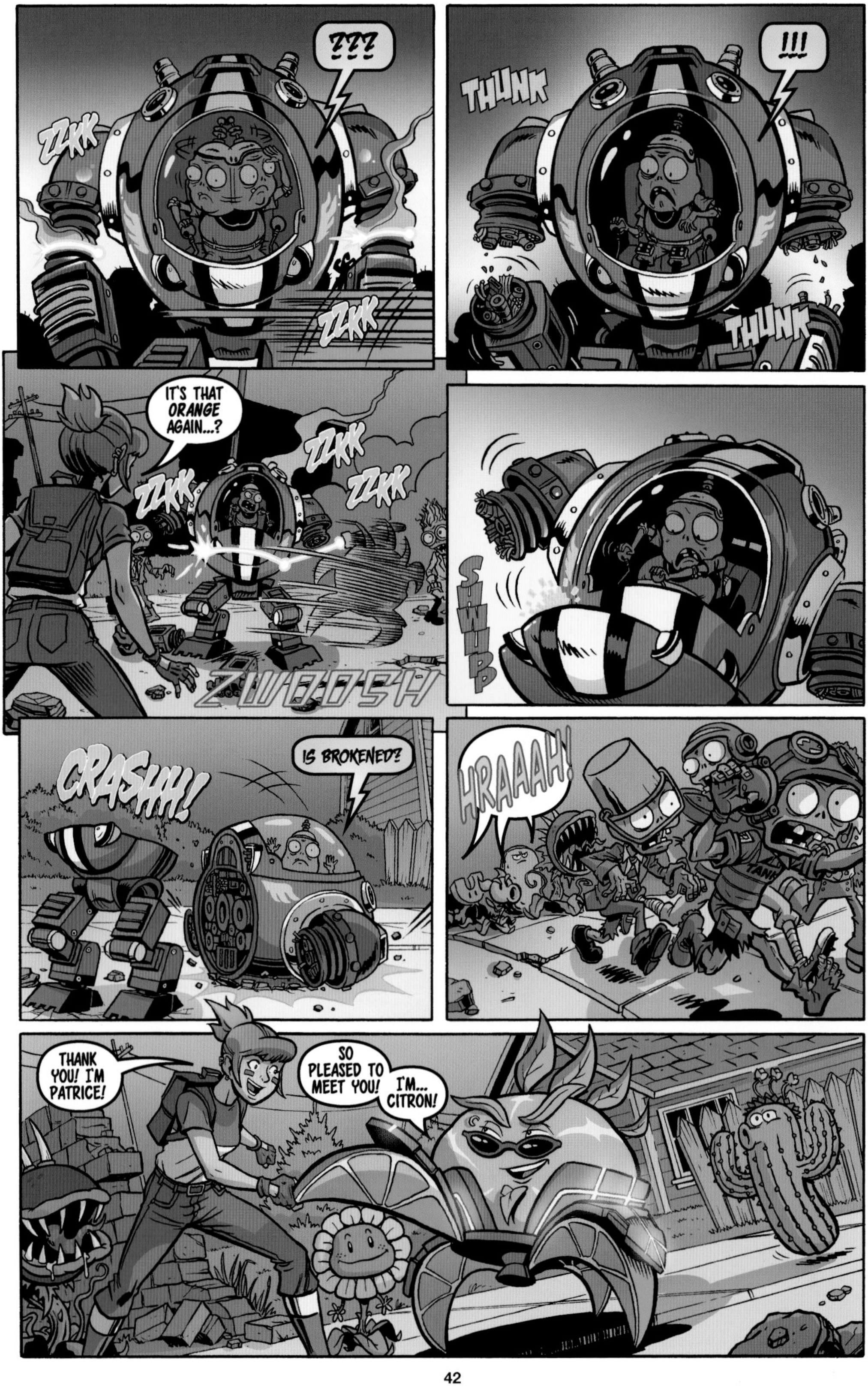
???
ZZKK
ZZKK
!!!
THUNK
THUNK
IT'S THAT ORANGE AGAIN...?
ZZKK
ZZKK
ZZKK
ZWOOSH
SHWUPP
CRASHH!
IS BROKENED?
HRAAAH!
THANK YOU! I'M PATRICE!
SO PLEASED TO MEET YOU!
I'M... CITRON!

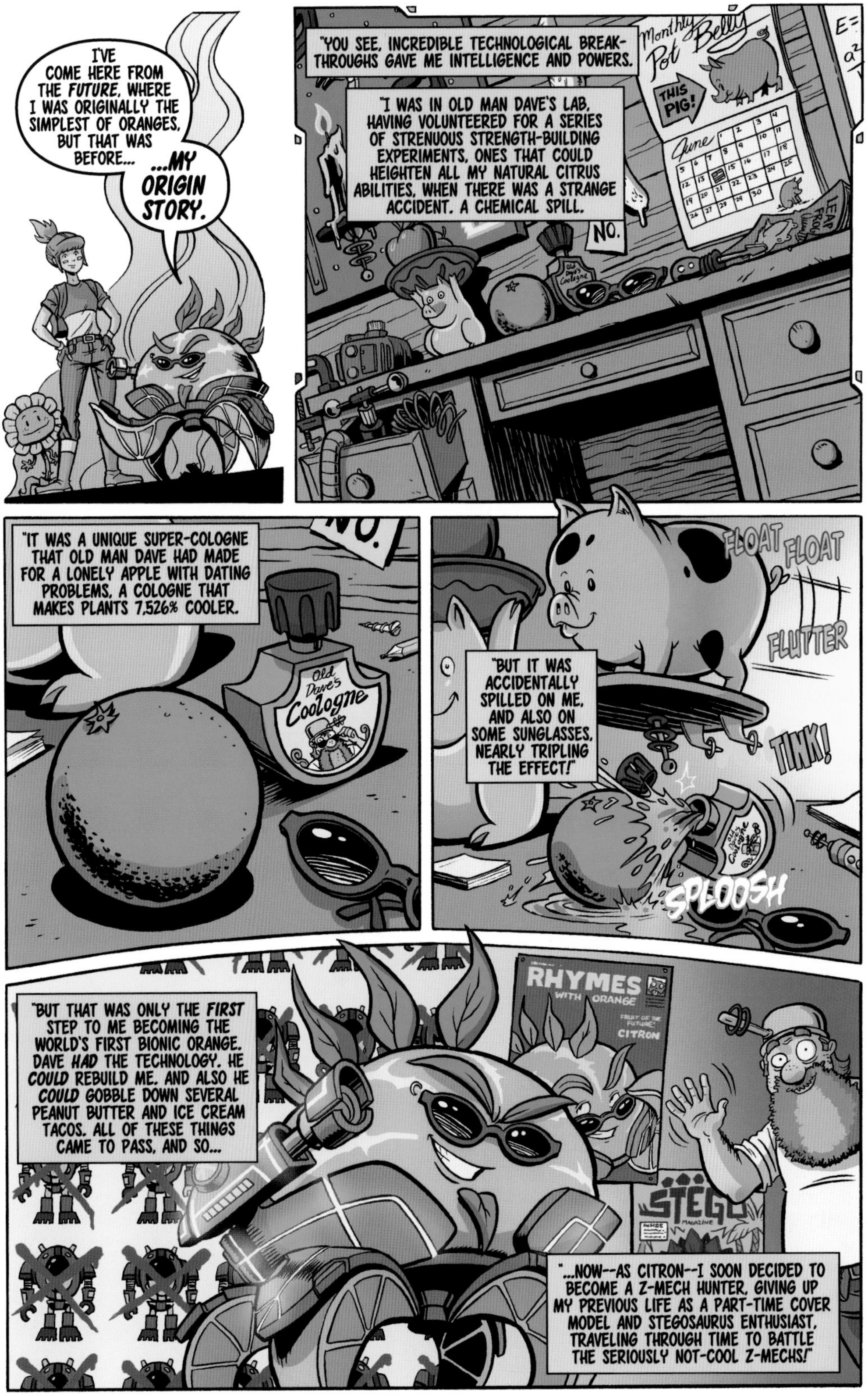
I'VE COME HERE FROM THE FUTURE, WHERE I WAS ORIGINALLY THE SIMPLEST OF ORANGES, BUT THAT WAS BEFORE...
...MY ORIGIN STORY.
"YOU SEE, INCREDIBLE TECHNOLOGICAL BREAKTHROUGHS GAVE ME INTELLIGENCE AND POWERS.
"I WAS IN OLD MAN DAVE'S LAB, HAVING VOLUNTEERED FOR A SERIES OF STRENUOUS STRENGTH-BUILDING EXPERIMENTS, ONES THAT COULD HEIGHTEN ALL MY NATURAL CITRUS ABILITIES, WHEN THERE WAS A STRANGE ACCIDENT. A CHEMICAL SPILL.
Monthly Pot Belly
THIS PIG!
June
NO.
Old Dave's Cologne
"IT WAS A UNIQUE SUPER-COLOGNE THAT OLD MAN DAVE HAD MADE FOR A LONELY APPLE WITH DATING PROBLEMS, A COLOGNE THAT MAKES PLANTS 7,526% COOLER.
Old Dave's Coologne
FLOAT FLOAT
FLUTTER
"BUT IT WAS ACCIDENTALLY SPILLED ON ME, AND ALSO ON SOME SUNGLASSES, NEARLY TRIPLING THE EFFECT!"
TINK!
SPLOOSH
"BUT THAT WAS ONLY THE FIRST STEP TO ME BECOMING THE WORLD'S FIRST BIONIC ORANGE. DAVE HAD THE TECHNOLOGY. HE COULD REBUILD ME. AND ALSO HE COULD GOBBLE DOWN SEVERAL PEANUT BUTTER AND ICE CREAM TACOS. ALL OF THESE THINGS CAME TO PASS, AND SO...
RHYMES WITH ORANGE
FRUIT OF THE FUTURE: CITRON
STEGO MAGAZINE
"...NOW--AS CITRON--I SOON DECIDED TO BECOME A Z-MECH HUNTER, GIVING UP MY PREVIOUS LIFE AS A PART-TIME COVER MODEL AND STEGOSAURUS ENTHUSIAST, TRAVELING THROUGH TIME TO BATTLE THE SERIOUSLY NOT-COOL Z-MECHS!"

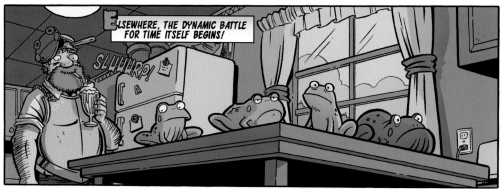

ELSEWHERE, THE DYNAMIC BATTLE FOR TIME ITSELF BEGINS!

SLUUURP!

BURRRP!

PUSH

AND SO...

DID... DID MY TIME PORTAL JUST CLOSE?

SHWOOP

NO MATTER. I'LL JUST CREATE ANOTHER.

TIME PORTAL CREATOR a product of Z-Tech

25¢

TINK! CHING

TIME PORTAL

HA! INSTANT TIME PORTAL!

TIME PORTAL CREATOR a product of Z-Tech

25¢

FWOOSH!

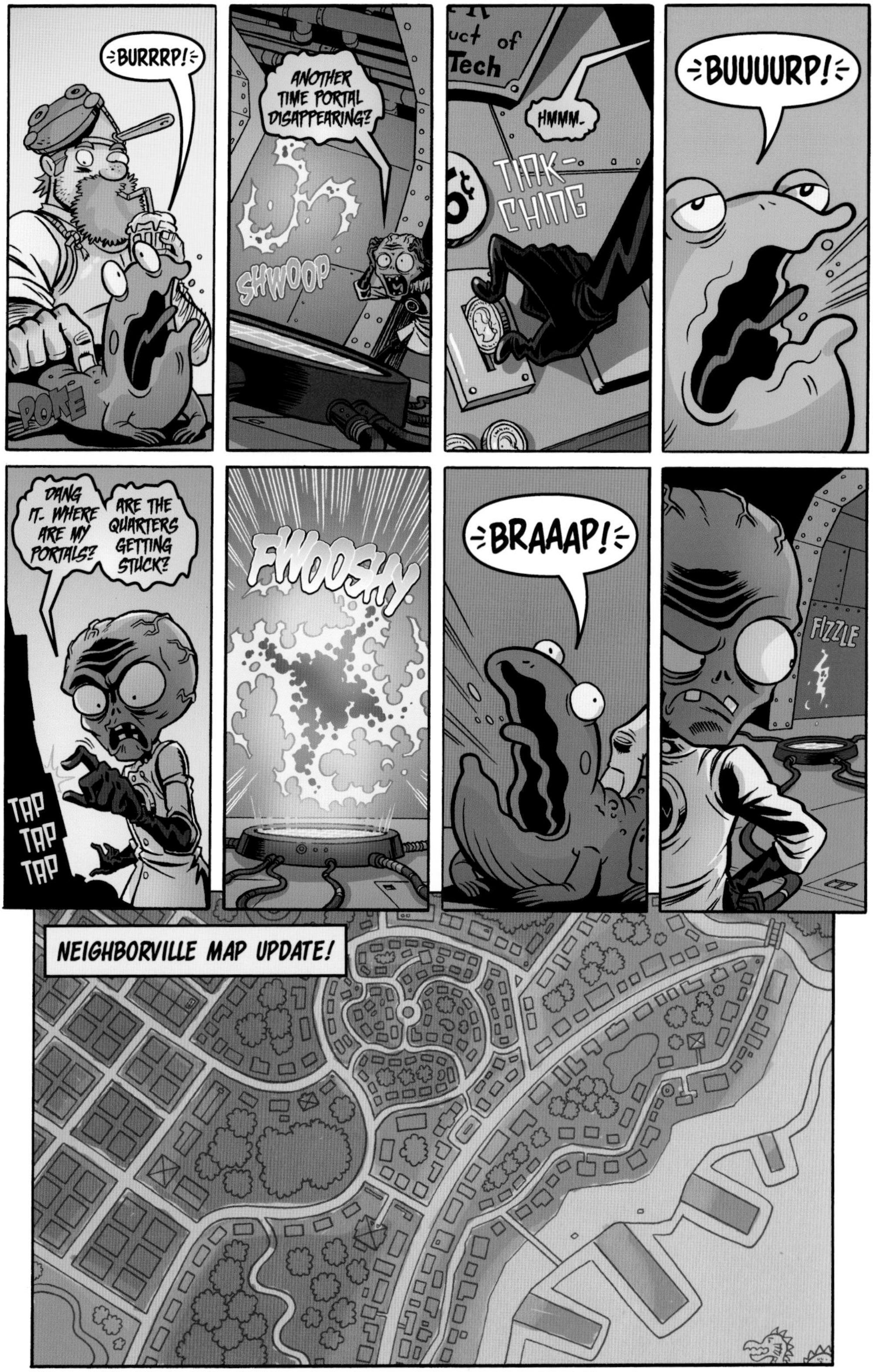
BURRRP!
POKE
ANOTHER TIME PORTAL DISAPPEARING?
SHWOOP
HMMM.
TINK-CHING
BUUUURP!
DANG IT. WHERE ARE MY PORTALS?
ARE THE QUARTERS GETTING STUCK?
TAP TAP TAP
FWOOSH!
BRAAAP!
FIZZLE
NEIGHBORVILLE MAP UPDATE!

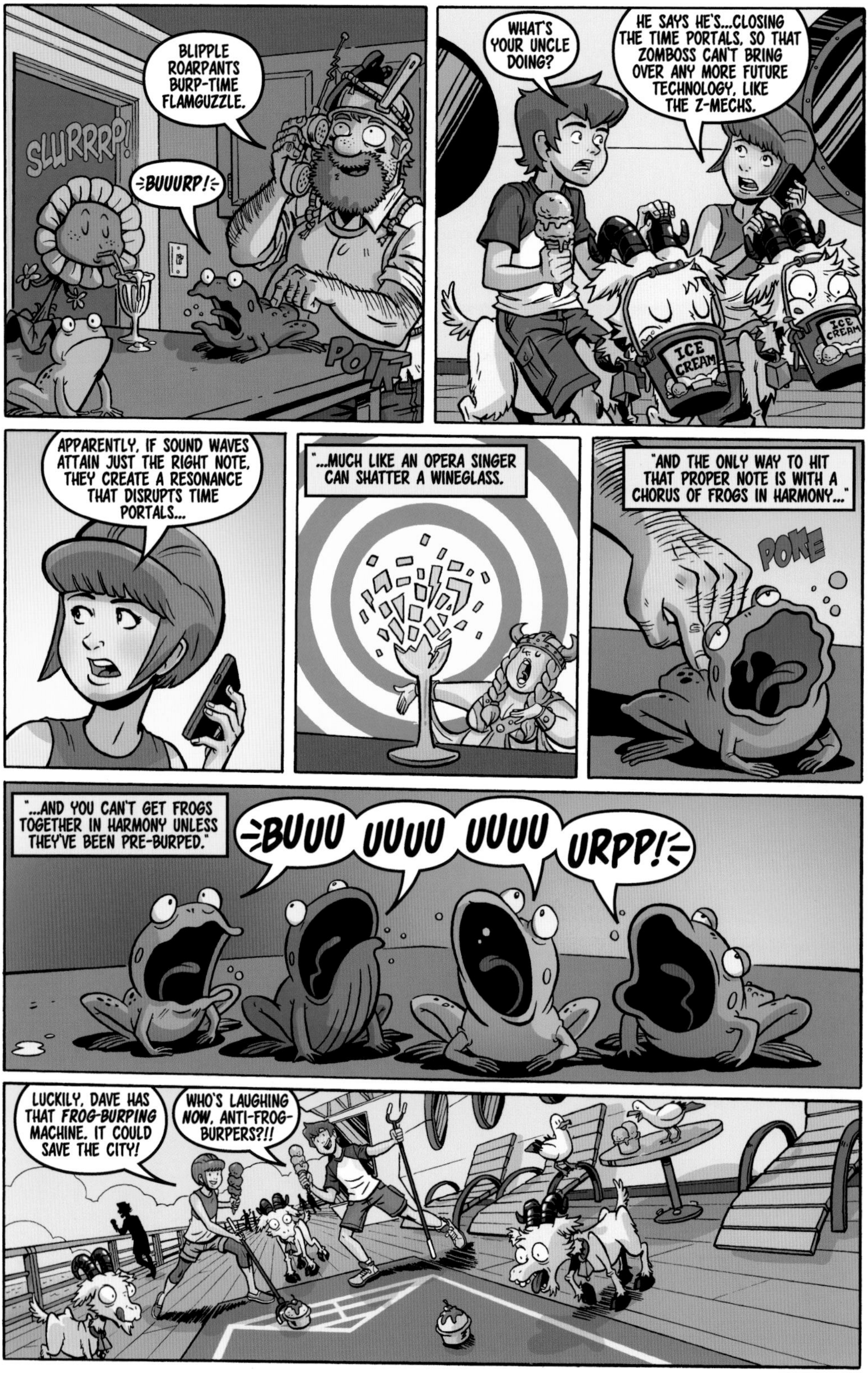
BLIPPLE ROARPANTS BURP-TIME FLAMGUZZLE.
SLURRRP!
BUUURP!
POKE
WHAT'S YOUR UNCLE DOING?
HE SAYS HE'S...CLOSING THE TIME PORTALS, SO THAT ZOMBOSS CAN'T BRING OVER ANY MORE FUTURE TECHNOLOGY, LIKE THE Z-MECHS.
ICE CREAM
ICE CREAM
APPARENTLY, IF SOUND WAVES ATTAIN JUST THE RIGHT NOTE, THEY CREATE A RESONANCE THAT DISRUPTS TIME PORTALS...
"...MUCH LIKE AN OPERA SINGER CAN SHATTER A WINEGLASS.
"AND THE ONLY WAY TO HIT THAT PROPER NOTE IS WITH A CHORUS OF FROGS IN HARMONY..."
POKE
"...AND YOU CAN'T GET FROGS TOGETHER IN HARMONY UNLESS THEY'VE BEEN PRE-BURPED."
BUUU
UUUU
UUUU
URPP!
LUCKILY, DAVE HAS THAT *FROG-BURPING* MACHINE. IT COULD SAVE THE CITY!
WHO'S LAUGHING *NOW*, ANTI-FROG-BURPERS?!!

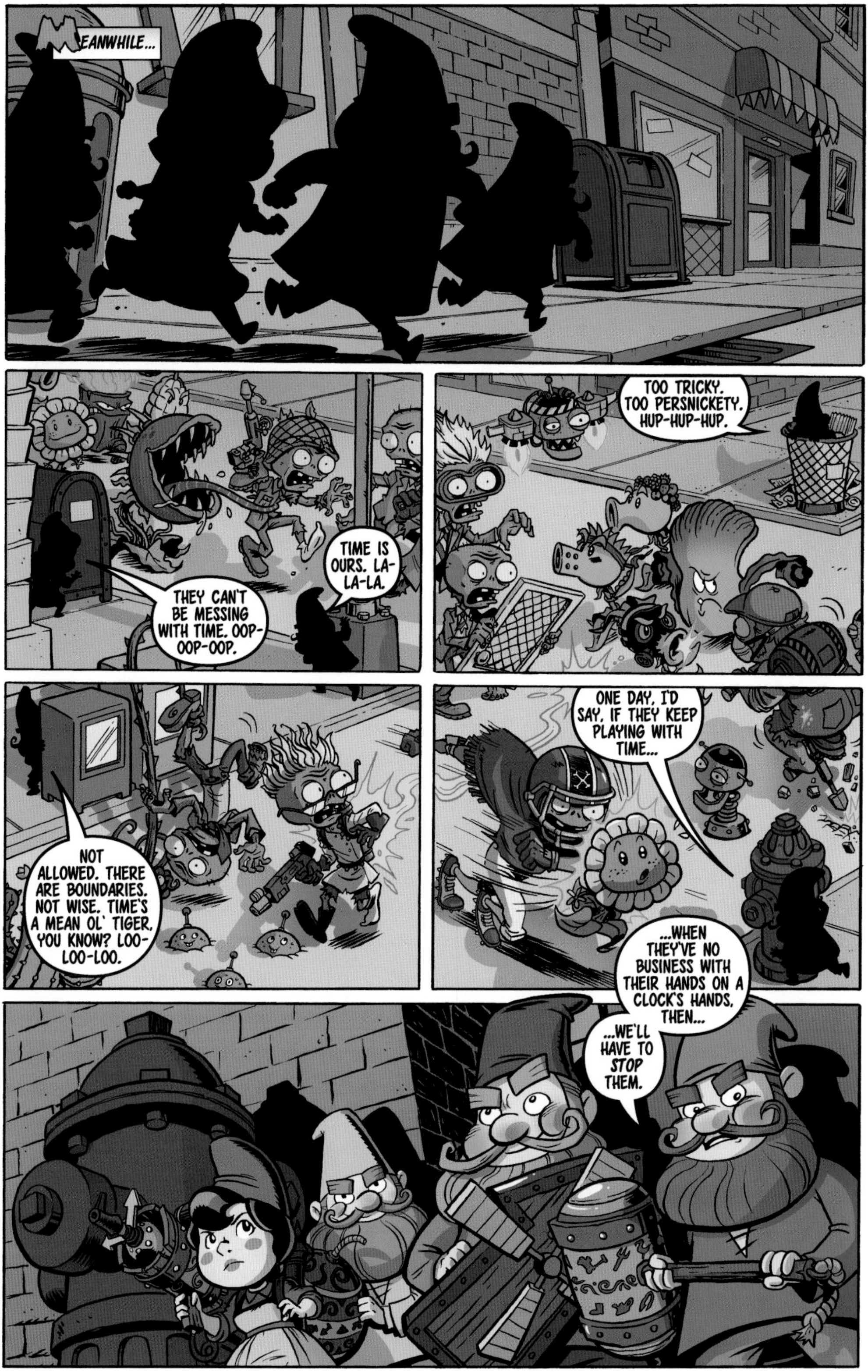
MEANWHILE...
THEY CAN'T BE MESSING WITH TIME. OOP-OOP-OOP.
TIME IS OURS. LA-LA-LA.
TOO TRICKY. TOO PERSNICKETY. HUP-HUP-HUP.
NOT ALLOWED. THERE ARE BOUNDARIES. NOT WISE. TIME'S A MEAN OL' TIGER, YOU KNOW? LOO-LOO-LOO.
ONE DAY, I'D SAY, IF THEY KEEP PLAYING WITH TIME...
...WHEN THEY'VE NO BUSINESS WITH THEIR HANDS ON A CLOCK'S HANDS, THEN...
...WE'LL HAVE TO STOP THEM.

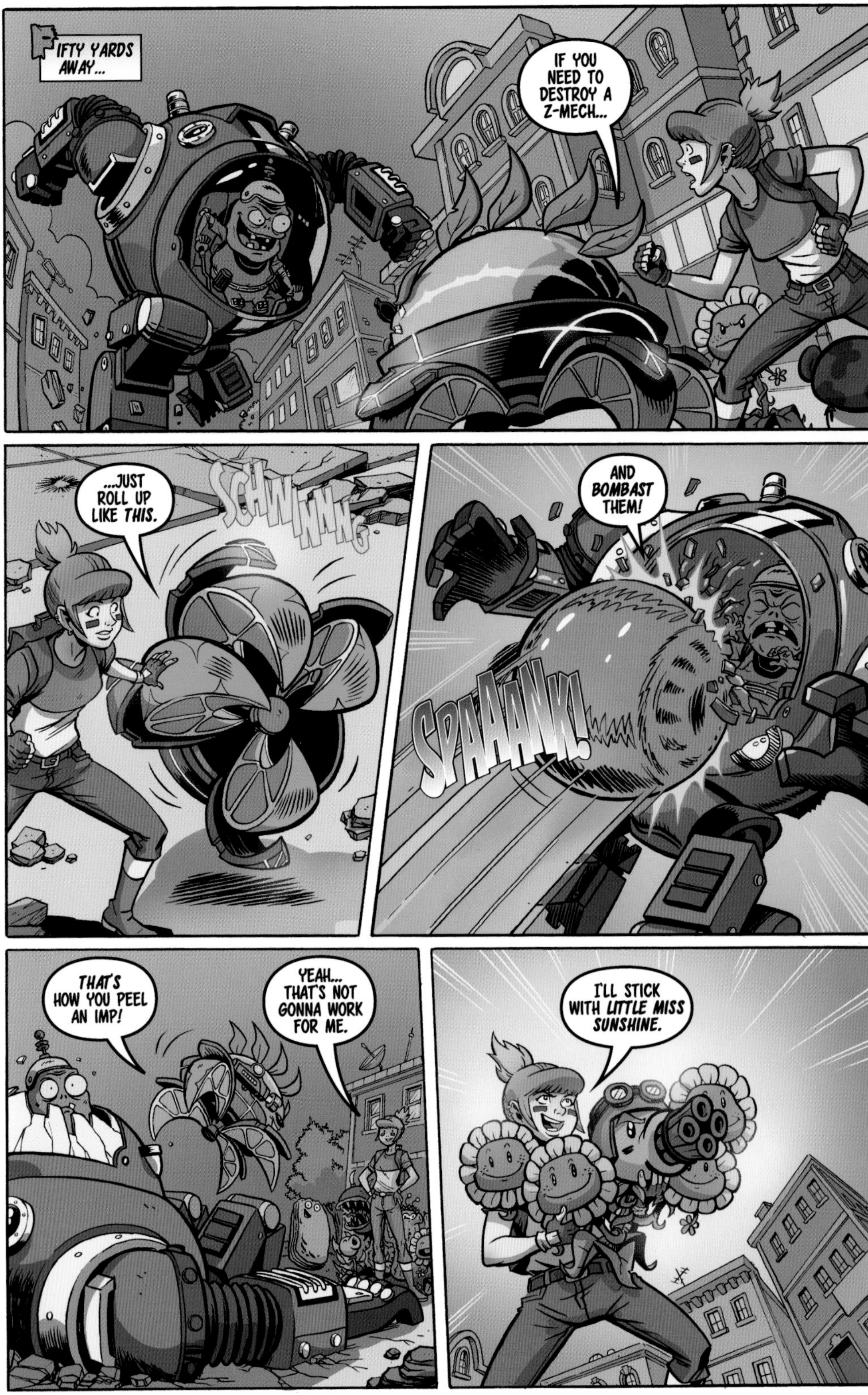
FIFTY YARDS AWAY...
IF YOU NEED TO DESTROY A Z-MECH...
...JUST ROLL UP LIKE THIS.
SCHWINNNG
AND BOMBAST THEM!
SPAAANK!
THAT'S HOW YOU PEEL AN IMP!
YEAH... THAT'S NOT GONNA WORK FOR ME.
I'LL STICK WITH LITTLE MISS SUNSHINE.

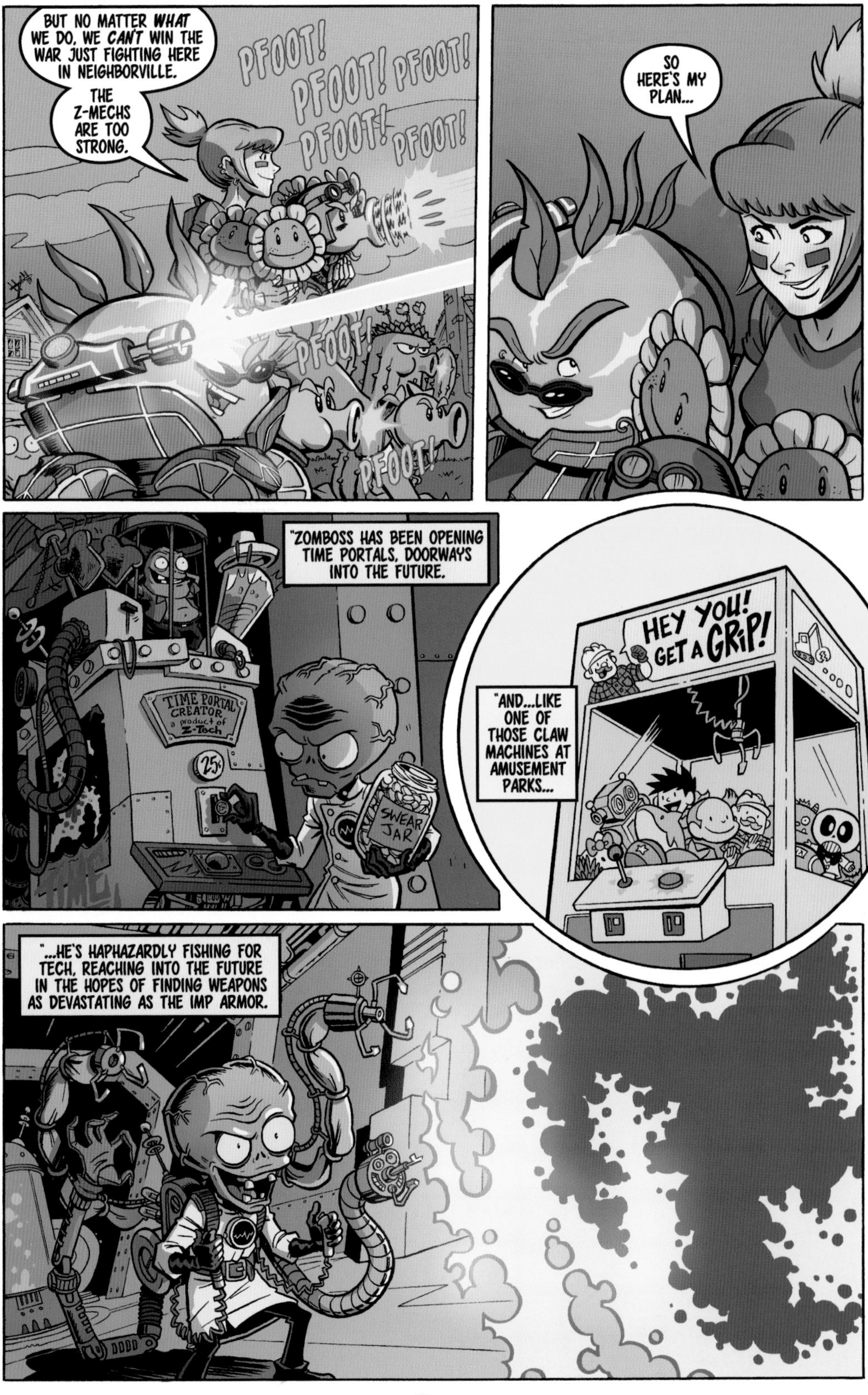
BUT NO MATTER WHAT WE DO, WE CAN'T WIN THE WAR JUST FIGHTING HERE IN NEIGHBORVILLE.
THE Z-MECHS ARE TOO STRONG.
PFOOT! PFOOT! PFOOT! PFOOT! PFOOT!
PFOOT!
PFOOT!
SO HERE'S MY PLAN...
"ZOMBOSS HAS BEEN OPENING TIME PORTALS, DOORWAYS INTO THE FUTURE.
TIME PORTAL CREATOR a product of Z-Tech
25¢
SWEAR JAR
HEY YOU! GET A GRIP!
"AND...LIKE ONE OF THOSE CLAW MACHINES AT AMUSEMENT PARKS...
"...HE'S HAPHAZARDLY FISHING FOR TECH, REACHING INTO THE FUTURE IN THE HOPES OF FINDING WEAPONS AS DEVASTATING AS THE IMP ARMOR.

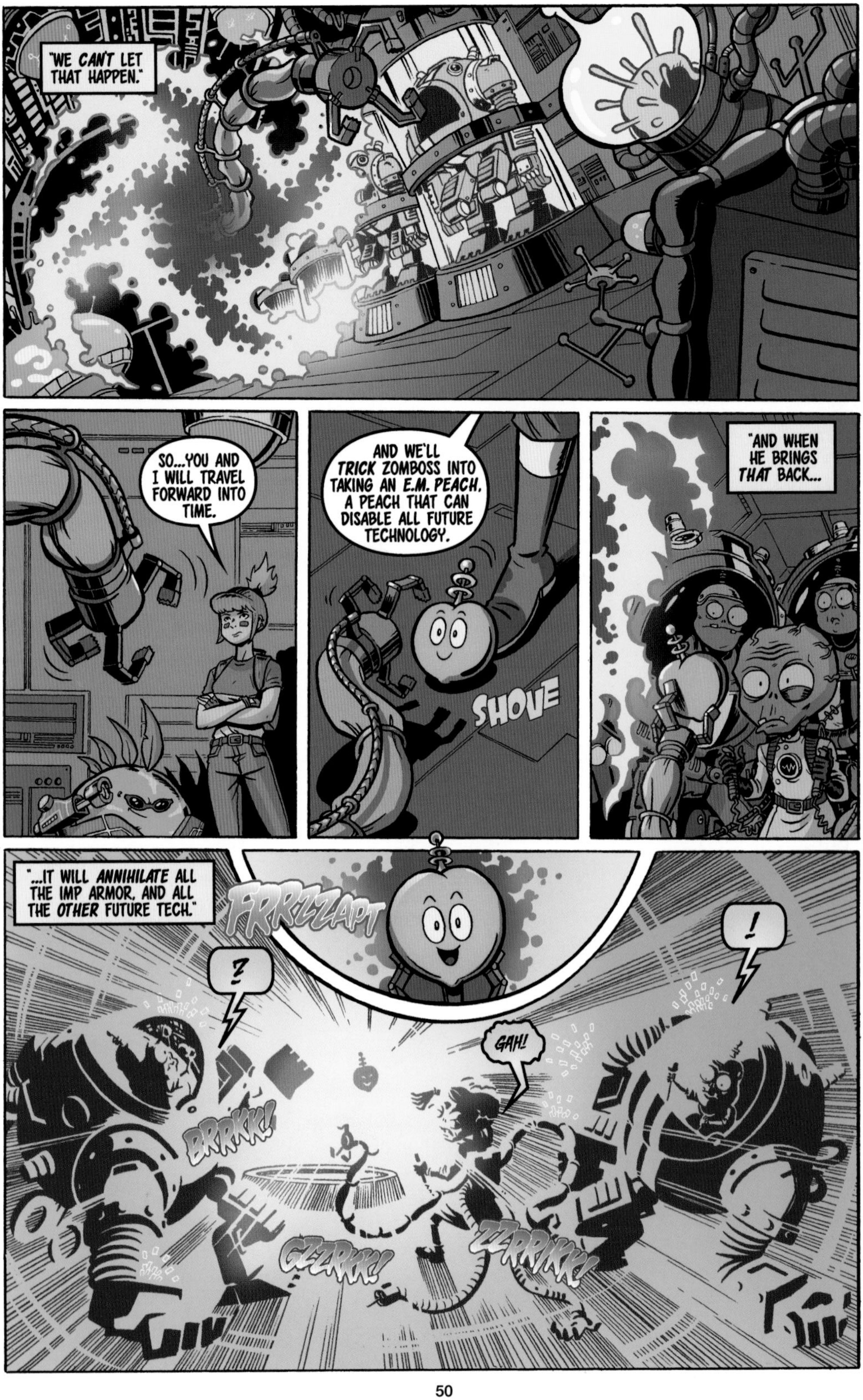
"WE CAN'T LET THAT HAPPEN."
SO...YOU AND I WILL TRAVEL FORWARD INTO TIME.
AND WE'LL TRICK ZOMBOSS INTO TAKING AN E.M. PEACH. A PEACH THAT CAN DISABLE ALL FUTURE TECHNOLOGY.
SHOVE
"AND WHEN HE BRINGS THAT BACK...
"...IT WILL ANNIHILATE ALL THE IMP ARMOR, AND ALL THE OTHER FUTURE TECH."
FRRZZZAPT
?
!
GAH!
BRRKK!
GZZRKK!
ZZZRRKK!

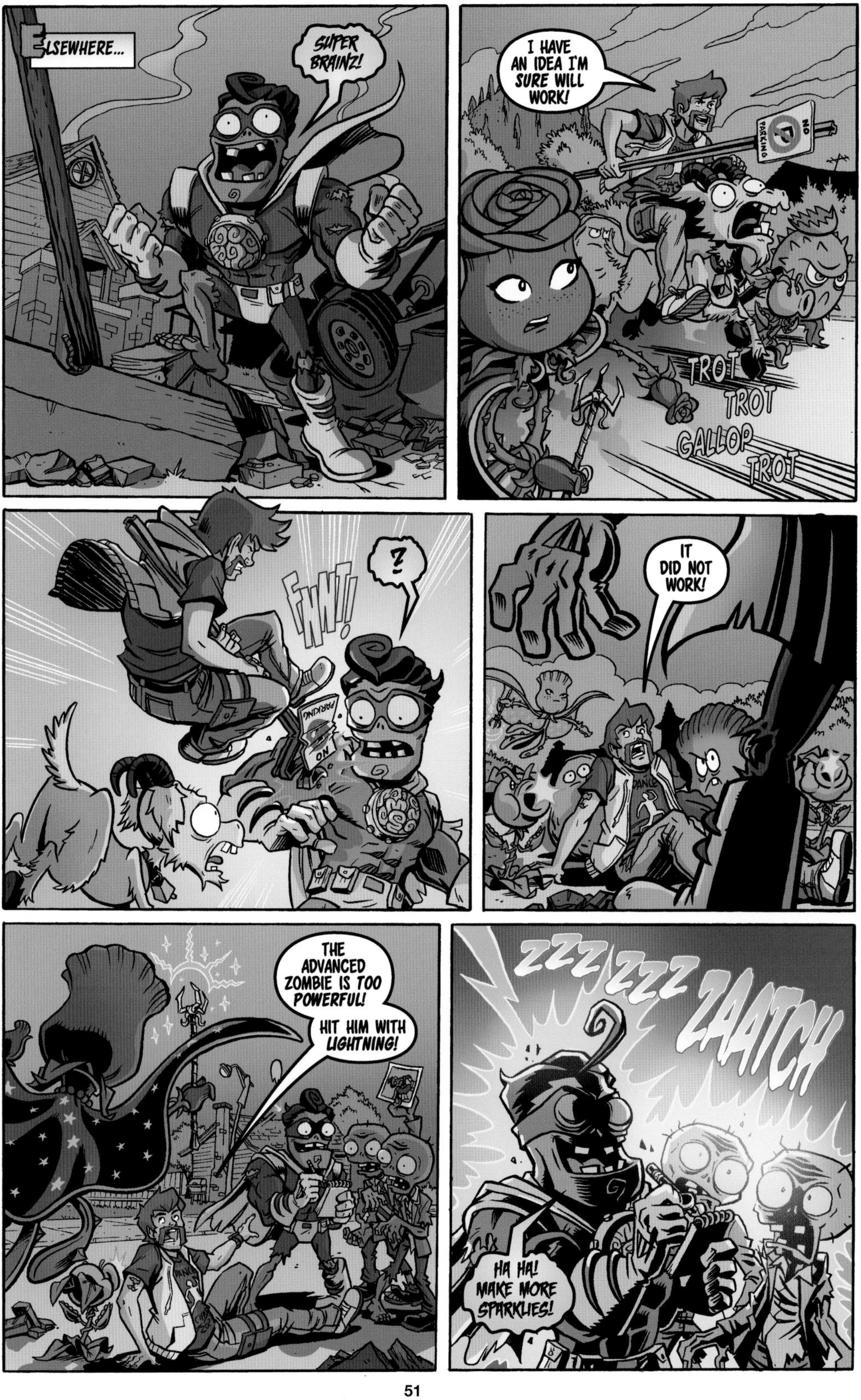
ELSEWHERE...
SUPER BRAINZ!
I HAVE AN IDEA I'M SURE WILL WORK!
NO PARKING
TROT
TROT
GALLOP
TROT
FWHT!
?
PARKING
NO
IT DID NOT WORK!
THE ADVANCED ZOMBIE IS TOO POWERFUL!
HIT HIM WITH LIGHTNING!
ZZZ ZZZ ZAATCH
HA HA! MAKE MORE SPARKLIES!

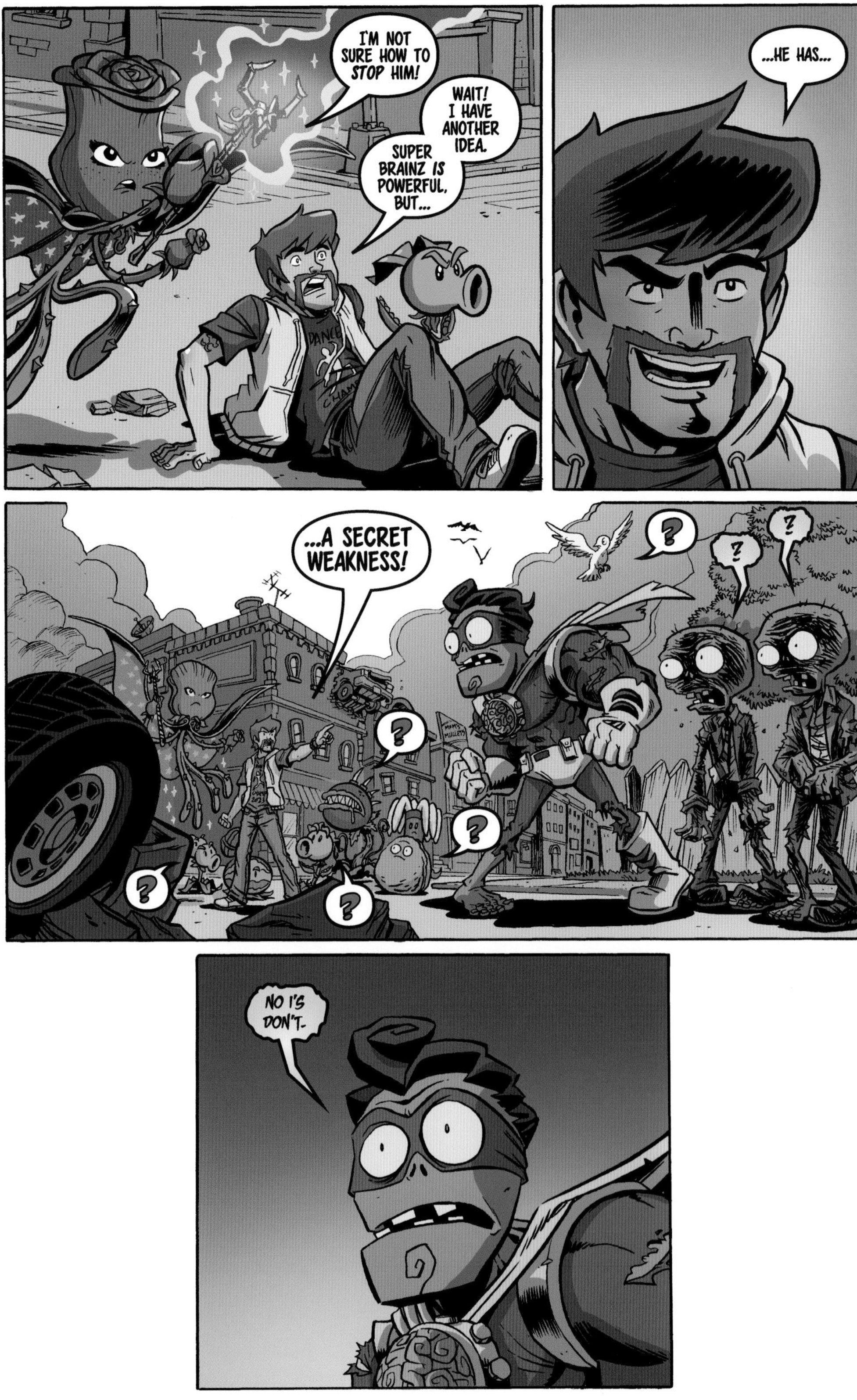
I'M NOT SURE HOW TO STOP HIM!
WAIT! I HAVE ANOTHER IDEA.
SUPER BRAINZ IS POWERFUL, BUT...
...HE HAS...
...A SECRET WEAKNESS!
?
?
?
?
?
?
?
NO I'S DON'T.

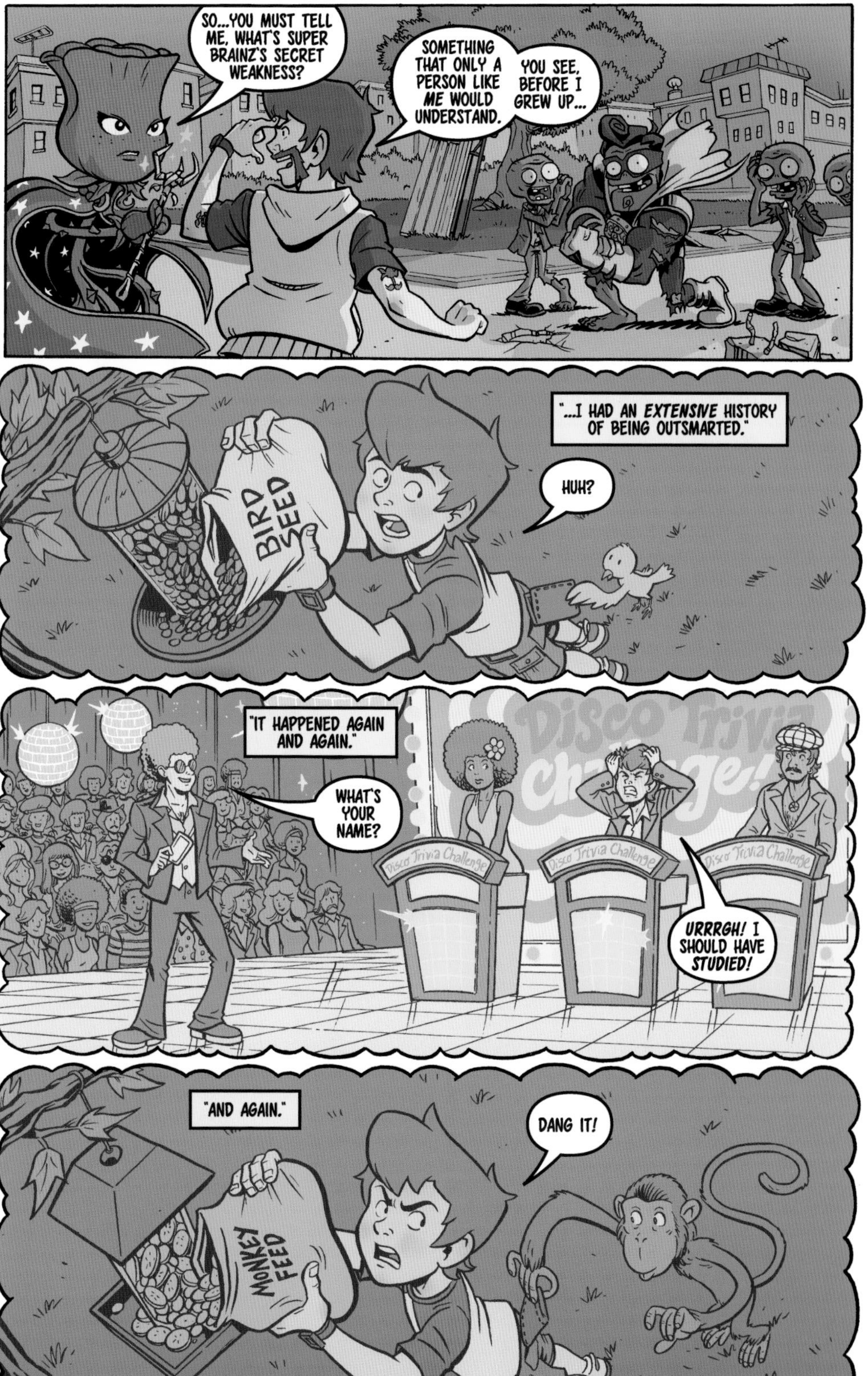
SO...YOU MUST TELL ME, WHAT'S SUPER BRAINZ'S SECRET WEAKNESS?
SOMETHING THAT ONLY A PERSON LIKE *ME* WOULD UNDERSTAND.
YOU SEE, BEFORE I GREW UP...
"...I HAD AN *EXTENSIVE* HISTORY OF BEING OUTSMARTED."
BIRD SEED
HUH?
"IT HAPPENED AGAIN AND AGAIN."
WHAT'S YOUR NAME?
Disco Trivia Challenge
URRRGH! I SHOULD HAVE *STUDIED!*
"AND AGAIN."
DANG IT!
MONKEY FEED

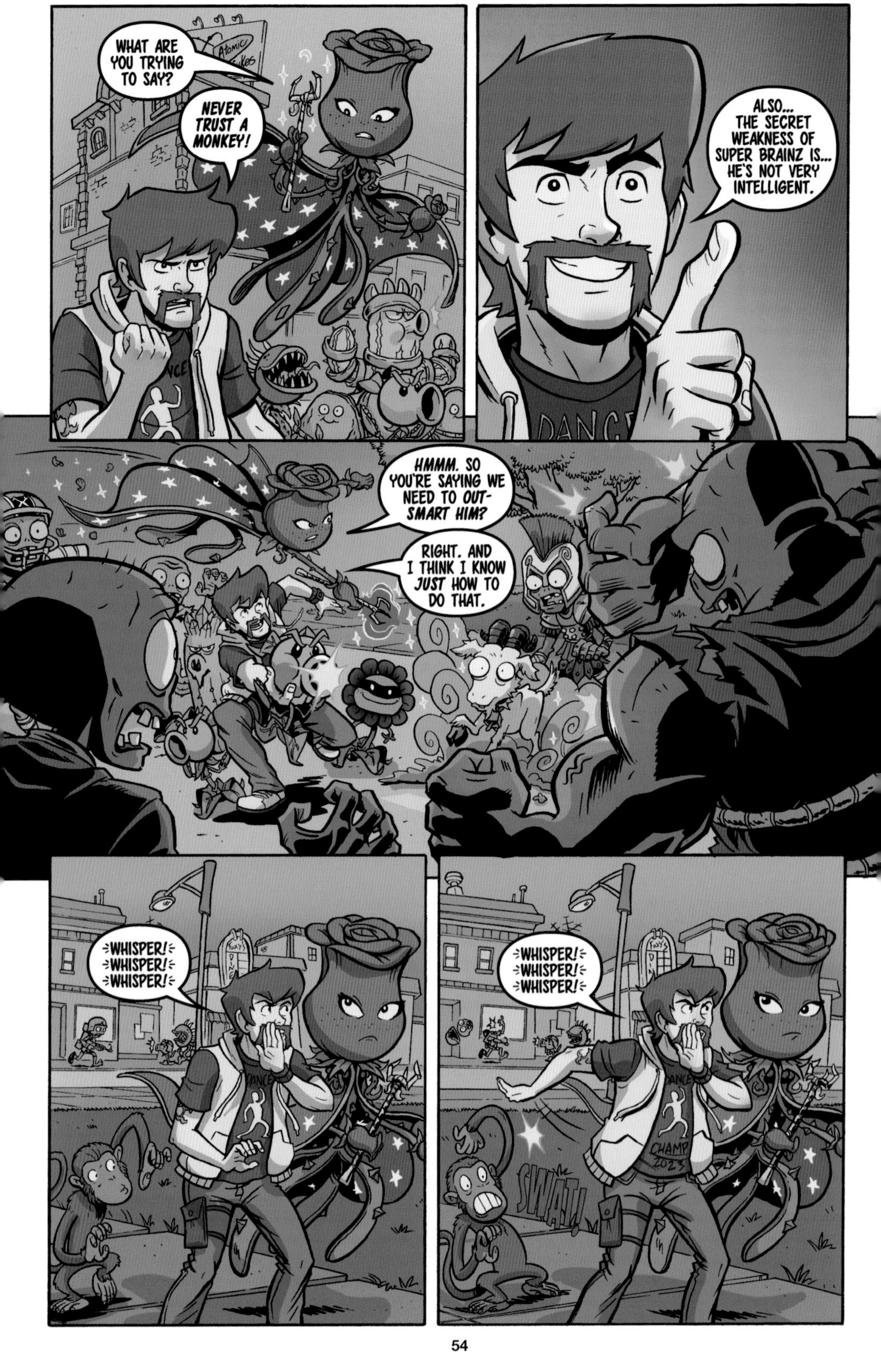
WHAT ARE YOU TRYING TO SAY?
NEVER TRUST A MONKEY!
ALSO... THE SECRET WEAKNESS OF SUPER BRAINZ IS... HE'S NOT VERY INTELLIGENT.
HMMM. SO YOU'RE SAYING WE NEED TO OUT-SMART HIM?
RIGHT. AND I THINK I KNOW JUST HOW TO DO THAT.
WHISPER! WHISPER! WHISPER!
WHISPER! WHISPER! WHISPER!
SWAT!

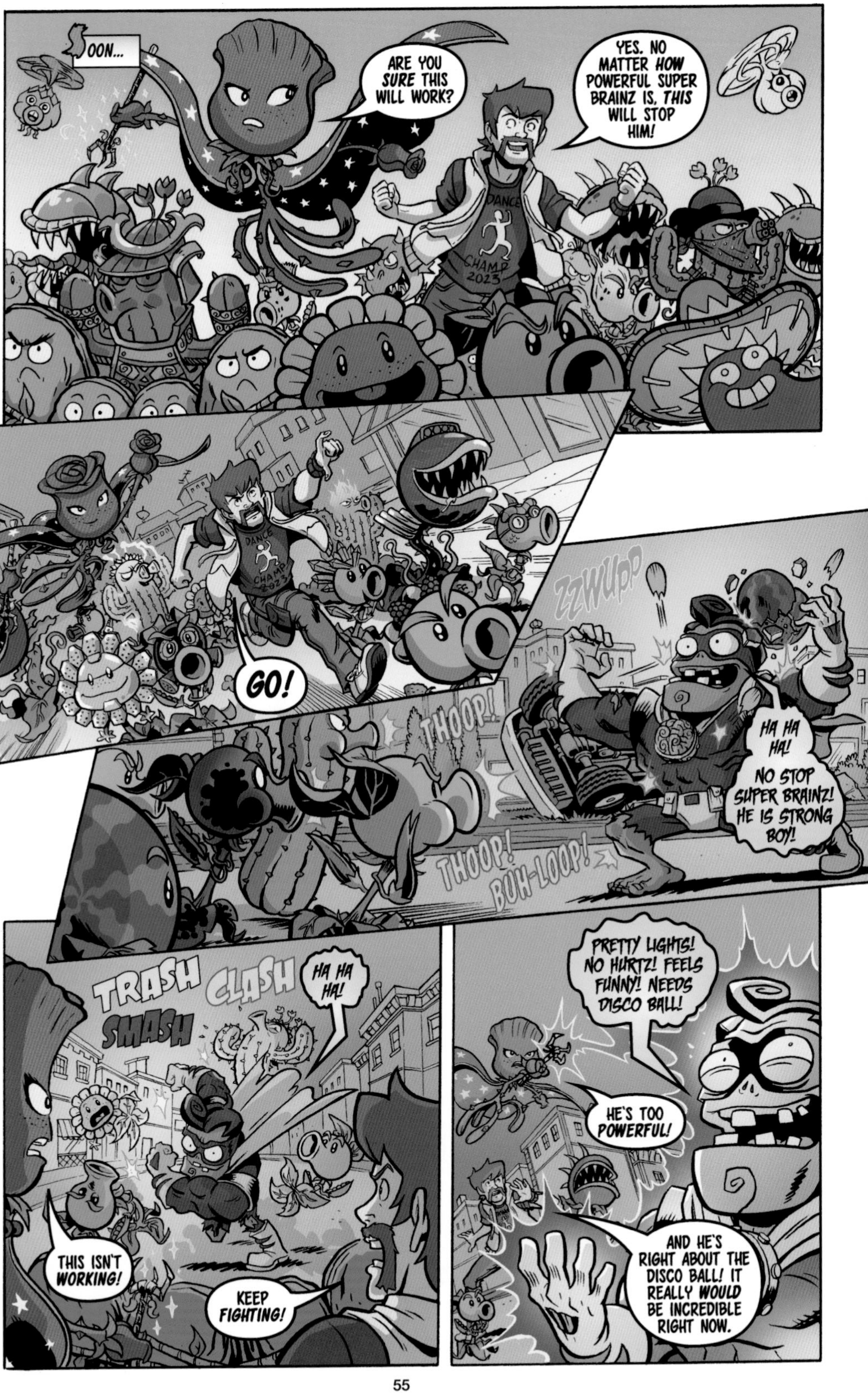
SOON...
ARE YOU SURE THIS WILL WORK?
YES. NO MATTER HOW POWERFUL SUPER BRAINZ IS, THIS WILL STOP HIM!
DANCE CHAMP 2023
GO!
ZZWUPP
THOOP!
THOOP!
BUH-LOOP!
HA HA HA!
NO STOP SUPER BRAINZ! HE IS STRONG BOY!
TRASH
CLASH
SMASH
HA HA HA!
THIS ISN'T WORKING!
KEEP FIGHTING!
PRETTY LIGHTS! NO HURTZ! FEELS FUNNY! NEEDS DISCO BALL!
HE'S TOO POWERFUL!
AND HE'S RIGHT ABOUT THE DISCO BALL! IT REALLY WOULD BE INCREDIBLE RIGHT NOW.

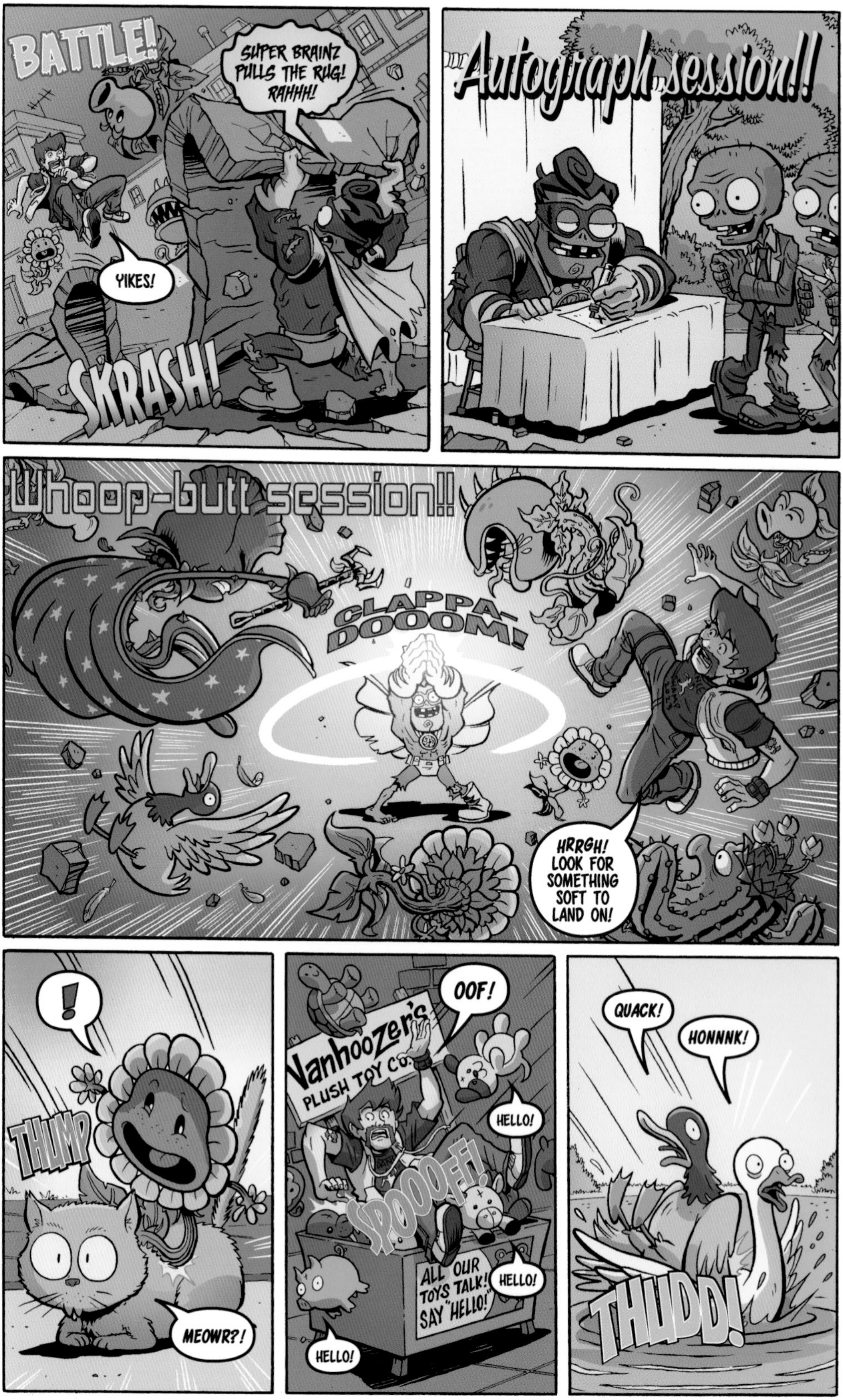
BATTLE!
SUPER BRAINZ PULLS THE RUG! RAHHH!
YIKES!
SKRASH!
Autograph session!!
Whoop-butt session!!
CLAPPA-DOOOM!
HRRGH! LOOK FOR SOMETHING SOFT TO LAND ON!
!
THUMP
MEOWR?!
OOF!
Vanhoozer's PLUSH TOY CO.
HELLO!
SPOOOF!
ALL OUR TOYS TALK! SAY "HELLO!"
HELLO!
HELLO!
QUACK!
HONNNK!
THUDD!

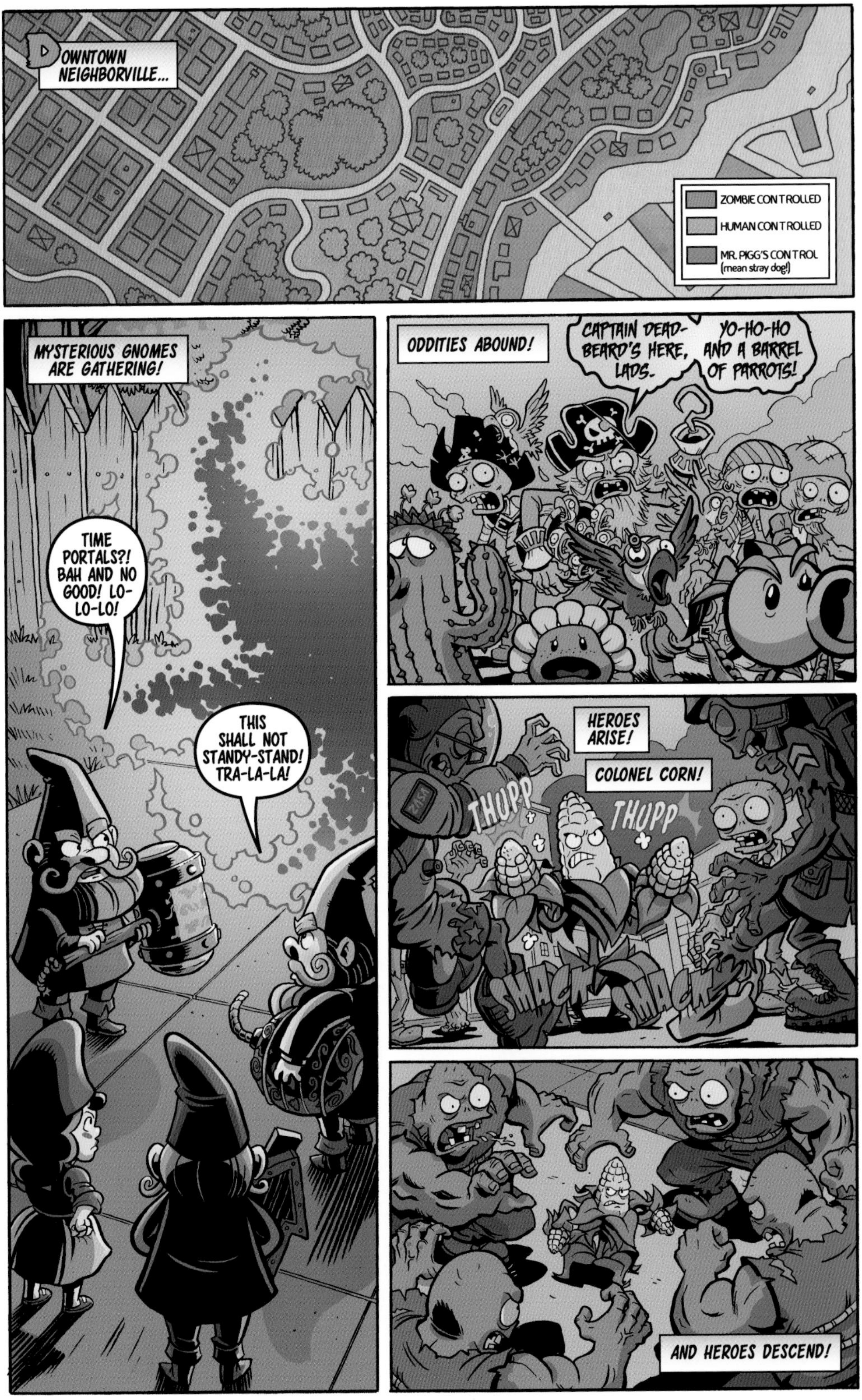
DOWNTOWN NEIGHBORVILLE...
ZOMBIE CONTROLLED
HUMAN CONTROLLED
MR. PIGG'S CONTROL (mean stray dog!)
MYSTERIOUS GNOMES ARE GATHERING!
TIME PORTALS?! BAH AND NO GOOD! LO-LO-LO!
THIS SHALL NOT STANDY-STAND! TRA-LA-LA!
ODDITIES ABOUND!
CAPTAIN DEAD-BEARD'S HERE, LADS.
YO-HO-HO AND A BARREL OF PARROTS!
HEROES ARISE!
COLONEL CORN!
THUPP
THUPP
SMACK
SMACK
AND HEROES DESCEND!

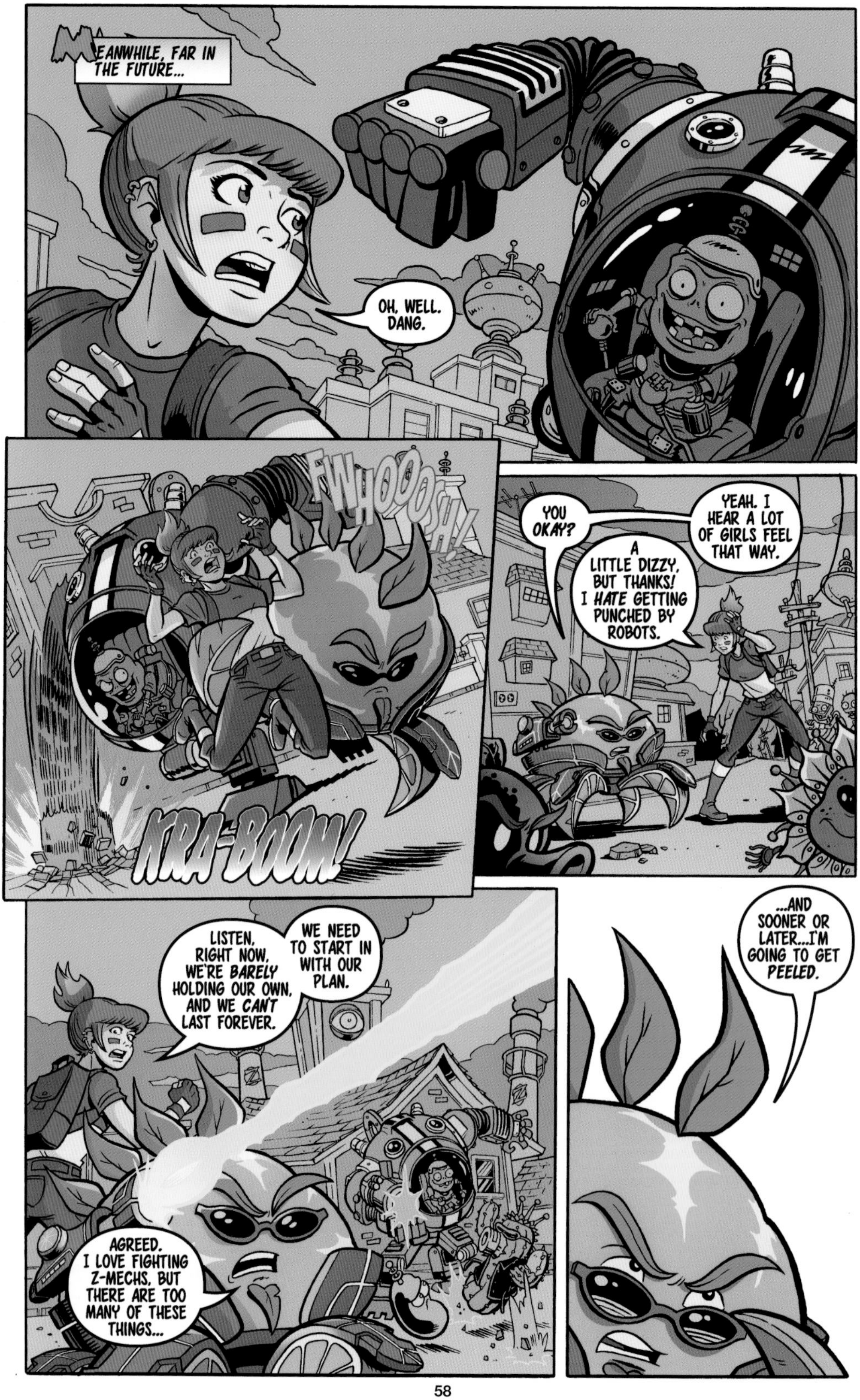
MEANWHILE, FAR IN THE FUTURE...
OH, WELL. DANG.
FWHOOOSH!
KRA-BOOM!
YOU OKAY?
A LITTLE DIZZY, BUT THANKS! I HATE GETTING PUNCHED BY ROBOTS.
YEAH. I HEAR A LOT OF GIRLS FEEL THAT WAY.
LISTEN, RIGHT NOW, WE'RE BARELY HOLDING OUR OWN, AND WE CAN'T LAST FOREVER.
WE NEED TO START IN WITH OUR PLAN.
AGREED. I LOVE FIGHTING Z-MECHS, BUT THERE ARE TOO MANY OF THESE THINGS...
...AND SOONER OR LATER...I'M GOING TO GET PEELED.

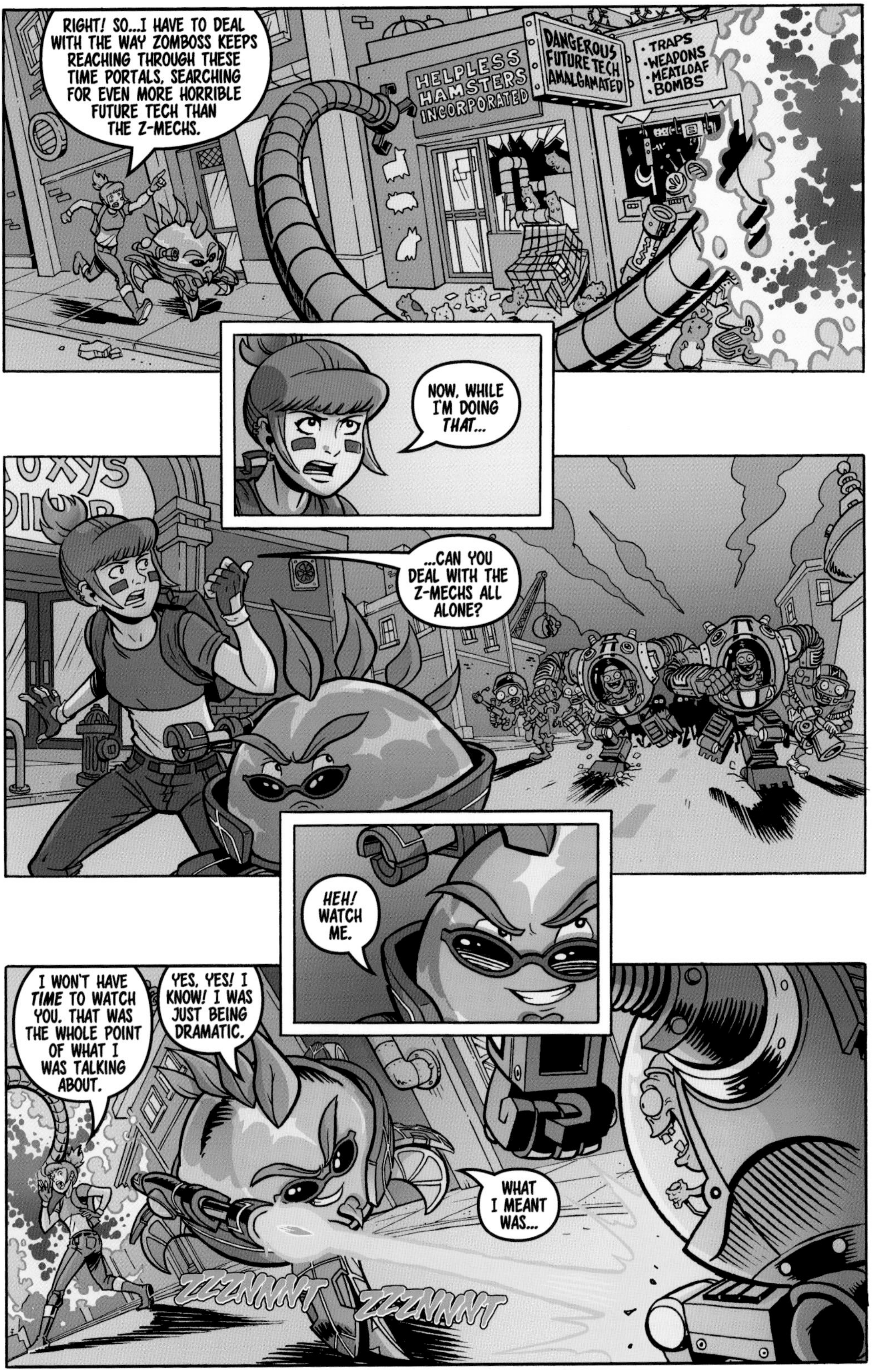
RIGHT! SO...I HAVE TO DEAL WITH THE WAY ZOMBOSS KEEPS REACHING THROUGH THESE TIME PORTALS, SEARCHING FOR EVEN MORE HORRIBLE FUTURE TECH THAN THE Z-MECHS.
HELPLESS HAMSTERS INCORPORATED
DANGEROUS FUTURE TECH AMALGAMATED
• TRAPS • WEAPONS • MEATLOAF BOMBS
NOW, WHILE I'M DOING THAT...
...CAN YOU DEAL WITH THE Z-MECHS ALL ALONE?
HEH! WATCH ME.
I WON'T HAVE TIME TO WATCH YOU. THAT WAS THE WHOLE POINT OF WHAT I WAS TALKING ABOUT.
YES, YES! I KNOW! I WAS JUST BEING DRAMATIC.
WHAT I MEANT WAS...
ZZZNNNT
ZZZNNNT

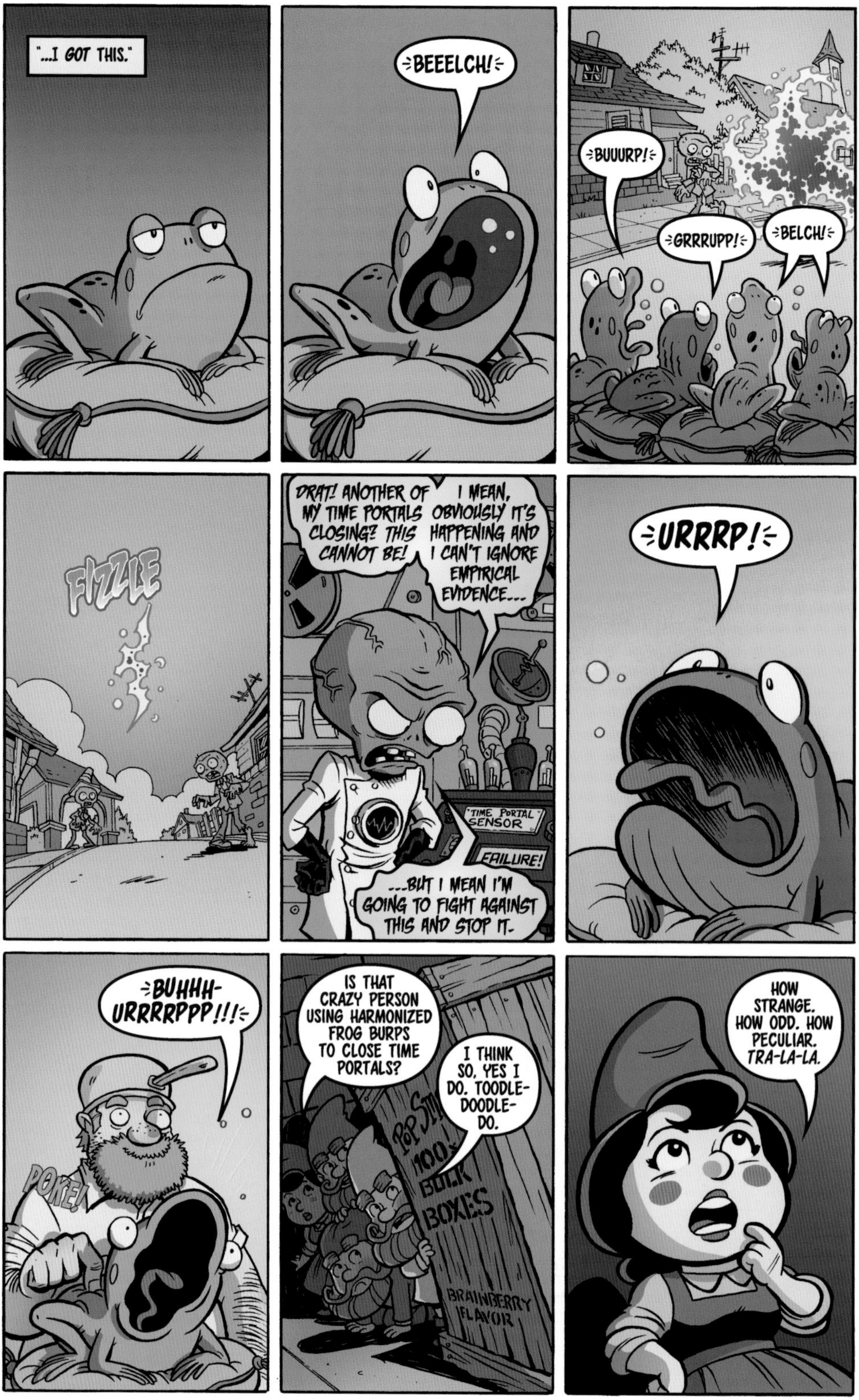
"...I GOT THIS."
BEEELCH!
BUUURP!
GRRRUPP!
BELCH!
FIZZLE
DRAT! ANOTHER OF MY TIME PORTALS CLOSING? THIS CANNOT BE!
I MEAN, OBVIOUSLY IT'S HAPPENING AND I CAN'T IGNORE EMPIRICAL EVIDENCE...
TIME PORTAL SENSOR
FAILURE!
...BUT I MEAN I'M GOING TO FIGHT AGAINST THIS AND STOP IT.
URRRP!
BUHHH-URRRRPPP!!!
POKE!
IS THAT CRAZY PERSON USING HARMONIZED FROG BURPS TO CLOSE TIME PORTALS?
I THINK SO, YES I DO. TOODLE-DOODLE-DO.
BULK BOXES
BRAINBERRY FLAVOR
HOW STRANGE. HOW ODD. HOW PECULIAR. TRA-LA-LA.

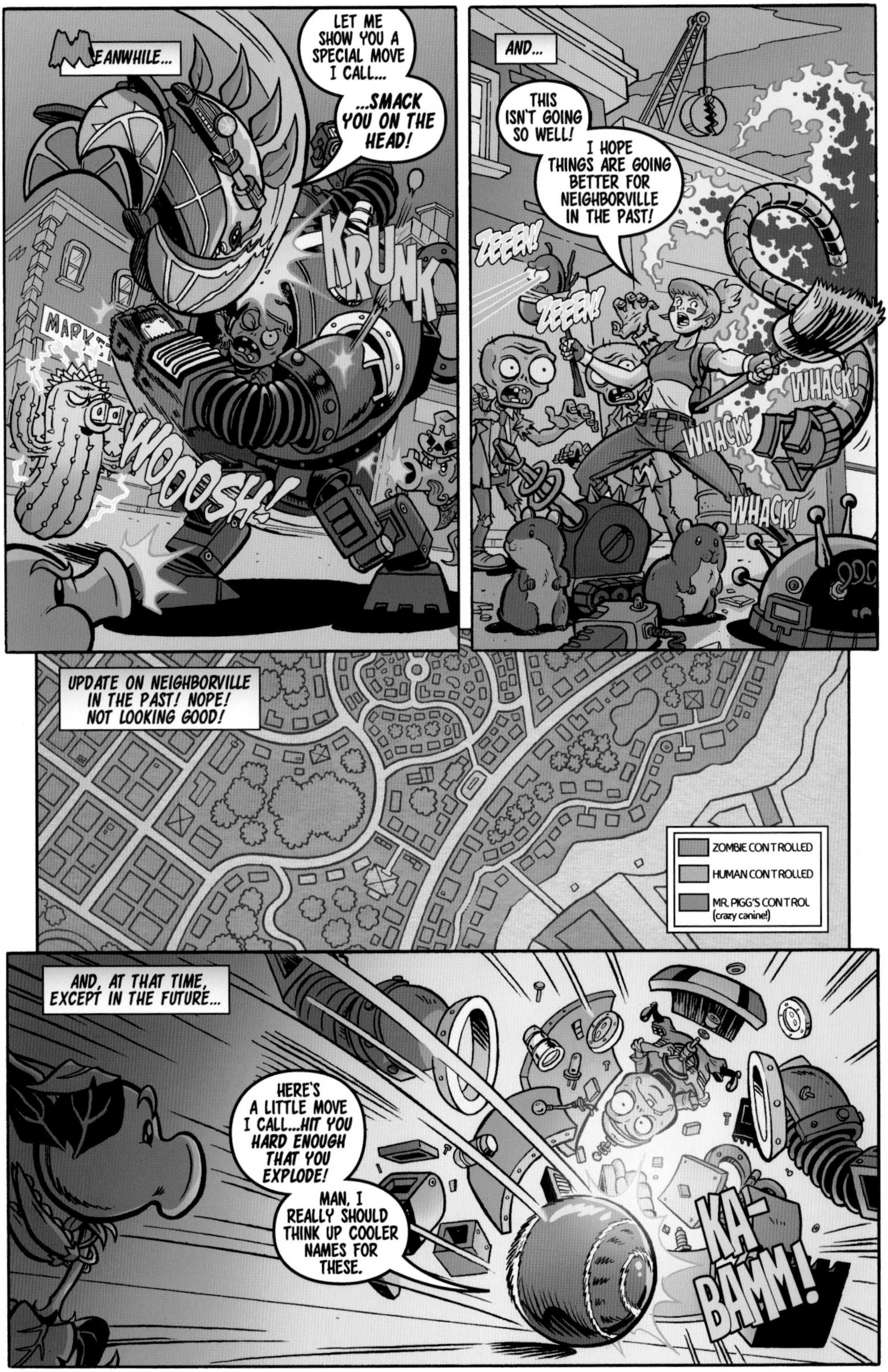
MEANWHILE...
LET ME SHOW YOU A SPECIAL MOVE I CALL...
...SMACK YOU ON THE HEAD!
KRUNK
WOOOSH!
AND...
THIS ISN'T GOING SO WELL!
I HOPE THINGS ARE GOING BETTER FOR NEIGHBORVILLE IN THE PAST!
ZEEEN!
ZEEEN!
WHACK!
WHACK!
WHACK!
UPDATE ON NEIGHBORVILLE IN THE PAST! NOPE! NOT LOOKING GOOD!
ZOMBIE CONTROLLED
HUMAN CONTROLLED
MR. PIGG'S CONTROL (crazy canine!)
AND, AT THAT TIME, EXCEPT IN THE FUTURE...
HERE'S A LITTLE MOVE I CALL...HIT YOU HARD ENOUGH THAT YOU EXPLODE!
MAN, I REALLY SHOULD THINK UP COOLER NAMES FOR THESE.
KA-BAMM!

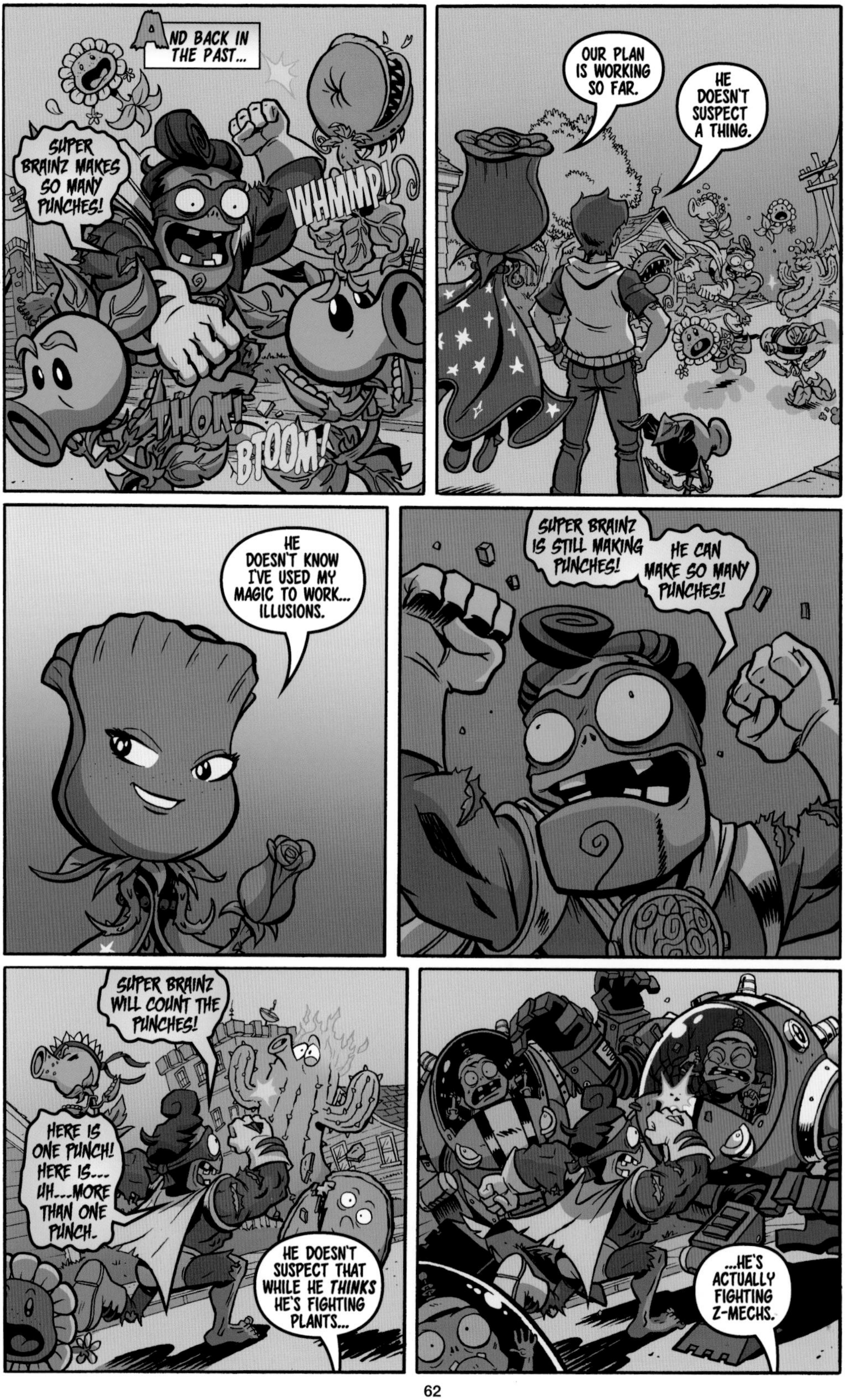
AND BACK IN THE PAST...
SUPER BRAINZ MAKES SO MANY PUNCHES!
WHMMP!
THOK!
BTOOM!
OUR PLAN IS WORKING SO FAR.
HE DOESN'T SUSPECT A THING.
HE DOESN'T KNOW I'VE USED MY MAGIC TO WORK... ILLUSIONS.
SUPER BRAINZ IS STILL MAKING PUNCHES!
HE CAN MAKE SO MANY PUNCHES!
SUPER BRAINZ WILL COUNT THE PUNCHES!
HERE IS ONE PUNCH! HERE IS... UH...MORE THAN ONE PUNCH.
HE DOESN'T SUSPECT THAT WHILE HE THINKS HE'S FIGHTING PLANTS...
...HE'S ACTUALLY FIGHTING Z-MECHS.

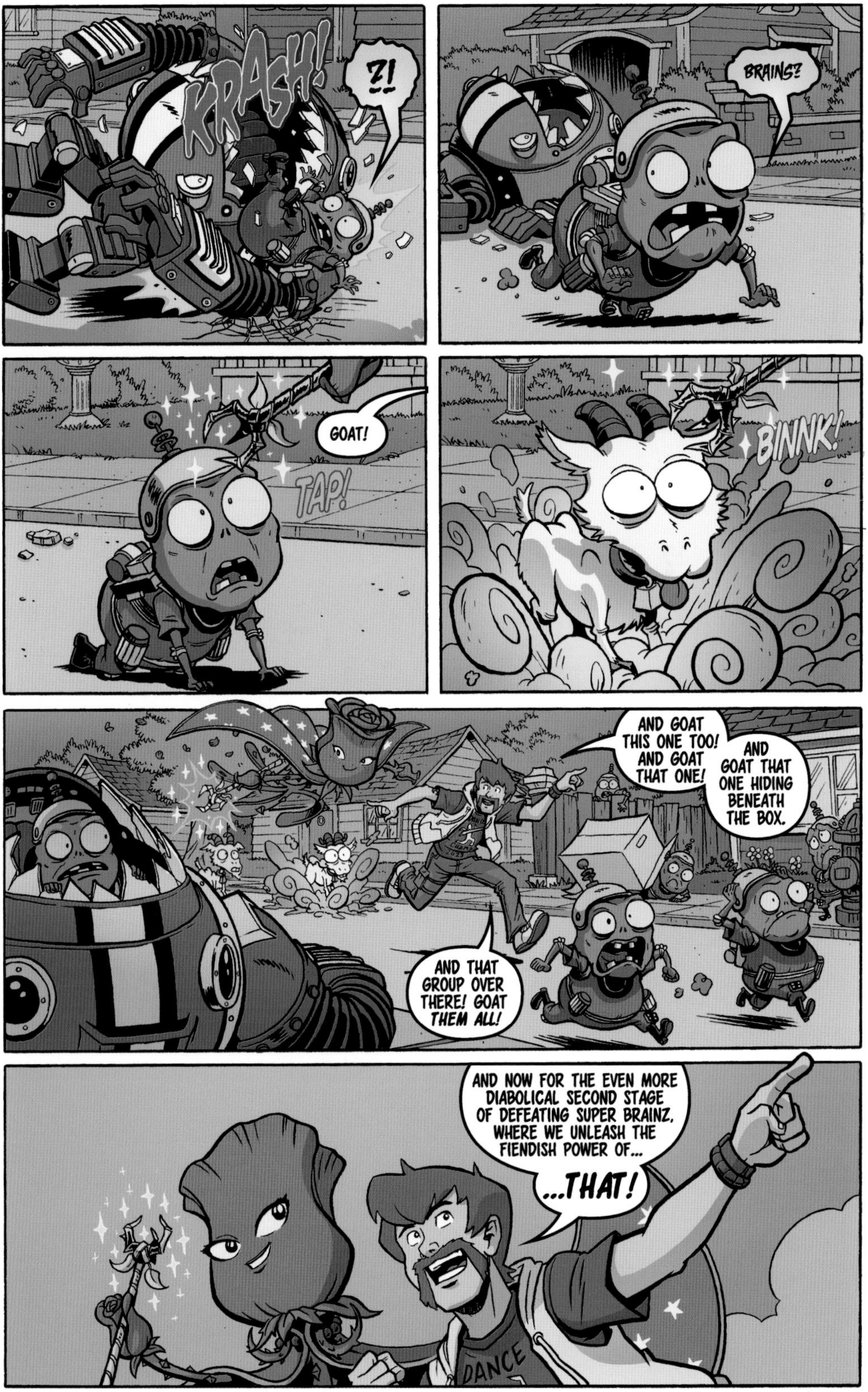
KRASH!
?!
BRAINS?
GOAT!
TAP!
BINNK!
AND GOAT THIS ONE TOO! AND GOAT THAT ONE!
AND GOAT THAT ONE HIDING BENEATH THE BOX.
AND THAT GROUP OVER THERE! GOAT THEM ALL!
AND NOW FOR THE EVEN MORE DIABOLICAL SECOND STAGE OF DEFEATING SUPER BRAINZ, WHERE WE UNLEASH THE FIENDISH POWER OF...
...THAT!
DANCE

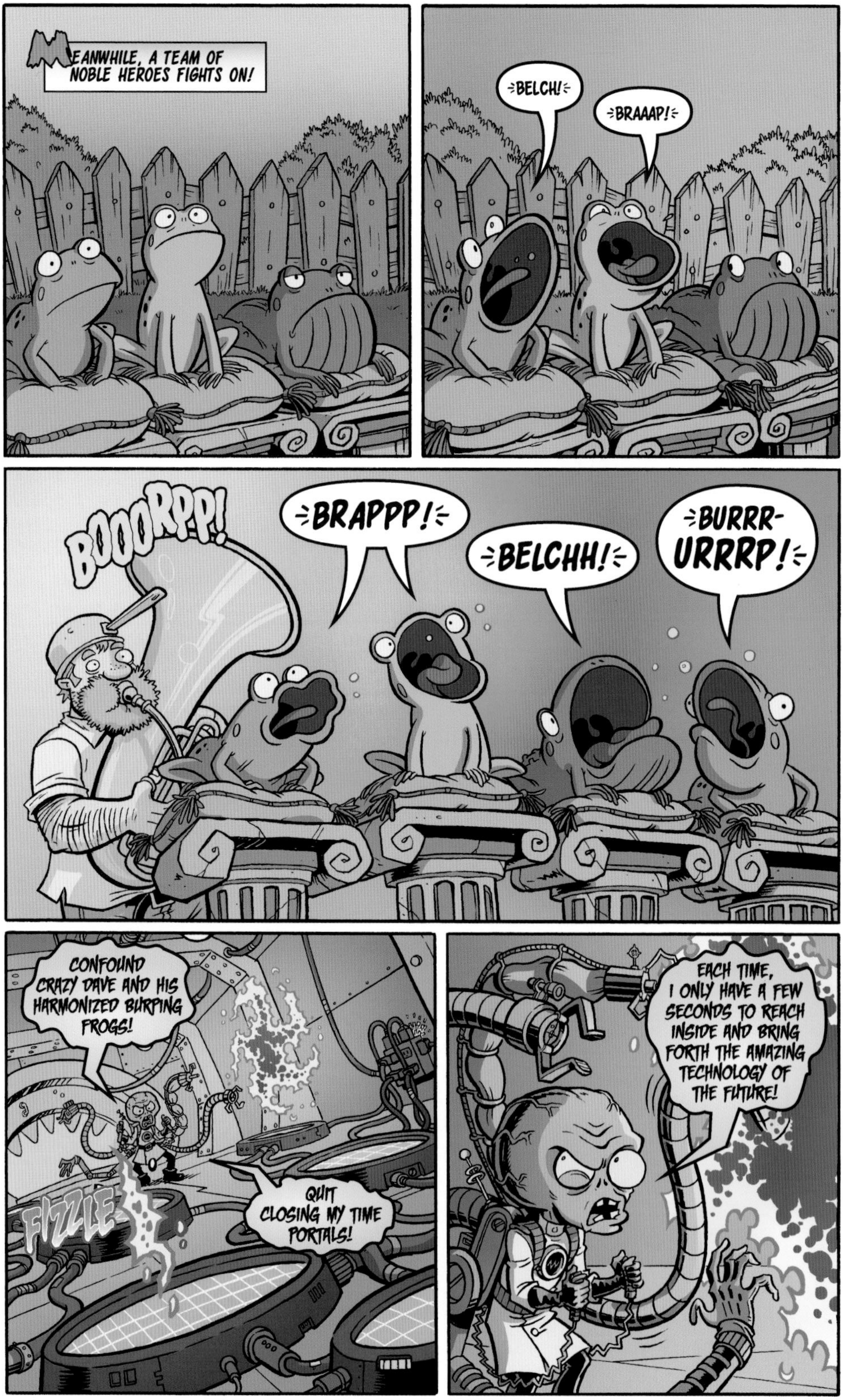
MEANWHILE, A TEAM OF NOBLE HEROES FIGHTS ON!
BELCH!
BRAAAP!
BOOORPP!
BRAPPP!
BELCHH!
BURRR-URRRP!
CONFOUND CRAZY DAVE AND HIS HARMONIZED BURPING FROGS!
FIZZLE
QUIT CLOSING MY TIME PORTALS!
EACH TIME, I ONLY HAVE A FEW SECONDS TO REACH INSIDE AND BRING FORTH THE AMAZING TECHNOLOGY OF THE FUTURE!

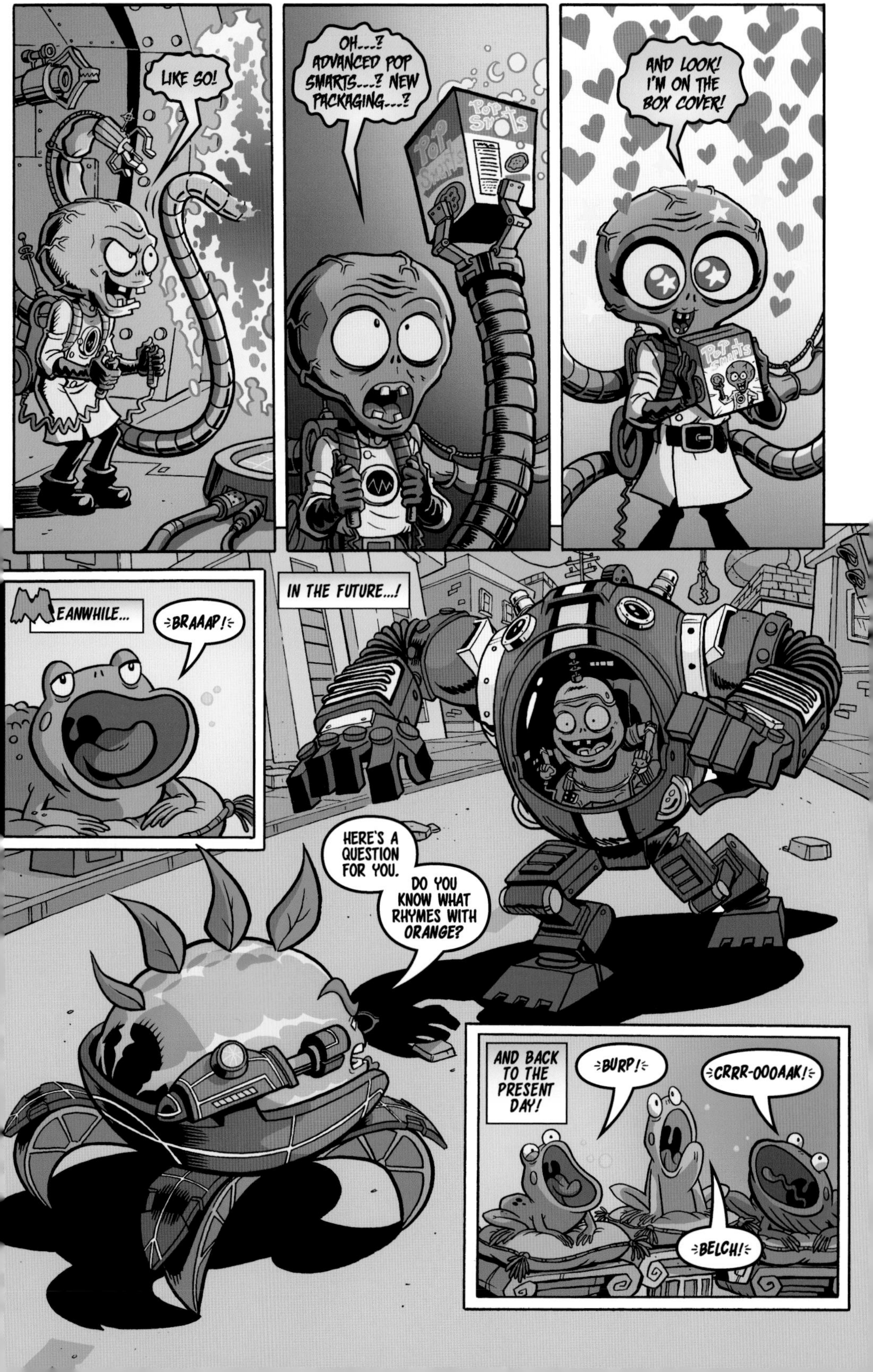
LIKE SO!
OH...? ADVANCED POP SMARTS...? NEW PACKAGING...?
POP SMARTS
AND LOOK! I'M ON THE BOX COVER!
POP SMARTS
MEANWHILE...
BRAAAP!
IN THE FUTURE...!
HERE'S A QUESTION FOR YOU.
DO YOU KNOW WHAT RHYMES WITH ORANGE?
AND BACK TO THE PRESENT DAY!
BURP!
CRRR-OOOAAK!
BELCH!

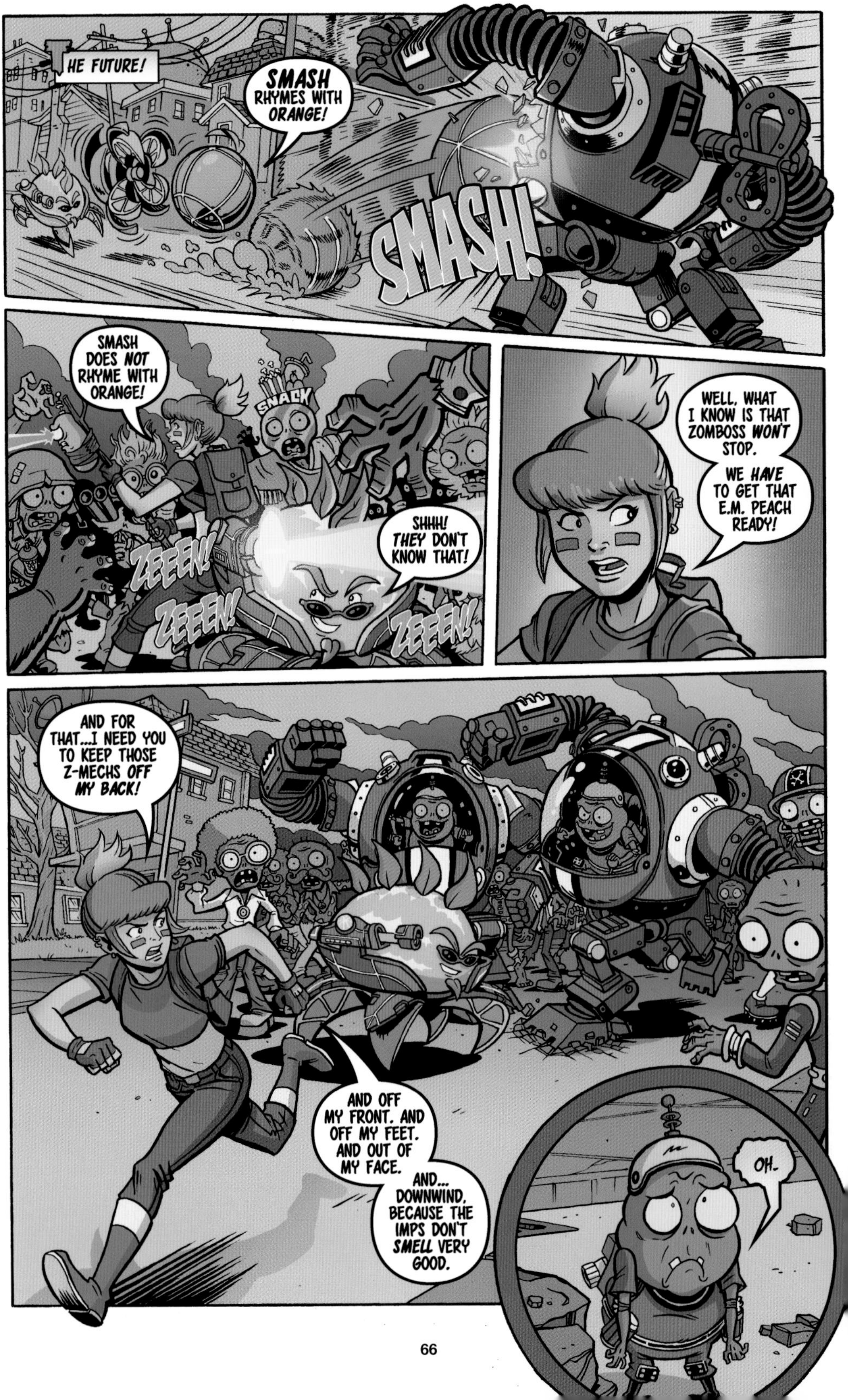
THE FUTURE!
SMASH RHYMES WITH ORANGE!
SMASH!
SMASH DOES NOT RHYME WITH ORANGE!
SNACK
ZEEEN!
ZEEEN!
SHHH! THEY DON'T KNOW THAT!
ZEEEN!
WELL, WHAT I KNOW IS THAT ZOMBOSS WON'T STOP.
WE HAVE TO GET THAT E.M. PEACH READY!
AND FOR THAT...I NEED YOU TO KEEP THOSE Z-MECHS OFF MY BACK!
AND OFF MY FRONT. AND OFF MY FEET. AND OUT OF MY FACE.
AND... DOWNWIND, BECAUSE THE IMPS DON'T SMELL VERY GOOD.
OH.

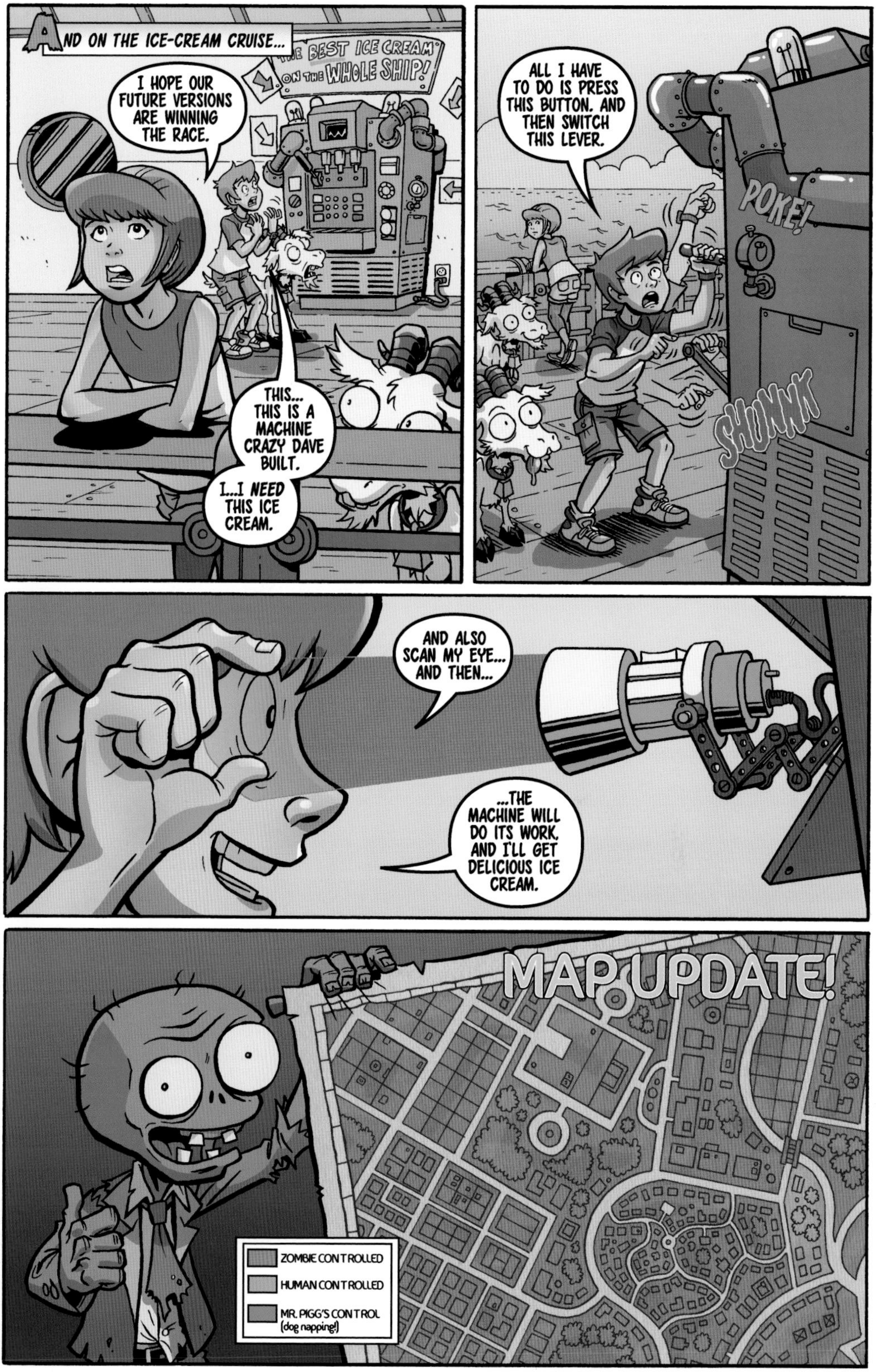
AND ON THE ICE-CREAM CRUISE...
THE BEST ICE CREAM ON THE WHOLE SHIP!
I HOPE OUR FUTURE VERSIONS ARE WINNING THE RACE.
THIS... THIS IS A MACHINE CRAZY DAVE BUILT.
I...I NEED THIS ICE CREAM.
ALL I HAVE TO DO IS PRESS THIS BUTTON. AND THEN SWITCH THIS LEVER.
POKE!
SHUNNK
AND ALSO SCAN MY EYE... AND THEN...
...THE MACHINE WILL DO ITS WORK, AND I'LL GET DELICIOUS ICE CREAM.
MAP UPDATE!
ZOMBIE CONTROLLED
HUMAN CONTROLLED
MR. PIGG'S CONTROL (dog napping!)

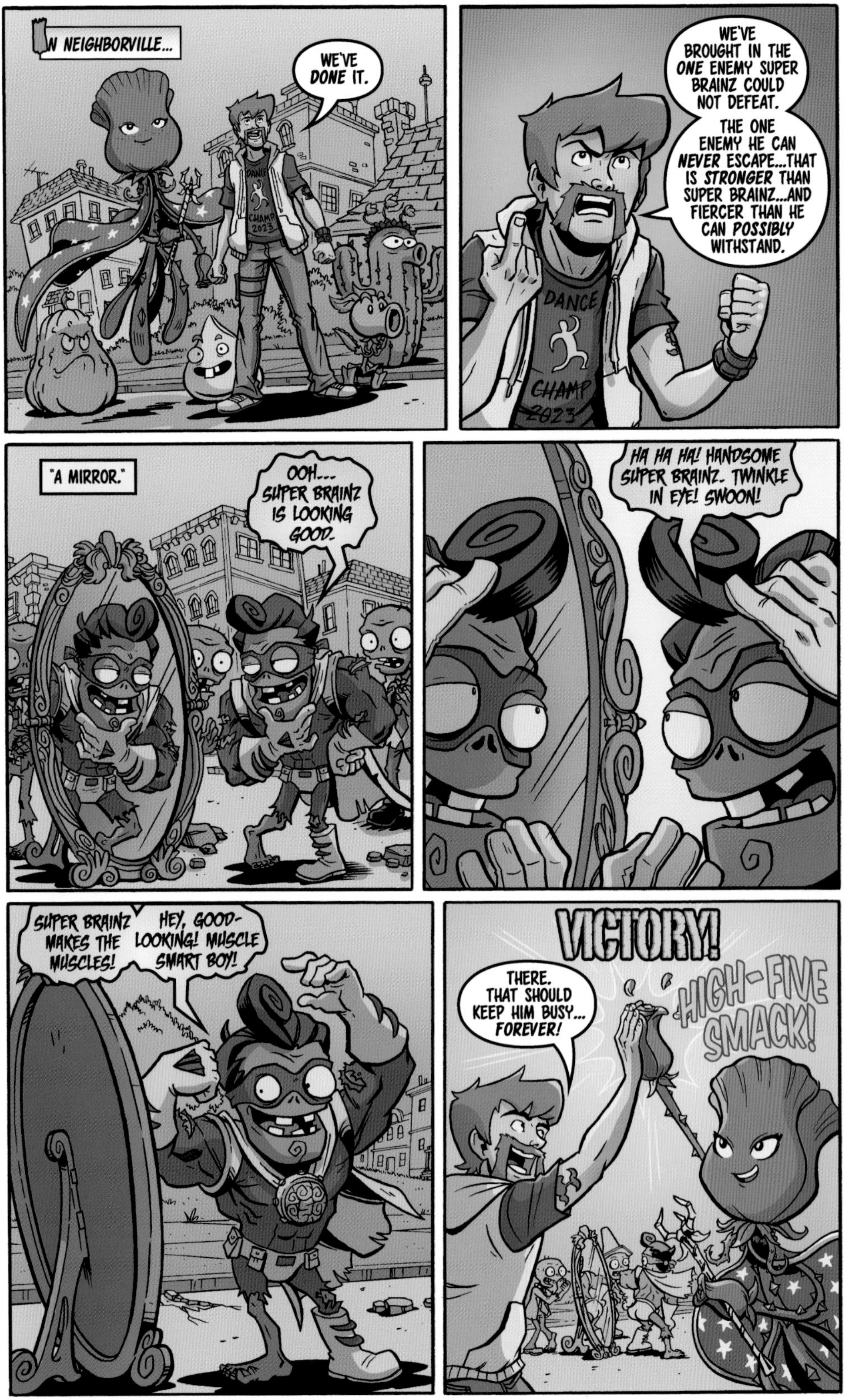
IN NEIGHBORVILLE...
WE'VE DONE IT.
WE'VE BROUGHT IN THE ONE ENEMY SUPER BRAINZ COULD NOT DEFEAT.
THE ONE ENEMY HE CAN NEVER ESCAPE...THAT IS STRONGER THAN SUPER BRAINZ...AND FIERCER THAN HE CAN POSSIBLY WITHSTAND.
"A MIRROR."
OOH... SUPER BRAINZ IS LOOKING GOOD.
HA HA HA! HANDSOME SUPER BRAINZ. TWINKLE IN EYE! SWOON!
SUPER BRAINZ MAKES THE MUSCLES!
HEY, GOOD-LOOKING! MUSCLE SMART BOY!
VICTORY!
THERE. THAT SHOULD KEEP HIM BUSY... FOREVER!
HIGH-FIVE SMACK!

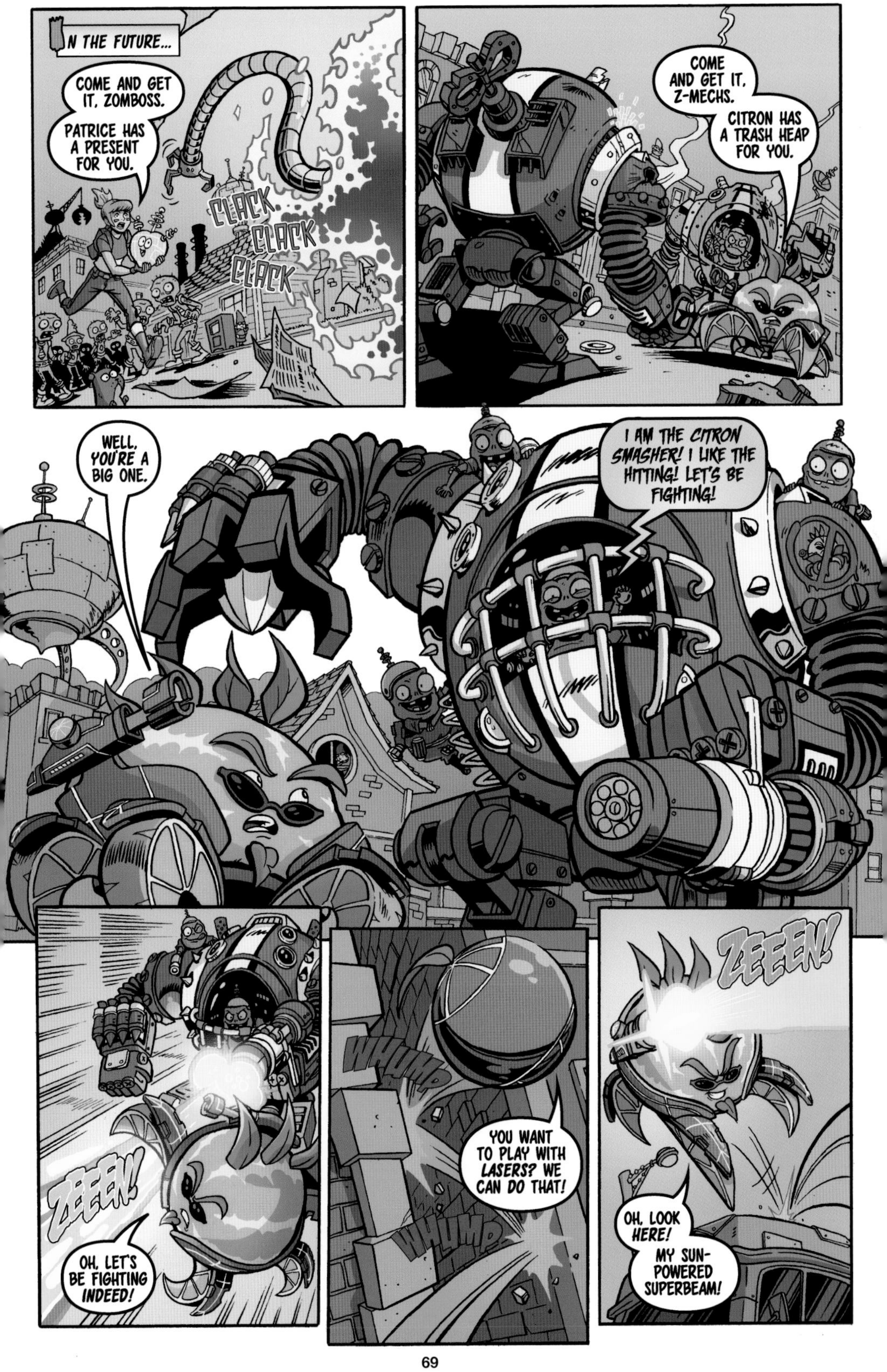
IN THE FUTURE...
COME AND GET IT, ZOMBOSS.
PATRICE HAS A PRESENT FOR YOU.
CLACK CLACK CLACK
COME AND GET IT, Z-MECHS.
CITRON HAS A TRASH HEAP FOR YOU.
WELL, YOU'RE A BIG ONE.
I AM THE CITRON SMASHER! I LIKE THE HITTING! LET'S BE FIGHTING!
ZEEEN!
OH, LET'S BE FIGHTING INDEED!
WHUMP
WHUMP
YOU WANT TO PLAY WITH LASERS? WE CAN DO THAT!
ZEEEN!
OH, LOOK HERE!
MY SUN-POWERED SUPERBEAM!

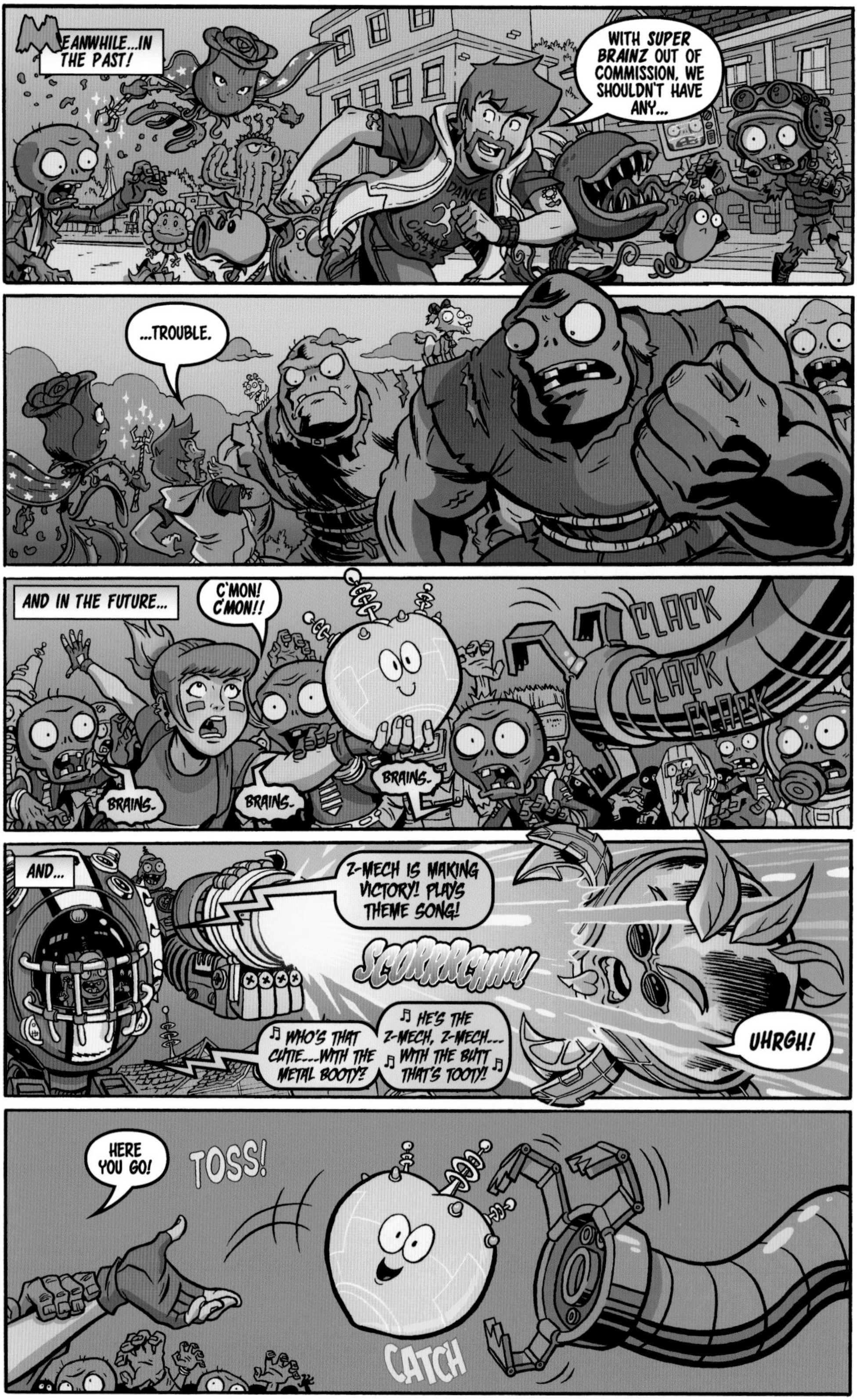
MEANWHILE...IN THE PAST!
WITH SUPER BRAINZ OUT OF COMMISSION, WE SHOULDN'T HAVE ANY...
DANCE CHAMP 2023
...TROUBLE.
AND IN THE FUTURE...
C'MON! C'MON!!
CLACK
CLACK
CLACK
BRAINS.
BRAINS.
BRAINS.
AND...
Z-MECH IS MAKING VICTORY! PLAYS THEME SONG!
SCORRRCHHH!
♫ WHO'S THAT CUTIE...WITH THE METAL BOOTY?
♫ HE'S THE Z-MECH, Z-MECH... ♫ WITH THE BUTT THAT'S TOOTY! ♫
UHRGH!
HERE YOU GO!
TOSS!
CATCH

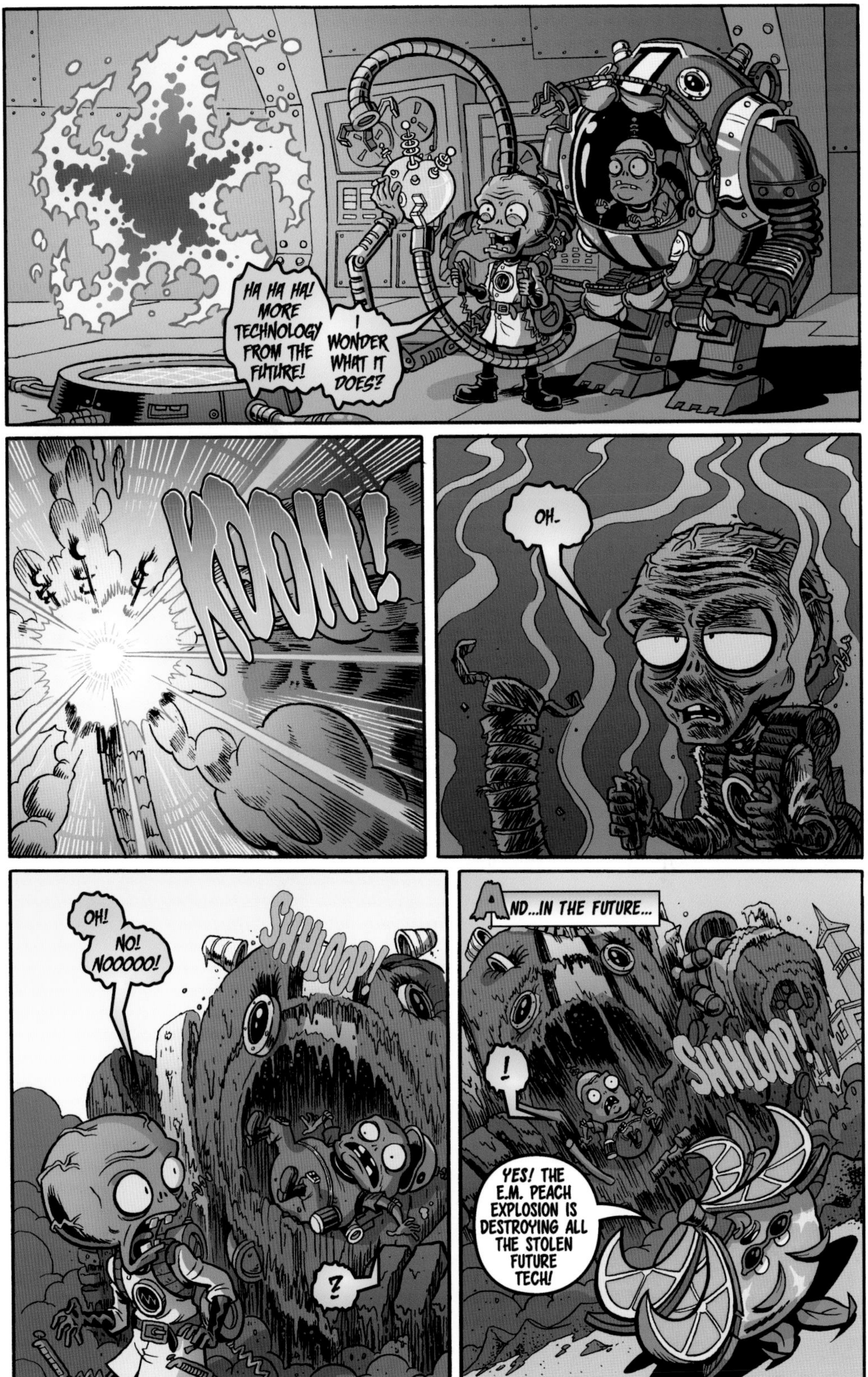
HA HA HA! MORE TECHNOLOGY FROM THE FUTURE!
I WONDER WHAT IT DOES?
KOOM!
OH.
OH! NO! NOOOOO!
SHHLOOP!
?
AND...IN THE FUTURE...
!
SHHLOOP!
YES! THE E.M. PEACH EXPLOSION IS DESTROYING ALL THE STOLEN FUTURE TECH!

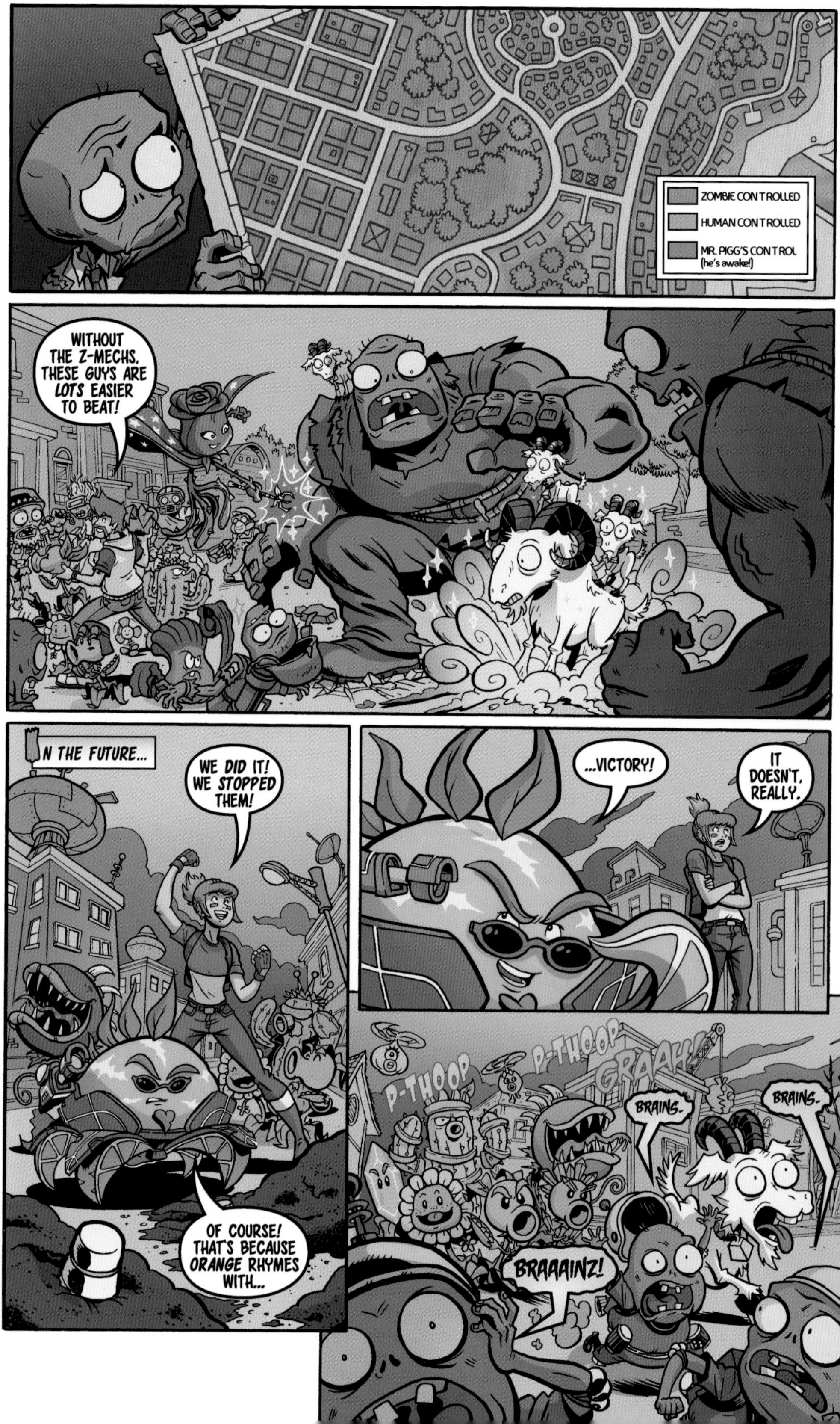
ZOMBIE CONTROLLED
HUMAN CONTROLLED
MR. PIGG'S CONTROL (he's awake!)
WITHOUT THE Z-MECHS, THESE GUYS ARE LOTS EASIER TO BEAT!
IN THE FUTURE...
WE DID IT! WE STOPPED THEM!
OF COURSE! THAT'S BECAUSE ORANGE RHYMES WITH...
...VICTORY!
IT DOESN'T, REALLY.
P-THOOP
P-THOOP
GRAAH!
BRAINS.
BRAINS.
BRAAAINZ!

MAP UPDATE!

ZOMBIE CONTROLLED
HUMAN CONTROLLED
MR. PIGG'S CONTROL
(That dog!)

A MINOR TRAGEDY!

WHAT HAPPENED TO THIS FUTURE-TECH ICE-CREAM MACHINE?

NOOOOOO!

MAP UPDATE!

ZOMBIE CONTROLLED
HUMAN CONTROLLED
MR. PIGG'S CONTROL
(ARF! ARF!)

A MINOR TRAGEDY!

TIME HAS RETURNED TO NORMAL, BUT THEY HAVEN'T HEARD THE LAST OF US.

TECHNICALLY, THEY HAVEN'T HEARD THE FIRST OF US YET.

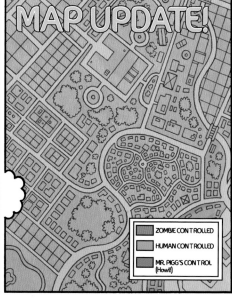

MAP UPDATE!

ZOMBIE CONTROLLED
HUMAN CONTROLLED
MR. PIGG'S CONTROL
(Howl!)

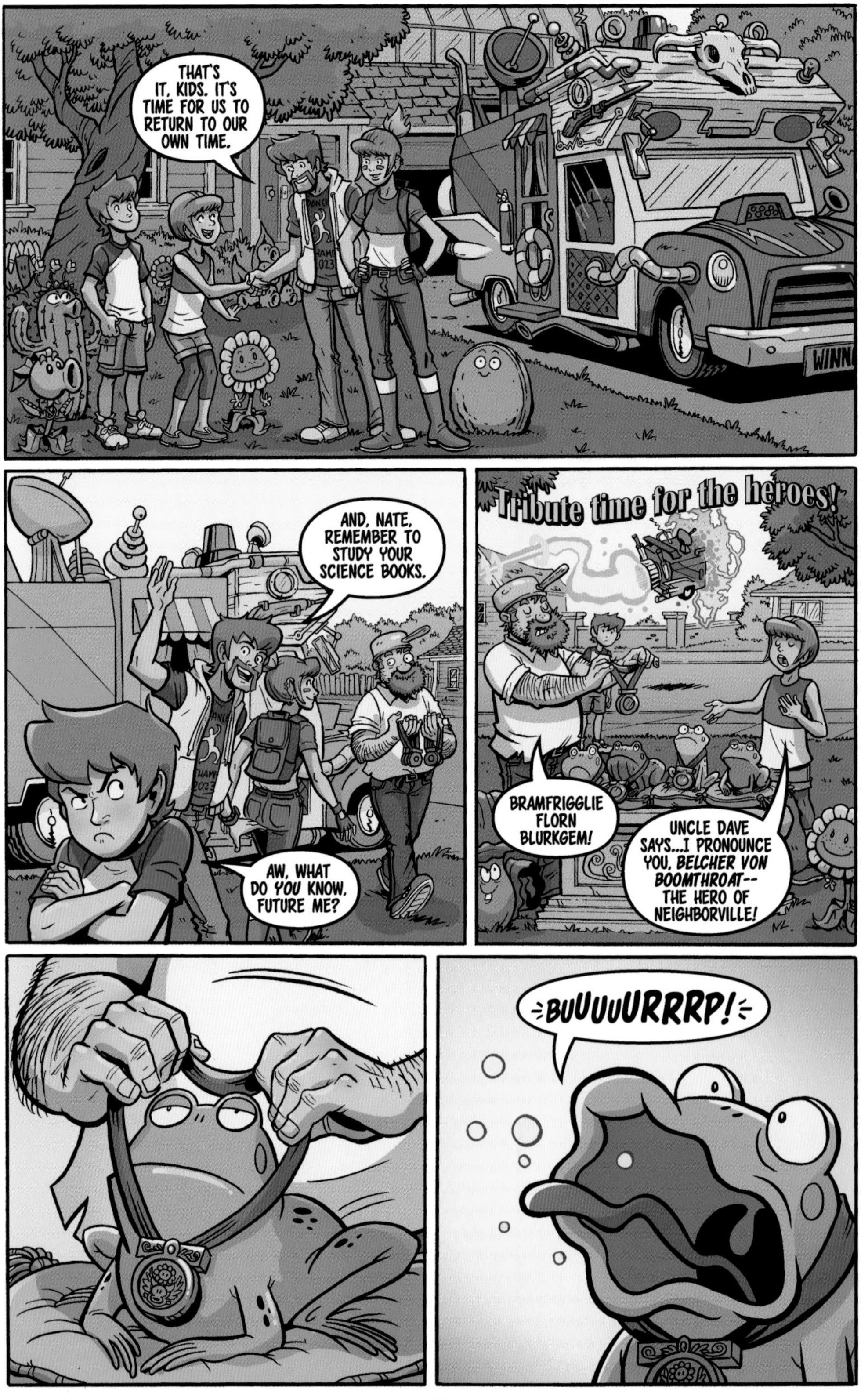
THAT'S IT, KIDS. IT'S TIME FOR US TO RETURN TO OUR OWN TIME.
WINN
AND, NATE, REMEMBER TO STUDY YOUR SCIENCE BOOKS.
AW, WHAT DO *YOU* KNOW, FUTURE ME?
Tribute time for the heroes!
BRAMFRIGGLIE FLORN BLURKGEM!
UNCLE DAVE SAYS...I PRONOUNCE YOU, *BELCHER VON BOOMTHROAT*--THE HERO OF NEIGHBORVILLE!
BUUUUURRRP!

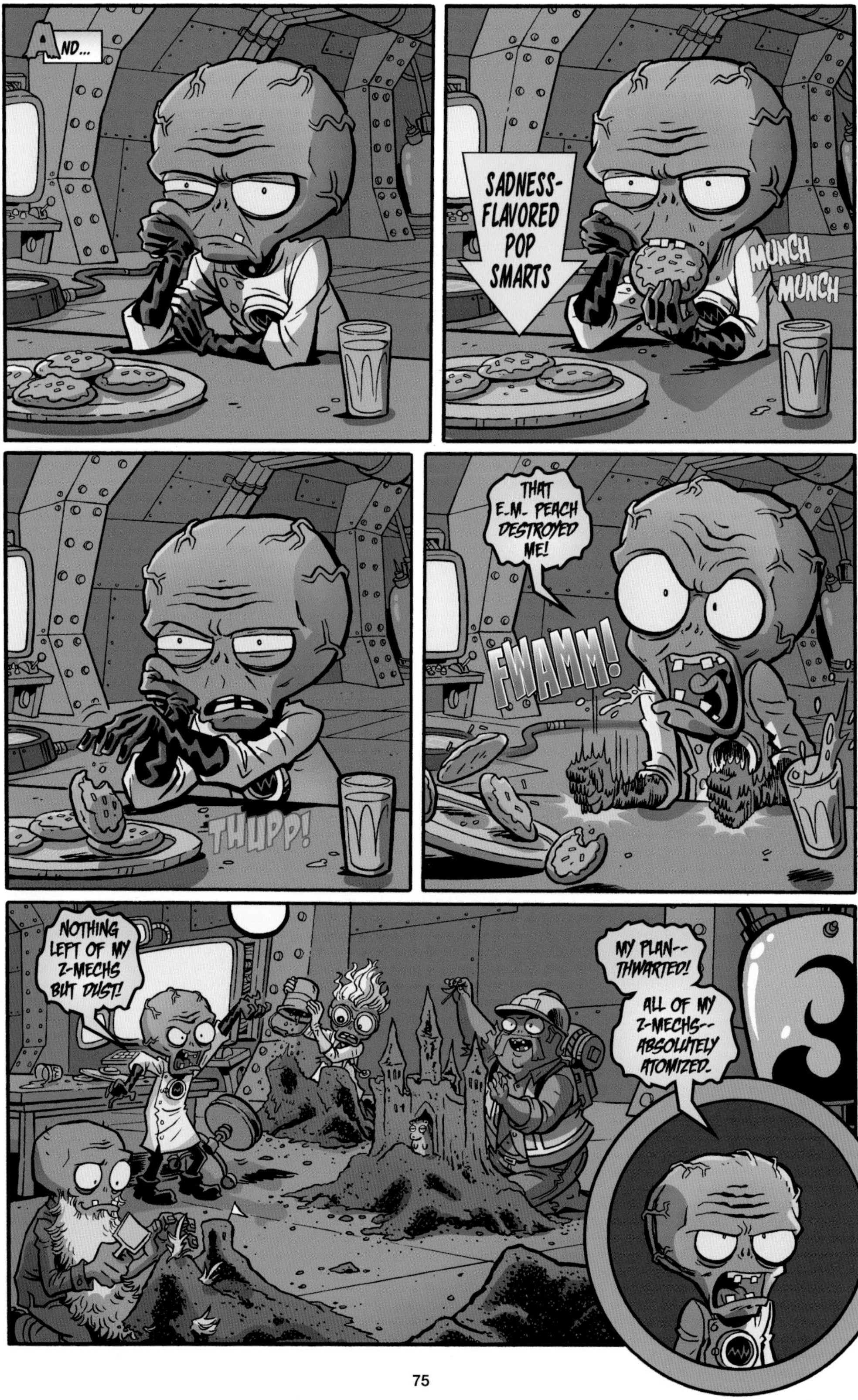
AND...
SADNESS-FLAVORED POP SMARTS
MUNCH MUNCH
THUPP!
THAT E.M. PEACH DESTROYED ME!
FWAMM!
NOTHING LEFT OF MY Z-MECHS BUT DUST!
MY PLAN--THWARTED!
ALL OF MY Z-MECHS--ABSOLUTELY ATOMIZED.

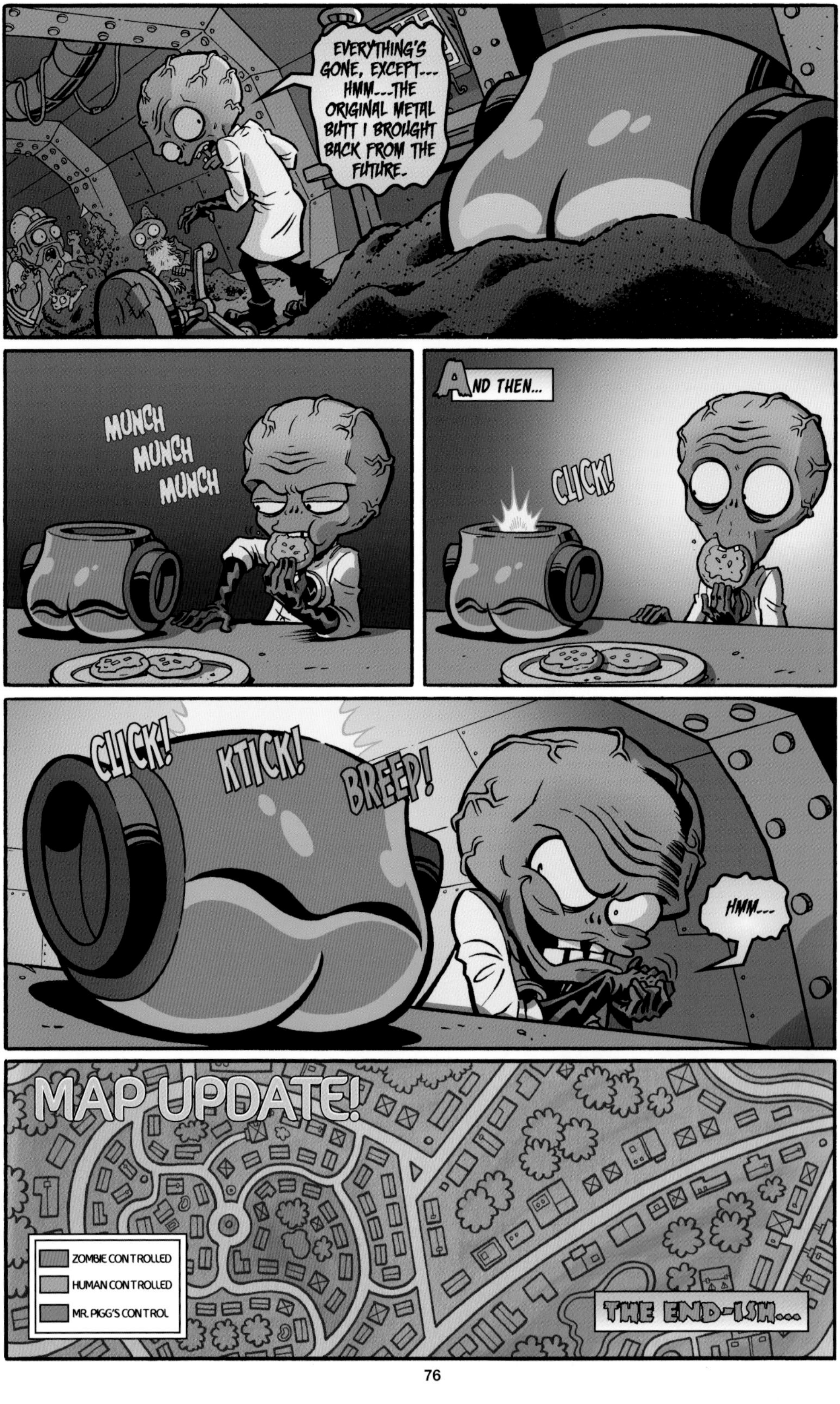
EVERYTHING'S GONE, EXCEPT... HMM...THE ORIGINAL METAL BUTT I BROUGHT BACK FROM THE FUTURE.
MUNCH MUNCH MUNCH
AND THEN...
CLICK!
CLICK!
KTICK!
BREEP!
HMM...
MAP UPDATE!
ZOMBIE CONTROLLED
HUMAN CONTROLLED
MR. PIGG'S CONTROL
THE END-ISH...

CREATOR BIOS

Paul Tobin

Jacob Chabot

Matthew J. Rainwater

Steve Dutro

PAUL TOBIN is a critically acclaimed freckled person who has a detailed plan for any actual zombie invasion, based on creating a vast perfume and cologne empire—both of which would be vitally important in a zombie-infested world. Paul was once informed he "walks funny, like, seriously," but has recovered from this childhood trauma to write hundreds of comics for Marvel, DC, Dark Horse, and many others, including such creator-owned titles as *Colder* and *Bandette*, as well as *Prepare to Die!*—his debut novel. His *Genius Factor* series of novels about a fifth-grade genius and his war against the Red Death Tea Society begins in March of 2016 from Bloomsbury Publishing. Despite his many writing accomplishments, Paul's greatest claim to fame is his ability to win water levels in *Plants vs. Zombies* without using any water plants.

JACOB CHABOT is a New York City–based cartoonist and illustrator. His credits include work for *SpongeBob Comics*, *Simpsons Comics*, Marvel Comics, *Hello Kitty*, and his own Eisner-nominated book *The Mighty Skullboy Army* (published by Dark Horse Comics). He also has almost all the achievements in *Plants vs. Zombies*

Garden Warfare, and if he could stop drawing for a minute, maybe he could finish them all!

Residing in the cool, damp forests of Portland, Oregon, **MATTHEW J. RAINWATER** is a freelance illustrator whose work has been featured in advertising, web design, and independent video games. On top of this, he also self-publishes several comic books, including *Trailer Park Warlock*, *Garage Raja*, and *The Feeling Is Multiplied*—all of which can be found at MattJRainwater.com. His favorite zombie-bashing strategy utilizes a line of Bonk Choys with a Wall-nut front guard and Threepeater covering fire.

STEVE DUTRO is a comic book letterer from northern California who can also drive a tractor. He graduated from the Kubert School and has been in the comics industry for decades, working for Dark Horse (*The Fifth Beatle*, *The Evil Dead*, *Eden*), Viz, Marvel, and DC. Steve's last encounter with zombies was playing zombie paintball in a walnut orchard on Halloween. He tried to play the *Plants vs. Zombies* video game once but experienced a full-on panic attack and resolved to stick with calmer games . . . like *Gears of War*.

ALSO AVAILABLE FROM DARK HORSE!

THE HIT VIDEO GAME CONTINUES ITS COMIC BOOK INVASION!

PLANTS VS. ZOMBIES: LAWNMAGEDDON
Crazy Dave—the babbling-yet-brilliant inventor and top-notch neighborhood defender—helps young adventurer Nate fend off a zombie invasion that threatens to overrun the peaceful town of Neighborville in *Plants vs. Zombies: Lawnmageddon*! Their only hope is a brave army of chomping, squashing, and pea-shooting plants! A wacky adventure for zombie zappers young and old!
ISBN 978-1-61655-192-6 | $9.99

THE ART OF PLANTS VS. ZOMBIES
Part zombie memoir, part celebration of zombie triumphs, and part anti-plant screed, *The Art of Plants vs. Zombies* is a treasure trove of never-before-seen concept art, character sketches, and surprises from PopCap's popular *Plants vs. Zombies* games!
ISBN 978-1-61655-331-9 | $9.99

PLANTS VS. ZOMBIES: TIMEPOCALYPSE
Crazy Dave helps Patrice and Nate Timely fend off Zomboss' latest attack in *Plants vs. Zombies: Timepocalypse*! This new standalone tale will tickle your funny bones and thrill your brains through any timeline!
ISBN 978-1-61655-621-1 | $9.99

PLANTS VS. ZOMBIES: BULLY FOR YOU
Patrice and Nate are ready to investigate a strange college campus to keep the streets safe from zombies!
ISBN 978-1-61655-889-5 | $9.99

PLANTS VS. ZOMBIES: GARDEN WARFARE VOLUME 1
Based on the hit video game, this comic tells the story leading up to the events in *Plants vs. Zombies: Garden Warfare 2*!
ISBN 978-1-61655-946-5 | $9.99

VOLUME 2
ISBN 978-1-50670-548-4 | $9.99

PLANTS VS. ZOMBIES: GROWN SWEET HOME
With newfound knowledge of humanity, Dr. Zomboss strikes at the heart of Neighborville . . . sparking a series of plant-versus-zombie brawls!
ISBN 978-1-61655-971-7 | $9.99

PLANTS VS. ZOMBIES: PETAL TO THE METAL
Crazy Dave takes on the tough *Don't Blink* video game—and challenges Dr. Zomboss to a race to determine the future of Neighborville!
ISBN 978-1-61655-999-1 | $9.99

PLANTS VS. ZOMBIES: BOOM BOOM MUSHROOM
The gang discover Zomboss' secret plan for swallowing the city of Neighborville whole! A rare mushroom must be found in order to save the humans aboveground!
ISBN 978-1-50670-037-3 | $9.99

PLANTS VS. ZOMBIES: BATTLE EXTRAVAGONZO
Zomboss is back, hoping to buy the same factory that Crazy Dave is eyeing! Will Crazy Dave and his intelligent plants beat Zomboss and his zombie army to the punch?
ISBN 978-1-50670-189-9 | $9.99

PLANTS VS. ZOMBIES: LAWN OF DOOM
With Zomboss filling everyone's yards with traps and special soldiers, will he and his zombie army turn Halloween into their zanier Lawn of Doom celebration?!
ISBN 978-1-50670-204-9 | $9.99

PLANTS VS. ZOMBIES: THE GREATEST SHOW UNEARTHED
Dr. Zomboss believes that all humans hold a secret desire to run away and join the circus, so he aims to use his "Big Z's Adequately Amazing Flytrap Circus" to lure Neighborville's citizens to their doom!
ISBN 978-1-50670-298-8 | $9.99

PLANTS VS. ZOMBIES: RUMBLE AT LAKE GUMBO
The battle for clean water begins! Nate, Patrice, and Crazy Dave spot trouble and grab all the Tangle Kelp and Party Crabs they can to quell another zombie attack!
ISBN 978-1-50670-497-5 | $9.99

PLANTS VS. ZOMBIES: WAR AND PEAS
When Dr. Zomboss and Crazy Dave find themselves members of the same book club, a literary war is inevitable! The position of leader of the book club opens up and Zomboss and Crazy Dave compete for the top spot in a scholarly scuffle for the ages!
ISBN 978-1-50670-677-1 | $9.99

PLANTS VS. ZOMBIES: DINO-MIGHT
Dr. Zomboss sets his sights on destroying the yards in town and rendering the plants homeless—and his plans include dogs, cats, rabbits, hammock sloths, and, somehow, dinosaurs . . . !
ISBN 978-1-50670-838-6 | $9.99

PLANTS VS. ZOMBIES: SNOW THANKS
Dr. Zomboss invents a Cold Crystal capable of freezing Neighborville, burying the town in snow and ice! It's up to the humans and the fieriest plants to save Neighborville—with the help of pirates!
ISBN 978-1-50670-839-3 | $9.99

PLANTS VS. ZOMBIES: A LITTLE PROBLEM
Will an invasion of teeny-tiny miniature zombies mean the party for Crazy Dave's two-hundred-year-old pants gets canceled?
ISBN 978-1-50670-840-9 | $9.99

PLANTS VS. ZOMBIES: BETTER HOMES AND GUARDENS
Nate and Patrice try thwarting zombie attacks by putting defending "Guardens" plants *inside* homes as well as in yards! But as soon as Dr. Zomboss finds out, he's determined to circumvent this plan with an epically evil one of his own . . .
ISBN 978-1-50671-305-2 | $9.99

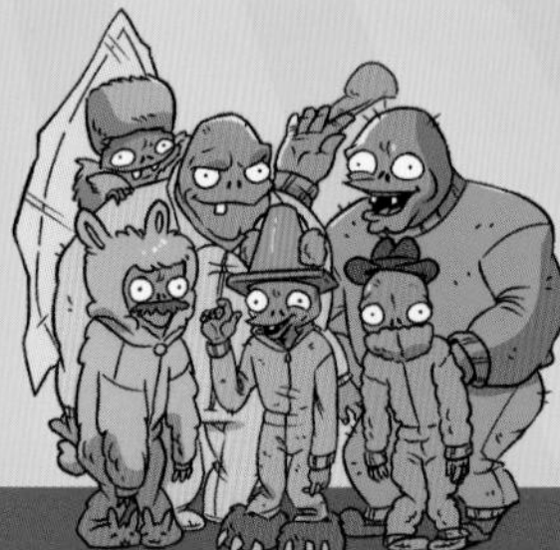

AVAILABLE AT YOUR LOCAL COMICS SHOP OR BOOKSTORE To find a comics shop in your area, visit comicshoplocator.com. For more information or to order direct visit **DarkHorse.com**

MORE DARK HORSE ALL-AGES TITLES

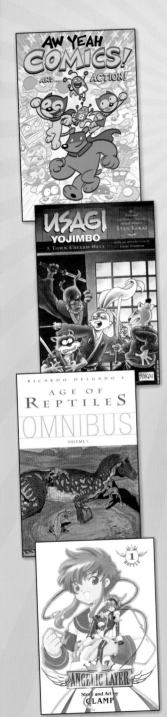

AW YEAH
COMICS!
AND...
ACTION!

AW YEAH COMICS! AND . . . ACTION!

Cornelius and Alowicious are just your average comic book store employees, but when trouble strikes, they are . . . Action Cat and Adventure Bug! Join their epic all-ages adventures as they face off—with the help of Adorable Cat and Shelly Bug—against their archnemesis, Evil Cat, and his fiendish friends!

ISBN 978-1-61655-558-0 | $12.99

USAGI
YOJIMBO
A TOWN CALLED HELL
STAN SAKAI
SAKAI

USAGI YOJIMBO

In his latest adventure, the rabbit *ronin* Usagi finds himself caught between competing gang lords fighting for control of a town called Hell, confronting a *nukekubi*—a flying cannibal head—and crossing paths with the demon Jei!

Volume 25: Fox Hunt
ISBN 978-1-59582-726-5 | $16.99

***Volume 26: Traitors of the Earth* | $16.99**
ISBN 978-1-59582-910-8

***Volume 27: A Town Called Hell* | $16.99**
ISBN 978-1-59582-970-2

RICARDO DELGADO'S
AGE OF
REPTILES
OMNIBUS
VOLUME 1

AGE OF REPTILES OMNIBUS

When Ricardo Delgado first set his sights on creating comics, he crafted an epic tale about the most unlikely cast of characters: dinosaurs. Since that first Eisner-winning foray into the world of sequential art he has returned to his critically acclaimed *Age of Reptiles* again and again, each time crafting a captivating saga about his saurian subjects.

ISBN 978-1-59582-683-1 | $24.99

1
BATTLE
ANGELIC LAYER
Story and Art by
CLAMP

ANGELIC LAYER BOOK 1

Junior-high student Misaki Suzuhara just arrived in Tokyo to live with her TV-star aunt and attend the prestigious Eriol Academy. But what excites Misaki most is Angelic Layer—an arena game where you control a miniature robot fighter with your mind! Can Misaki's enthusiasm and skill take her to the top of the arena?

ISBN 978-1-61655-021-9 | $19.99

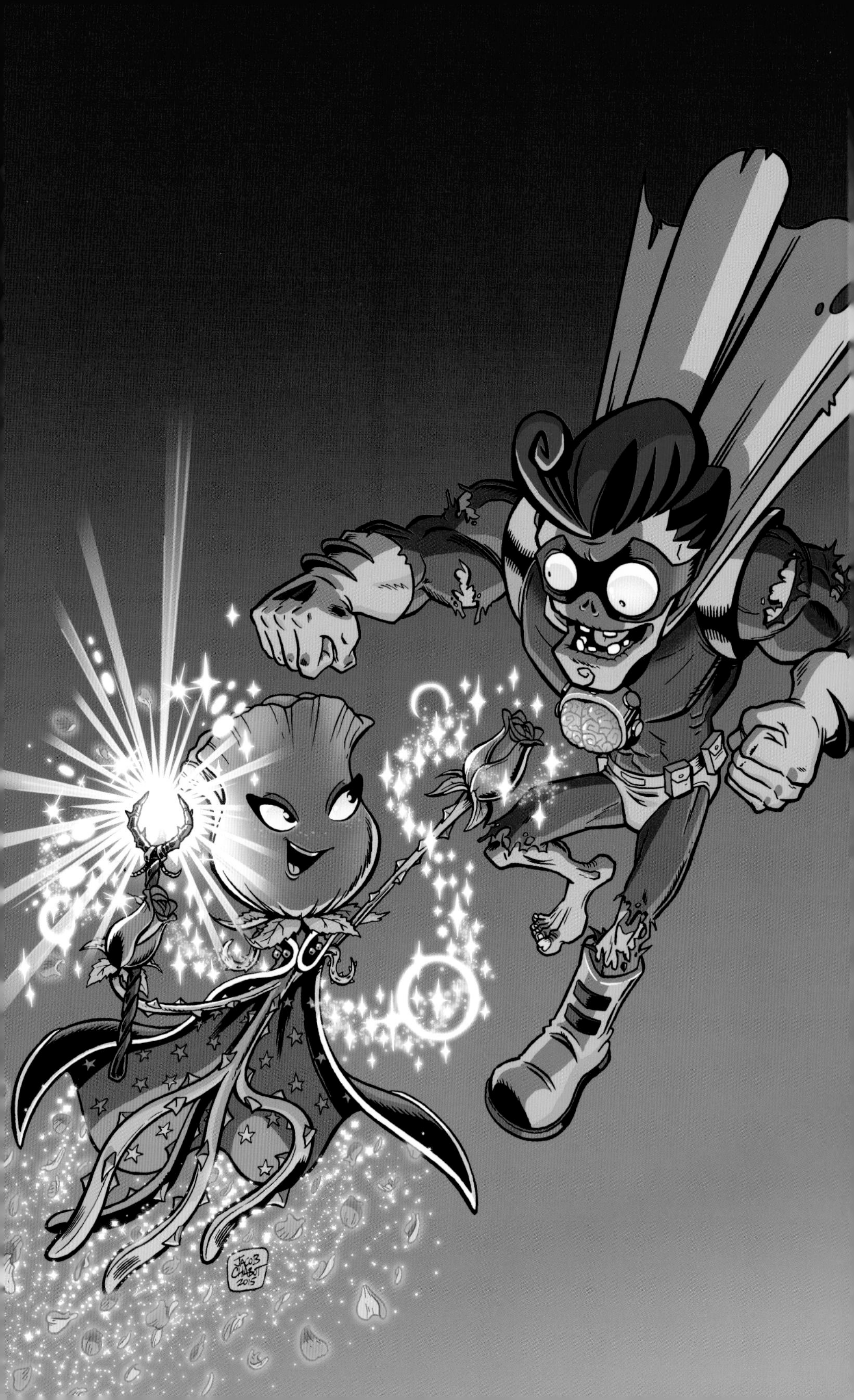
JACOB CHABOT 2015

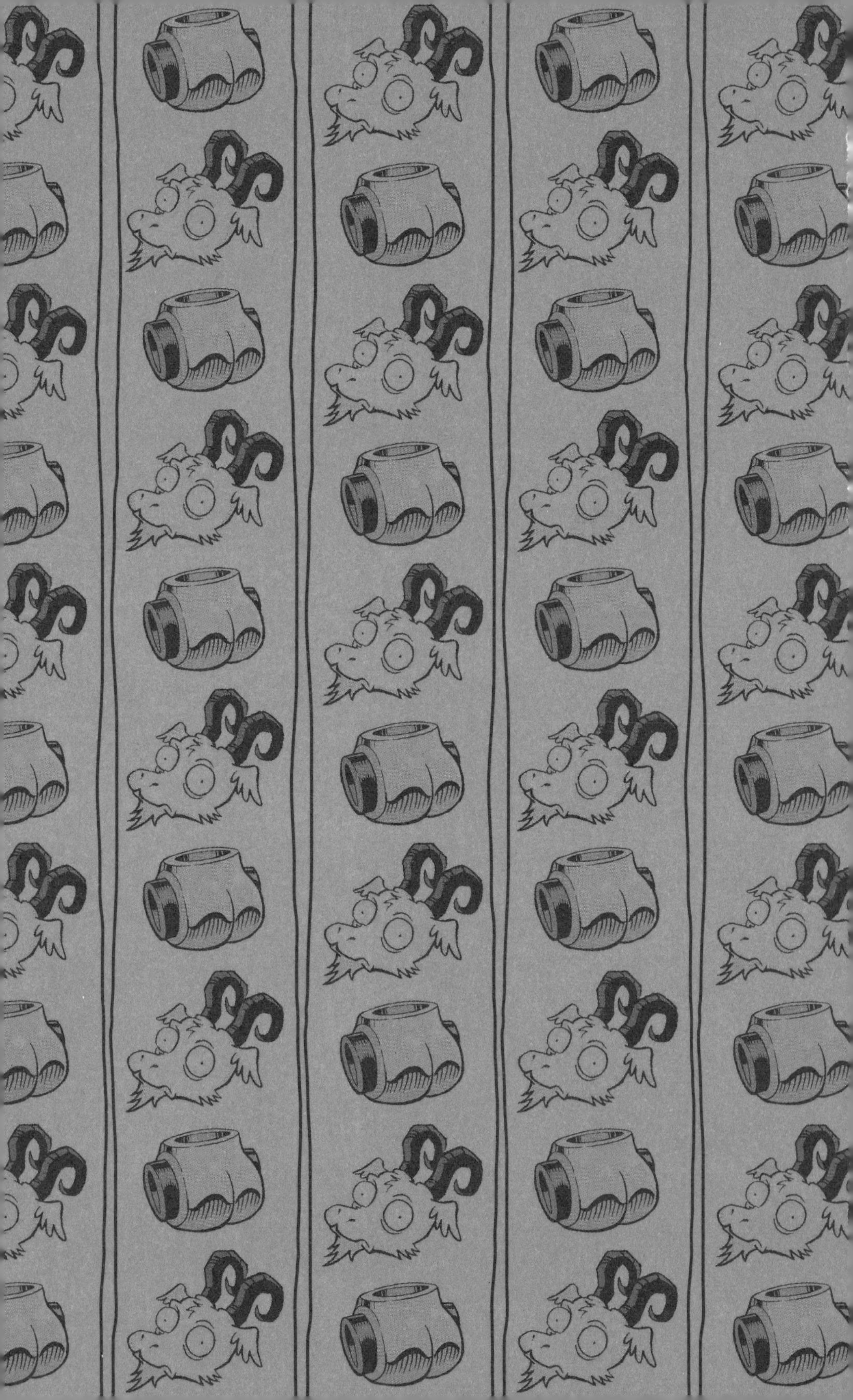